Toast Soldiers

TOAST SOLDIERS

Stories

Bruce Meyer

CROWSNEST BOOKS

Crowsnest Books
www.crowsnestbooks.com

Distributed by the University of Toronto Press

ISBN: 9780921332800 (paperback)
ISBN: 9780921332817 (ebook)

Cataloguing Information available from Library and Archives Canada

This is a work of fiction. Names, characters, places, events, and incidents are either the products of the author's imagination or used in a fictitious manner. Any resemblance to actual persons, living or dead, or actual events is purely coincidental.

Cover design and illustration by Raz Latif.

Printed and bound in Canada

for Kerry and Katie

"Sometimes," said Pooh, "the smallest things take up the most space in our heart."

A.A. Milne

Every lover is a soldier.

Ovid

CONTENTS

Toast Soldiers

OLD SOLDIERS DO DIE, and when Toby's passing left the bridge quartet a man short so only Keith, Mortimer, and Morrison, remained of the four directions, Keith could not tell Mortimer from Morrison, though they were all veterans of the Market Garden fiasco in Holland. What made matters even more confusing for Keith was that Mortimer and Morrison, both bald, bespectacled, and togged in navy cardigans and white shirts, kept switching places between East and West. Keith sat dejectedly at dinner the night Toby died. Toby had been the most faithful of friends, someone who he could rely on, someone whose eyes he could read, and who never betrayed a secret from the past. Toby's empty chair reminded Keith of the horror of watching Oxley fall from the underside of the Waal Bridge in Nijmegen.

Having Toby with him in the elder home meant Keith was not alone with his memories. Both had been attached to xxx Corps. When the two flirted with the women in residence, they said they weren't lying when they claimed they were triple x. It was a soldier's joke that masked the nightmare the two shared. Nijmegen lay in ruins from a night of Allied bombing when the Lancasters and Halifaxes missed the train station and wiped out eight hundred locals. The Germans described the air raid as wanton destruction of the city, and it turned the population against Montgomery's men long before the first Sherman tank rolled into the streets.

Keith lost his best buddy, George, on the first day of Operation Market Garden as xxx Corps entered the city. September 19, 1944. The road in had been a beautiful walk. The trees were full and bursting with that last, fine moment that marks the apex of a long, hot summer. Keith and George could see the hump-back of the bridge up ahead as its girders spanned the river. There was no resistance to their progress. The clack of the tank treads, the sounds of men talking amongst themselves, gave the entry into Nijmegen an air of a country hike, more like a training exercise. As they passed one house, a man rushed out his front door with glasses of ale for them and offered the two pals a toast as liberators and saviors. Another woman ran up and hugged them both. It was a beautiful day. George shouldn't have died the way he did.

The road in gave Keith and George a false sense of acceptance, so when they came upon a girl with auburn pigtails as she sat in the shell of what had been a baked goods shop on the main street, they paused, looked in the shattered doorway and smiled at her and she smiled back. She was seated beside a fire and holding a pannekoek press in her left hand. The aroma of the cinnamon and the airy batter steaming drew George into the shop. The girl set the pan down on a block of stone and, as George held out his hand to receive the bread, she smiled with a thin mouth tilted to one side, almost in an expression of wry wit, a knowing look in her eye, and raised an antique revolver and shot George between the eyes. Keith drew a bead on her with his rifle and fired back, catching the girl in the side of her head as the pigtails snapped around it. The smile on the girl's face as Keith looked through the sight never left him. Toby had been the one resident of the home who understood what the pain in that smile held for Keith. Toby had been up the road following the pair of friends. He appeared on the scene of Keith bent over George's body and, as the girl began to move her arm, groaning in a low moan, it had been Toby who delivered the coup de grace with his bayonet. The girl sighed, and the odd, thin, tilted smile disappeared from her face. Keith wept. Toby pulled at his arm drawing Keith from the scene, and wordlessly motioning with his head that they had to keep moving forward. Keith looked back at the empty entrance that framed the moment. Toby never spoke of the moment in the bakeshop on the road into Nijmegen, but sometimes, when their hands at bridge were difficult and Mortimer and Morrison were getting the better of them at cards, Toby would look up from his hand and nod to Keith with reassurance that whatever the circumstances they would press on together.

Now that Keith was without his confidant, he was bothered by Toby's empty place at the table. It kept reminding him of the doorframe of the bakeshop, the empty frame that might have held a Dutch landscape or a laughing cavalier that remained forever empty. That evening at dinner, small things made Keith weep – the attendant removing Toby's plate and cutlery when she realized he wasn't coming for dinner, the water glass that she did not lift away from the empty place, and the indent of the chair that was still shaped to the outline of Toby's back – and though the staff did their best to comfort him, Keith could not tell them what was wrong. He imagined the tug of Toby's arm pulling him from the ruins of the bakery.

The next morning was no better. A new chef arrived and replaced the regular English breakfast of fried eggs and bacon with a softboiled egg and thin fingers of bread that he called "toast soldiers." The square-cut strips, the toast soldiers, reminded Keith of the field biscuit that George, and Toby, and Oxley, ate when they stopped for rations beneath an old, twisted elm. His hand shook as he dipped the soldiers in the broken yolks. Keith loathed softboiled eggs. He detested the shells even if he only ate them halfway. They reminded him of ruins.

The toast soldiers arrived for breakfast on the same day as Kepler. Kepler caused Keith to rage inside. Not only did the newcomer refuse to play bridge so that the fourth direction remained empty during the afternoons of gentlemanly card games, but the fellow refused to speak English. He was inscrutable. The dining room woman sat the silent man in Toby's place. To Keith, the German was an interloper, a spy, someone who had come to extract information from the others at the table. "Tell him nothing," Keith whispered to Mortimer and Morrison. "That man is a bloody spy. Give him no intelligence. If he asks anything of you, tell him you don't speak German. Tell him only your name, rank, and serial number. Loose lips sink ships, chaps."

Keith's contempt for Kepler was instantaneous. It began at breakfast the moment the man sat down in Toby's empty chair. Kepler handed the small dish of marmalade to the server, raised his hand, and waved it off, not wanting it on the table."Hold on a minute there," Keith shouted as if the server could not hear. "It is my right as an Englishman to have my marmalade. You put it back at once!"

"*Nein*," said Kepler, and shoved it toward the server. The dining room attendant didn't know what to do. With a motion of his finger, Kepler indicated that the attendant should leave the marmalade on the table of a woman at the other side of the room, pointing to her and wagging his finger. Was Kepler ingratiating himself to the woman at the expense of Keith's marmalade? It wasn't Kepler's marmalade to give. Keith's daughter-in-law had brought it to him from Scotland. Keith loved his Golden Shred. He claimed it was his 'king's breakfast.'

The woman on the other side of the room who received the Golden Shred marmalade was Helen. No one knew much about her. She never spoke at meals, never conversed with the other residents, and never invited anyone to sit with her during the afternoons in the lounge when Keith and his friends were occupied with their games of bridge. Helen was enigmatic. She was small and white-haired. She wore a pink cardigan each day. Keith surmised she had more than one because she spilled her tea down her front one day at lunch and by late afternoon the sweater appeared brand new. Around her neck, she wore a lace collar like those a tourist might purchase in Ireland, though the patterns were not Irish. Whenever Keith walked by the woman, she would clutch her lace collar tightly at her throat almost to the point of choking herself. The collar business made Keith uneasy because it made Helen uneasy. And because Helen never spoke, many concluded she had suffered a stroke. The attendants seated her at the 'quiet' ladies table.

What made Keith even more curious about Helen was her smile – a mackerel smile, tight-lipped, and tilted slightly to one side. Keith saw no expression of pleasantry in it. The look was more an expression that she knew something about him, and she wasn't going to tell him what it was. The only person Keith trusted with secrets was Toby and, now that Toby was gone, he did not relish the thought that others knew more about him than they should. He wracked his brains to remember where he had seen that smile before, but he could not place it. And when her eyes followed him as he wheeled himself across the lounge on his rollator, or in moments when he saw her watching him and studying him with her narrow eyes squinting not from bad eyesight but from an anger behind them, Keith could not quite fathom why he felt doubly troubled by the woman's presence.

Each afternoon during the old soldiers' bridge games, Helen sat in a wing chair beside the window of the lounge and appeared to be reading, though she never turned a page, and the book was always open in her lap. Other residents suggested she was mute, perhaps hard of hearing or completely deaf, so Keith tested her one day, moving a footstool into Helen's path as she entered the room and then pointed out, just in time, that she ought to look where she was going. She stopped, pushed the footstool aside, and glared at Keith. She heard him fine and dandy. She heard everything. She was on Keith's "watch what you say around her" list along with the new man, Kepler. Her manners and her mannerisms hinted at a European background. She certainly knew some English, at least enough to navigate around a footstool, Keith noted to Mortimer and Morrison. One of the two balding veterans responded that it shouldn't be any concern of Keith's, though five minutes later he couldn't remember if Morrison or Mortimer had commented. The damned fools were mirror images of each other and, now that Toby was gone, telling the two apart, even if they had served in the Market Garden campaign, grew far more difficult by the day.

"Damned foreigners," Keith said to an orderly who was settling him to bed one night. "Can't trust any of them."

"I am from Poland," replied the young woman as she stood erect and smoothed her blue, striped smock and glared at Keith. "Am I not to be trusted?"

"We almost lost our England trying to save you from the bloody Germans and those godless Russians, and thank us? Ha! When you thought you were in the clear, you ran off and joined the damned Russians even after they killed all your officers in some blighted wood. You don't know what's good for you, eh?" The young woman left his room and slammed the door after her. She noted on Keith's chart that his paranoia and mental deterioration were becoming more pronounced.

Keith, on the other hand, felt he had good reason to be suspicious of those around him. With Toby gone he had no one to watch his back for him. He was certain that Kepler knew English, and so he tried to get a rise out of the new arrival.

Dummkopf had done the trick. Over breakfast, a meal without his beloved dish of golden marmalade on the table to dress his toast soldiers for battle, Keith began to sing. "Dummkopf, O silly Dummkopf, with a suicidal sociopath for a father..." Kepler stood up, shook his fist at Keith, and was searching at the edge of his plate for a fork but only managed to grab a spoon when an attendant restrained him.

"Keith," said the young Polish woman, "you know better than that. Apologize to Mr. Kepler for your incorrigible behavior."

"Only if he apologizes to you, my dear, for invading Poland!" Then the manager appeared from her office and stepped in to bring peace to their time, holding up a sheet of paper like Neville Chamberlain and shouting, "Let us have some peace, at least." Keith chortled, then begged the manager to remove the "Nazi pariah" who scoffed at the trio when they tried to play bridge in the afternoon without a fourth. Realizing she was dealing with a table of veterans, the manager told him, "Just be a good soldier and put up with the chap. You know. Like in the old days. Stiff upper lip."

"My dear," Keith replied, "in the old days, we leveled Dresden for what those bastards did to Coventry." He was told to be quiet, or he would be confined to his room, his barracks as Keith called them.

Keith hated being manipulated. He was considered a leader among the other residents. They respected him, and not without cause, though they whispered behind their hands that they couldn't see the point in dragging out the war any longer. Keith heard what they were saying. Some of them had lost the ability to whisper. But despite the war being dredged up, Keith still had the respect of most of the residents. He was someone they looked up to. He'd won an MM in Holland and risen to the rank of Captain by the end of the whole mess. Within the first week of Kepler's arrival, no one in the dining room wanted to be seated, seen with, or seen speaking to the German. They felt a loyalty to Keith.

"Look," said the manager. "He's harmless. He just wants to be with you all. One of the gang."

At each meal, Keith and Kepler exchanged hostile stares as if they were leveling arms at each other at close range in a stand-off, neither even troubling to ask the other to pass the salt as they ate. Mortimer and Morrison pretended Kepler wasn't there and talked about him in the third person. They wanted to protect Keith. He'd earned his marmalade, they said. But the marmalade incident angered Keith and he wouldn't let the matter drop. He told the server that he was refusing to eat his toast soldiers, let alone dip them in his shell-shocked egg yolks, until his Golden Shred was returned.

The worst of Keith's suspicions were confirmed the day the men were given their showers. While he waited in his wheelchair, Keith watched Kepler being lifted into the plastic bath seat, and when the German's upper right arm was exposed, Keith saw a patch of grafted skin on the man's bicep.

"That new man, Kepler, he's SS," Keith grumbled out loud in the lounge the next afternoon when only silent Helen was there. Keith didn't realize he was alone with her, and she did not look up from the page that never turned. "I saw the skin graft. That's where the Waffen men were tattooed. I saw them for myself. I saw those SS marks on the Panzer men at Nijmegen."

The next morning at breakfast, as the softboiled eggs and toast soldiers were put in front of him, Keith hollered at the server. "I want my damned marmalade back! It's over there with that silent woman," and he pointed accusingly at Helen as if she had taken it.

The server tried to placate Keith. "Mr. Kepler thinks sweets are a sign of weakness."

"Rubbish! Damnable lies! Bring it back now," Keith demanded as everyone turned to look.

Kepler smiled. The woman remained mute. She simply stared straight ahead as the server relented and carried the marmalade dish to Keith's table. He reached out with his knife and spread it on his toast soldiers without looking up. Keith felt he had won a small, though hard-fought, victory; but he would have to remain vigilant. "That Kraut is out to get me," he confided to Mortimer or Morrison.

A spate of warm weather arrived after what had been a long, rainy, and cold summer. The staff decided that the morning activity for everyone would be some air on the patio. The sunshine, they told everyone as breakfast began, would do them good. Before the eggs and toast soldiers were served, Keith raised his hand and asked what day it was.

"September 19th," the Polish orderly replied.

"This was the day," Keith announced to everyone in the dining room, "that I lost my best friend, George, as we entered Nijmegen. We'd grown up together. We'd had our first pint at a pub at the end of our street. We enlisted together. We fought side by side as mates through some of the worst of it until some little totsie in a second-rate pastry shop shot him dead. Terrible business. Terrible business. It was also the day of a very bloody battle. I would have kept killing except that we ran out of ammunition and bloody Germans." Tears began to well in his eyes and his shoulders heaved up and down with sobs.

Mortimer spoke up. "It was the day Keith won his MM while attempting to remove explosives from the Waal Bridge." Everyone applauded except Kepler and Helen. They kept their hands folded in their laps.

The orderly then declared, "Later in the day, with or without the benefit of spirits, we shall toast our soldiers. Is that agreeable with you, Keith?" she said, leaning over him in a patronizing manner. "Toast soldiers?" she repeated with emphasis on each word and an odd interrogative upturn at the end of her phrase as if she had decided that Keith was deaf. Then breakfast was served.

Keith looked for his marmalade. It was gone again. "Where is my bloody spread?" he asked.

Kepler smiled. "You will get what is coming to you today."

The German reached into the pocket of his shirt and produced a photograph.

Keith was astounded that Kepler spoke English, though with a thick accent.

"I have something to show you, Keith. I was stationed in Nijmegen in 1944. I was probably one of the ones shooting at you from the other side of the bridge. You and your RAF friends ruined that beautiful city. In one night, I lost the love of my life and her parents. There they are," Kepler said as he tapped the photograph several times insistently with the tip of his index finger then shoved it across the table to Keith. "See them? See how beautiful she was? I am the officer in the photograph, and yes, the one in the SS Panzer uniform. That is me when I was young and in love."

Keith looked at him astonished. "You shouldn't even be in this country, you bloody SS blighter. I'll have you thrown out." Mortimer and Morrison stared at Kepler, and one of them tightened his fist around the handle of his fork as if ready for hand-to-hand combat.

"The oldest girl," continued Kepler, "I loved the oldest one. Her parents ran a bakery on the main road from the south into the center of the city. You know the street. You may even remember the bakery. Her name was Marie. My Marie. Your airmen killed her. And the second sister. You know her. You shot her while she sat in the ruins of the family shop. She was making pannekoek to greet the British and American soldiers."

"That little bitch shot my friend George, so I killed her for what she did. I blew her bloody brains out and my friend Toby finished her off, God rest his soul." Keith looked at the photograph. The two girls were smiling the same smile, a mackerel smile tilted slightly to one side, sly and knowing. Keith wanted to believe the smile was sinister, but there was nothing sinister about three girls sitting in a garden with a soldier in a black uniform.

Kepler reached across the table. "I'll take that back. As for the third and youngest sister? When Holland was liberated, the partisans paraded her in the streets and shaved her head. She was made a public disgrace. There was nothing people wouldn't do to ruin her. And why? Because her sister had loved a German? I thought you chaps were fighting for love and justice and all the garbage you spewed out in your propaganda films, your Vera Lynn songs about Little Johnny in his bed. You are weaklings. You know neither great love nor great pain."

"You bastards all deserved to die. None of you had any real feelings. It was so bloody staged, so Nuremberg Rally-ish." Keith stared at the photograph before pushing it back to Kepler. "I wish I had killed you at Nijmegen, but it seems you suffered a fate worse than death, if losing someone you love dearly is the worst pain you can imagine. I know because I loved my pal, George. So, you were in love with Marie, and she died in the air raid. I shot the next one, you say."

"Kristijana."

"So you say. Kristijana. And the third one?"

The Polish girl fetched the dish of marmalade from Helen's table and laid it in front of Keith.

"About bloody time. My toast soldiers are getting spoiled," Keith said. He snatched the golden spread and slathered it upon the fingers of toast. The toast soldiers were lined up on his plate like bodies that Keith had witnessed, shattered lives waiting to be cast into mass graves after the town had been liberated, stiff, almost faceless, and nameless figures. And for what? All so some insane leader could drive an enraptured nation into the jaws of hell? "You were all demons," Keith shouted.

Keith bit into the toast. He finished his first soldier, then took up another. As he pushed the egg away in its little cup, overdone again, a strange tightness took hold of his chest. His hands shook. He dropped the knife and the toast soldier. He banged with his fist on the table and reached for his throat and began to gag. The Polish girl came running to his assistance as he slumped forward. Kepler sat smiling.

"Herr Keith, you keep wanting to fight a war that is over. Me? I surrendered just after your General Montgomery crossed the bridge. I didn't want to go back to Germany. My heart was in

Holland. I laid down my weapons. I have been a civilian all these years. I fight no more."

When the ambulance came, Keith was loaded onto a gurney. A heart machine beeped between his legs. Mortimer and Morrison stood up and saluted him. Keith tried to raise his hand to return the salute, but the cord on the oxygen monitor was too short. But as he passed Kepler, he saw Helen standing slightly behind the German with her hand on his shoulder. She slipped her other hand into the German's and smiled, her lips closed, her mouth tilted to one side as if she knew a secret.

Oglevie

Just before he'd been tossed out from the city club, the trainer warned Oglevie there would be only mush between his ears if he fought another bout. He offered Oglevie the chance to be a plumber's assistant, but Oglevie threw the trainer to the floor and told him to go to Hell. He'd tried to coach a young heavyweight how to use a left uppercut but when the kid couldn't understand what was being said through fattened lips and slurred words, Oglevie knocked the kid to the mat sending the pupil to hospital to have his jaw wired shut for three months.

When Oglevie looked in the mirror, he did not see the smiling good-for-a-bright-future small-town boy who had captained his high school boxing team to the county championship, or the lithe body and toned washboard torso that invited a beating, but the rearranged face of a stranger that he didn't recognize when he shaved.

When the bus dropped him in the town named for his ancestor and pulled away, he could not recall the old haunts being so haunted. Paint peeled from the storefronts. Weeds grew up between cracks in the sidewalk. Dust clouds chased after the bus as if it were their last chance to escape. There had been a blind man who sat on the steps of the town hall and recited the names of former mayors and then asked for a quarter or a dime, but no one remembers what happened to him. Then the hall had been taken over by squatters before it burned down and took with it all the records of what Oglevie had been.

The gym where Oglevie had trained for three months immediately following his high school graduation was down at the end of the main street if he turned right and followed a one-sided road along the river where the store backs had been shaded by willows on summer afternoons. After settling into a basement room in a house that had a "Room for Rent" sign in the window, Oglevie decided to explore a past he thought he had forgotten. The sun was setting on the dusty summer evening. The air was full of flies.

He found the gym door ajar and wedged his way in. Oglevie tried hard to remember the gym as it once was. The training room with the ring, barbells, and punching bags, was always filled with dust. When the light of a setting sun flooded in the windows of the workout room there was a feeling that each illuminated column was a road to heaven waiting to be traveled. He had been alone in the gym on a night exactly like the night he returned to town, and he said it was a moment of holiness when the light came in between the parted branches of the willow trees beside the river and beckoned him to pursue his dreams.

"There are only two ways out of this ring," his hometown trainer, Babs, had yelled in Oglevie's face. "One is to be carried out and the other is to climb out intact with something to show for all your pain. You have to decide which it is going to be, laddie! There's a fighter in there, but you have to cut the path for him through your hubris or both of you will die," the old man hollered in Oglevie's face. "The fighter in you will die and take you with him."

The gulf between his hometown and his path to fortune widened with each day. He hadn't had enough money to come home for his mother's funeral. His father wrote to him to say he was moving farther west to find work, though he didn't say where, and the image of the man he had idolized blurred into the sweat and smell of greased leather gloves, the onion aroma of men's bodies, and the salty metallic taste of blood that ran from his nose and filled his mouth when he was too slow to duck a punch.

Only one gym in the city agreed to take Oglevie on, and only if he stayed long into the night after the other fighters had gone home, to mop the floors and spread sawdust on the taut canvas of the ring. If the world of pain between the ropes would not come clean, he would take a galvanized bucket and a bristled brush and kneel before the stained patches to scrub them clean. With every hard stroke that felled him, he felt himself growing stronger.

The longer he hung around the gym, the more he changed, both in mind and appearance. One day, not long before Oglevie quit the city gym and spent his savings on the bus ticket back to where he had come from, he looked in the mirror and didn't recognize himself.

"Do I look like a monster?" he asked me one afternoon.

I am one of those bartenders who practices honesty much to the disappointment of my customers, but because I have the only joint in town where someone can buy a drink, they always come back. Being honest is not the safest thing either. My elderly uncle who bequeathed me the bar said I ought to avoid answering rhetorical questions. But I told Oglevie what I saw.

"I see a guy who's taken his punches. I see a face that's still there though rearranged as an artist might shuffle things to make a statement about the human condition or something. It's all still there but in an artistic kind of way. I could say you're a work of art or I could say you're just some piece of work. Either way, you know what you are better than I, and appearances can be deceiving."

"I'll tell you this once and you're not to tell anyone else. I left the city because the last time I went to the boxing club, someone had drawn a caricature of me and taped it to a punching bag, and I knew I couldn't take it anymore. I'd had my bouts. I even won a couple though no one gives a damn about welterweights except maybe me. The smaller guys are the cannon fodder of a boxing card. Everyone remembers heavyweights, even the ones who don't amount to anything. My bouts were against kids just like me who had gone to the city to punch their way to fame and fortune, and there I was knocking their teeth out in the ring, and I realized I was striking blows, left hooks, and right jabs, against the mirror of myself and maybe against myself. The last kid, I think I hit him so hard he didn't wake up for a week. I thought he was dead, but what died was the vision of what I wanted to become. I hit that kid harder than I'd hit anyone in years because I wanted to hurt myself. I wanted to roll my pain into one punch and feel it in every sinew of my body. I realized that for every guy I knocked out there was a name that would never appear again on a card, and I was killing myself."

"To thine own self be true?" I asked.

He smiled. I think he thought I was joshing him. I was, and I laughed so he'd know we both saw the absurdity of his situation – the pain, the constant beating without reward, and the failure, although I didn't want to mention that. Someone in pain doesn't need to have their suffering enlarged or even ennobled. They need reassurance that the hard knocks are part of some grander plan and to learn from them.

He'd once been the town hero. That was a long time ago. Now he was just a stranger, one of the drifting shadows who stepped off the late bus from the city, a shadow in the square looking around for a place to stay for the night. There are none except for the rooms I rent above my bar. They come into my place, and they all look bewildered as if their eyes are saying they don't want to be where they've ended up.

I knew who this stranger was but thought it best to give Oglevie his anonymity, though he puzzled me. Maybe he *was* the fallen hero, the guy who goes out to the horizon as far as he can go and comes back because he learns the world is flat and people fall off the edge or the ocean is too vast and deep. There are plenty of reasons, and none of them are about defeat. Most of the lessons are about pain – the pain of fear, the fear of pain. I know, I'm rambling.

Maybe he came back because he had learned something awful about the world, the truth perhaps – that the world is only too willing to beat a person up either for sport or a few dollars or just for the hell of it. I figured I wouldn't press any further with the questions. I'd done my Good Samaritan thing. I offered Oglevie something better than sleeping in the square on a park bench. I told him he could have a room above my bar, The Horseshoe, in exchange for picking up glasses and jugs off the tables, washing up in the kitchen, pulling beers when I was busy making a sandwich, and running a broom around the floor when the place needed it. The job was for as long as he wanted it, though one question kept nagging me.

"I saw you get off the bus. You were playing with a dog in the shadows of the moonlight, but as you followed the mutt to the square, you knelt down and began playing and rubbing his belly. You don't have a dog with you now. What was that all about? Do dogs just run up to you like that?"

"You know about Arty?"

"I was locking up and I turned from the door and saw you and a dog. The town is full of strays. Then I heard you shouting his name. I thought he had come with you on the bus."

"Arty was this dog that liked me, a puppy before I left. He was brown and white and lived next door with a family named Jespersen."

"The old man owned the hardware store, but the bolts rusted around him, so he just walked away from his house and his business, and he and his wife went to live with their daughter," I said.

"Yep. The kid was a real brat," Oglevie replied as he swirled the last mouthful in his glass but didn't drink it. "She wasn't good to that dog. A puppy needs to be loved but loved within limits. A little dog like that shouldn't be set up high in a tree and told to jump down. It could break its leg. It shouldn't be hit with a stick or have the hose turned on it with cold water. Arty was the kind of dog I would have liked to have had. He dug under the fence and came into our backyard. Mr. Jespersen would beat the poor thing, but day after day he'd appear first thing in the morning in our yard, and I'd play with him in the grass – puppy play, tug a rope kind of play. I'd pick him up in my arms, stroke him behind the ears and smooth my hand over his eyebrows and forehead, and tell him in a soft voice he was a good dog."

"I can't say anyone missed the Jespersons when they left."

"The strange thing is that an old dog with the same coat hobbled up to me when I got off the bus last week. He had his head down and his coat was mangy. The dog looked as if the world had sucked the life out of him. His head was low. He had something wrong with one of his back legs like someone had hit him or kicked him or run into him with a car. He looked so old and tired even in the moonlight."

"How long were you gone?" I asked.

"Almost fifteen years"

"That's a long time for a dog to hang on."

"Yeah, a long time. Almost impossible for a dog to hang around that long, especially an abused dog. I put down my suitcase as he began to wander away with his tail between his legs. That's when I shouted his name. I yelled it at the top of my lungs, 'Arty! Arty! Good boy! Come!' And you know what? He came limping back to me. I sat down on the pavement, and I rubbed his head and stroked him, and he rolled over on his back so I could rub his tummy. And it was Arty, though not the Arty I had known. It was the Arty the world had finished with. He sat up, extended his front paw, and I shook it just like I had taught him when I told him we were pals. And when I was through rubbing his chest and gut, he rolled over and stared at me, probably in disbelief because I was staring at him the same way – I mean, how long had I been gone? And he licked my hand, and then he crossed his front paws, and closed his eyes."

"He died?"

"Yep. Right there. I dug a place for him with my bare hands, scraping the earth open until my fingers bled, right over there in the square beneath an oak tree. I wanted to carve his name on the tree but figured someone would come along and dig him up. He didn't deserve to go to the town dump. He deserved a kingly burial at the roots of an oak. I removed his collar and there on the tags, beneath all the grime and dirt, was his name. It was Arty. He'd waited until I came home."

Oglevie looked up from his beer.

"I know this is a lot to ask because you'd have to shut down the bar for an evening, but there's a card over in Fairfield and I phoned the guy who was running it and asked if I could be part of the bout. I don't know what got into me. I've been out of the ring for a while, but I want to go for it, give it one last shot. I can't get the fighter out of my system."

"Go for it," I said. "But don't get killed. You want me to take you to your funeral?"

"That's just it. I don't have any way to get there."

Fairfield was about a half-hour west. It wasn't a big city, but it was big enough to draw people away from small towns such as Oglevie and big enough to draw good-sized crowds to the arena on Sunday nights.

"Are you sure you should be climbing back into the ring? I mean, maybe you're rusty for a reason. Maybe time just said, 'enough is enough' because you've had enough."

After giving Oglevie the back-and-forth and the I'll-have-to-think-about-it routine, I relented. Sunday nights were slow to dead. It wasn't as if people were lined up outside my bar to catch a cool one after praising the Lord all day. I'm not even sure there were enough folks around to muster a good Amen.

The next week, I drove Oglevie to Fairfield Arena. The place stank, as arenas always do in the off-season, with the smell of sweat and refrigeration coolant from the ice plant. There is always a ghost in an empty arena, a spirit of seasons past and seasons to come, that is caught between lost hopes and bright dreams. In the middle of the surface where the Fairfield Fire played hockey after the snow fell in late October, the organizers had set up the canvas and ropes, and when I ran my hand across the surface to see if the mat was forgiving to knocked-out fighters, I could smell the odd aroma of blood and bleach.

The first two bouts didn't last long. Some club from the city eight hundred miles away had bused in their ringers. The local guys tried to fight but they didn't stand a chance. Before the third bout got underway, a pimply local kid who I am certain was punching above his weight walked to the center of the ring, raised his right glove, and shouted, "We who are about to die salute you." The kid knew what he had coming. He lasted fifteen seconds before his coach emerged from the corner and dragged the body by an arm and a leg to his corner the way I'd seen a man pick up the corpse of his dog from the middle of the highway.

Oglevie's moment was next. I walked over to his corner. There was a guy with him in the ring who I'd never seen before and, as I tried to ask Oglevie if he wanted to go through with the punishment, the 'coach' told me to get lost.

"I'm his friend," I said. "I'm only trying to help him. I don't want to see him get hurt. These guys from the city – they're just killing the farm boys to run up their bout count."

Oglevie shrugged. The bell rang.

At the end of the first round, Oglevie was bleeding badly and spat his mouth guard into his glove. The 'coach' who had been brought in by the organizers stuffed rolls of dental cotton up Oglevie's nose, patted him on the back as the bell rang, and said, "There he is. Go get him."

Oglevie lasted five rounds. He punched hard. He landed some good blows. When he was hit, a spray of sweat and blood from his head flew into the seats. He was giving the audience a spectacle, a carnival of pain and catastrophe, and I sat there wondering how much punishment my guy could take.

I am certain the fifth round went too long. By the time the bell should have rung, Oglevie was doubled over, yet he kept taking a pounding, refusing to leave his feet. No matter how defiant his body was, I saw his eyes close, not wincing but calm as if he had fallen asleep beside the stream that ran back of his old gymnasium. He was smiling. His mind wasn't in the ring. His mind was dreaming of the willows and the brook, the cool breeze on a sweltering summer evening that rustled the drooping fronds, and for an instant, I wondered if he had become one of those willows in his mind as the relentless battering tore into his ribs and upper gut and knocked the side of his head backward and forwards and side to side.

Then, he fell.

He was still smiling when he hit the canvas.

At two in the morning, he woke in the recovery room of the hospital. I had volunteered myself as next-of-kin because as far as I knew he had none. He was alone in the world with his pain and his stoic resolve, and both had almost killed him.

His mouth was stuffed with cotton. His body was swaddled in white bandages and his eyes were black and swollen and surrounded by a puffy face twice its size and he tried but could not sit up. I told him I'd stick around and keep him company. I had no idea a human being could have so many broken things inside him, but Oglevie set a record for Fairfield Hospital.

Each day for the next three weeks, I closed the bar for the afternoon and made the drive to Oglevie's hospital bed. He told me how much he appreciated me being there. I told him being alone was no fun. He'd nod and we'd stare at each other, me in the corner chair and Oglevie propped up in an antiquated steel-tube hospital bed. We didn't say much. I didn't know what to ask and if I found something to ask him, he'd shrug. He probably didn't know how to answer. That's what friends do. They share silences.

When he was released, we had a long, silent drive back to our town, but just as we approached the outskirts as the sun set over the fields where the harvesters were making their way through the green legumes and the yellow canola, he asked if we could go by The Horseshoe so he could have a beer. He reached into his jacket pocket and pulled out a stack of twenties.

"I'm good for a while."

"You almost got killed," I said. "Is that money worth your life?"

"It's not the money. It's the fight. Everyone dies making a living and some of us work hard at getting ourselves killed."

We laughed. I opened the bar, turned on the television, lit the small, yellow, buzzing neon *OPEN* sign in the window, and pulled him a draught. As he sat there, I realized Oglevie, the town and the man, hadn't changed. Both took a pounding. Both embraced pain and loss and degradation in one form or another, and both picked up where they left off, no better for having won a victory no one cared about and no wiser for having suffered a defeat.

I was open the next afternoon and Oglevie sat on his perch. He'd moved in upstairs. The baseball season was nearing its end. The crops had come in. Things were changing in their changeless ways as they always did.

"Good to be back?" I asked.

He shrugged. "Sure, I guess." He was focused on the game. That final bout had rearranged his nose so that his profile was only complete when he turned his head to the right. I wanted to tell him I hoped he wouldn't fight anymore, if only for his own good, but figured he didn't want to hear that from me. A fighter is a fighter, not just for a month or a year or as a passing fancy but for his entire life, and the hardest bout is usually the last one, the final leg on the journey home when the universe targets the noblest of fighters and tries to tear them apart. If they are lucky, they land on the shores of home, battered, broken, with nothing to show for where they have been other than the experience they've taken in along the way. Oglevie had taken a battering. The universe had done its worst. Now he was home.

I didn't know where the question came from, but he asked me, "Why is this place called The Horseshoe? I don't see a lot of luck around here."

I shrugged. "Maybe because I keep faith with the absurd notion that the horseshoe my uncle nailed over the bar *is* lucky, that it is pointed in the right direction and that it is holding something in store, building up its magic so someday things will change, that I will change, and my life will change."

Oglevie winked at me. "Don't lose faith," he said.

When he finished his second beer, I asked him if wanted another and he put his hand over the top of the glass and said he'd had enough, that there was something he had to do, and if it didn't work out, he'd be back on the stool in half an hour and if it did he'd see me around. Oglevie turned and waved goodbye. I'd never seen him do that and I was concerned for him. Though I had gotten to know him, I couldn't read him. Maybe his face was too altered for me to see the signs of what he was thinking or the smile in the corners of a mouth too damaged for me to see.

It was dark inside the bar and the sun was in full blaze outside on a hot autumn afternoon – the kind of day that blinds a person and makes them squint until their eyes adjust. I could see the heat shimmering off the sidewalk. I decided I'd see where he was going so I hung my head out The Horseshoe's front door.

Oglevie made his way along the block and stopped in front of the bakery, one of the few businesses still open in town. The owner bakes breads and cookies and displays local crafts such as pottery and scarves. She knits and weaves during the winter when the remaining residents of the town don't venture out much.

There is a sign above the place, *Oglevie's Pennies-a-Cup*, because besides selling bread, lemon squares, and crafts by local artisans, the bakery also has a few tables where a person can sit down, grab a sandwich, and sip a cup of coffee. It is brightly lit. The sun pours in through two display bay windows.

For some reason, the owner displays a sailboat in one bay window though we're nowhere near any significant body of water, and in the other bay presents a large dollhouse. Every month she rearranges the tiny furniture and gives a prize of a free coffee and lemon square to the first person who can tell her what's different about the tiny house. She's a small woman who is very fussy and who polishes each table with a white linen cloth the moment someone comes in and sits down. I asked her once why she kept the doll house in the window.

"It's for dreams to live in," she said very matter-of-factly.

"And the sailboat?"

"That's for when my dreamboat will return."

"What's your dream boy like?" I asked.

"He's got the loveliest eyebrows. They're so expressive when he talks. And when he smiles his eyes light up and the corners crinkle with sunshine."

"Good luck in this town," I told her. "There's the guy over on the bank stoop just waiting for someone to take him in."

She sighed. "That old man's been my suitor every day. He comes in and sings to me. Sometimes he brings his friend, and they sing but they're rowdy and I don't let them in anymore. I just have to keep saying no. I tell him lies and when he thinks he's caught me out on something I unweave the fabrications and start an entirely new line of fibs."

I haven't eaten there. Something about the owner who is a baker and weaver who keeps a tiny house for dreams to live in doesn't sit right with me. When people come into The Horseshoe, they come to get away from life, but I know they can't go far because all the hard realities follow them in the door. I've got one wall decorated in old wasp nests which are kind of frightening but make for good conversation pieces, and another wall where I display my collection of ax heads that I've picked up at farm auctions and lane sales.

There's a darkness to my place, a darkness where folks can hide and are not seen if they don't want to be. No one knows if they're there. They can put some coins in the jukebox and the loud music drowns out their conversation. They play sad songs, the kind of songs someone would sing if they were in a state of despair or drunk and regretful, though I don't let the drunks leave in their cars. There are no dreams in The Horseshoe, only illusions. I had a fruit machine for a while, but the government people made me take it out. It left a blank spot on the wall where it stood and black rubber ring marks on the floor. I don't recall anyone ever getting lucky.

But when I went to the door, blinded at first, and looked down the street to see where Oglevie was going, I saw him standing in front of the bakery window. He appeared to be talking through the glass, pointing, and gesturing to someone on the other side and nodding enthusiastically. I could see a hand reach into the dollhouse bay and hold up a miniature bed as he nodded enthusiastically as if to say, "Yes, that's it, that's the secret I've been hiding in plain view," and then, seeing his reflection in the glass, Oglevie straightened his jacket, ran his fingers through his hair to make himself presentable, hiked up his belt, and went inside the bakery to claim his prize.

The Promised Land

All the houses on Oppenheimer Crescent contained some form of homage to the bomb. The bomb had its own sense of style. Atoms were beautiful. They were small models of the solar system. Planets revolved around the sun the way electrons revolved around the nucleus of an atom, only faster – so fast no one could see them, though everyone knew they were there.

Atoms were evident in schoolyard games where someone in the middle of a circle would reach out and touch the others as they ran amok as near to the center as they dared go without being tagged 'it.' If someone were caught by the person in the center, everyone would yell "Boom!"

Toby wanted to play Atom hockey after he finished hockey school and learned not to skate on his ankles. If he was good, he could go on to Atoms where boys could skate and pass and never fought their way across the ice on the edges of their skate boots. Atoms could stickhandle. They were cool. At the end-of-season dinner, the Atoms were awarded jackets with the team crest on them. Novices were only given sew-on felt patches that came apart in the wash. Being an Atom carried a sense of permanence.

Everywhere Toby looked in his house, there were visual homages to the atom, as if the home were a temple where the particle was worshipped. The cutlery they used to put food in their mouths had three starbursts of exploding atoms on the handles. The chandelier beneath which they ate their meals was a large nucleus with brass tubes surrounding the center, and on each brass tube shone electrons of glowing energy that came from power generated by a nuclear reactor. The banister uprights on the staircase were metal rods piercing grey wooden spheres. The sad part of atoms, Toby thought, was that they had to be destroyed to release what was inside. They were the sad-eyed piñata donkey that seemed so helpless and trusting at the birthday party. Atoms were the toys the universe had already outgrown and set out on garbage day.

The terrazzo floor in the front hall was inlaid with a design of an atom being shattered by jagged lightning bolts of inexplicable electricity – a reminder as he left the house every day that he could unleash the future, though he would have to discover how to split an atom to unleash the time it held.

The bomb that shattered the oxygen atom had leveled cities and ended wars, though no one mentioned how many had died in the momentary flashes above the Japanese cities or the few whose ashen shadows remained on the walls when the dust settled. Now, the hydrogen atom was being split in tests in the desert of Nevada. The skies glowed orange at sunset as they never had before. Something wonderful was happening every day.

His mother was expecting again. Toby was the oldest. He had a sister, Clara, who was warned not to be obnoxious – whatever that meant – when she teased Toby because she didn't understand what it meant to be the oldest child in the family, and Dougie who was his younger brother who loved watching medical shows and swore he would become a doctor. Dougie wasn't much fun to play with. A great uncle had given him a stethoscope and when they played soldiers in the backyard, Dougie wanted everyone to be wounded so he could listen to their hearts. Most of the neighborhood kids would tolerate Dougie for a little while, but when they were shot by the lousy Krauts, and Dougie insisted they lie still and be treated, they became impatient with him.

The family lived on Oppenheimer Crescent in a knot of suburban avenues with names such as Little Boy Drive and Niels Bohr Circle and Ernest Rutherford Way. His parents moved to Oppenheimer Crescent when the subdivision opened during the Cold War when the world divided like a shattered atom into the Communist East and the Capitalist West and could, at any moment, explode into a thanatotic cataclysm.

Toby's father was an architect. He had designed the subdivision, and the pattern of intertwining streets was meant to mimic the coils of a brain. "Everyone is going to need brains," their father told them, "if we're going to survive the Cold War." And if a war was cold, did that mean other wars had been hot? Toby imagined flashes coming out of the barrel of a gun the way it did on the cowboy shows he wasn't permitted to stay up and watch, though his father said his favorite program was Gunsmoke.

Toby heard one of the older neighbors say, "If there's smoke, there's fire." The man was a veteran who sat on his porch and chain-smoked. Most of the parents told their kids to stay away from Stan because he'd suffered a breakdown during the war, and they weren't to ask him about it in case he became violent. A pair of army boots sat just inside the door of Stan's garage and were filled with cobwebs. And if the previous wars had been fought with guns, the one now would be fought with atomic bombs. It didn't make sense. "The war was cold," Toby's father said, "because no one wanted to fire first. The first to fight will be obliterated."

Toby was told he was a lucky boy to grow up in the free world, watched over by the power of mass destruction, and oh how he wished God would hear his words of thanks as they bowed their heads for grace around a dinner table each evening lit by the eternal glow of a chandelier wrought in the shape of a nucleus with electrons of bright, unshaded Christmas tree bulbs spinning around it to enforce the metaphor that energy was light. Let nothing betray our way of life and our path to eternal light, his father intoned to God and Toby knew what that meant.

Each Amen left a strange stirring in his stomach and even farther below in his underwear as the naked Christ hung on a cross in church, a Christ who died for Toby's sins made him feel ashamed enough to crawl out of his own skin. Christ was naked when no one else was permitted to be naked in public. Christ could not be touched, though Toby wished he could be touched by Christ and feel the pleasure of the Son of God. Reverend Gill said it was a sin, but to Toby it was holiness. Oh, sweet Jesus, Toby would say as he lay on his bed in his underpants when he was changing into his pajamas before saying his prayers and humming "Jesus Bids Us Shine" until the darkness made him give up dreaming and he let the world go dark.

In school, he watched a Social Studies movie where a bald man with glasses and a clipboard explained why the children of Toby's age would never live in darkness. They had unlimited energy. Electricity was the new birthright. Light. Lots of light. Light was made by Niagara Falls pouring endless white water over the lip of the precipice and falling into the green swirl below. Water surged into shafts called penstocks to drive enormous, drowned wheels of turbines, and light would fill every corner of darkness in their lives. Let there be light!

There was oil. More oil than the students could imagine. It would power cars. Cars had fins and looked like jets or spaceships. The inside of Toby's father's car was decorated in images of exploding atoms. Gas stations with attendants who resembled soldiers in their neat and clean blue uniforms and peaked caps waited on every corner. As a car entered the gas station lot, the vehicle's tires would drive over an air hose and a bell in the station would ring 'ding-ding' and the attendant would tip the brim of his peaked cap to salute hello. And where did it all come from? It sprang uncontrollably from the ground and sprayed through a metal tower into the air. A fountain of the future. When the teacher was out of the room for a moment, Toby set the projector on reverse, and oil was sucked back into the well and everyone laughed.

And then the students were shown the ultimate vision of the future: a movie about yellow cake. The movie was titled "The Miracle of Light." Uranium was mined from deep in the Earth by men with bulldozers moving through tunnels to the rhythm of inspiring music. Those miners held the key to the future. The man with the glasses and clipboard held a palmful of flaxen crushed rock to the camera and broke the dried clod of uranium ore between his fingers and told everyone in the darkened classroom the future was nuclear energy. A woman in an apron lifted a golden cooked turkey from an oven as her children smiled. A young girl switched on a reading lamp over the shoulder of a man who was supposed to be her father, and the man smiled at her and pointed to something in the magazine because he could see now.

Then the movie cut away to a blinding light: a rising mushroom cloud swirling into the sky, parting the clouds, and spreading its arms the way naked Christ spread his arms announcing, "Boys and girls, you live in an age of miracles, and the new promised land is just beyond tomorrow because Nuclear Power is your ultimate gift." A swimming pool containing uranium rods reflected the girders of a steel-beamed ceiling and reminded Toby of the recreation center at the heart of his community. Steam rose from round cooling towers. This, said the voice from the projector, was a controlled nuclear reaction. Nuclear reactions had to be controlled. They took the beautiful little atoms and smashed them, and that destruction reminded Toby of the night his father rubbed two sugar cubes together and created a blue glow between his fingers. Nothing could unsettle Toby's world.

Yet danger was part of life whether he realized it or not. A cartoon of a smiling electron circling a happy neutron was smashed by a hammer and a light bulb glowed. Some of the kids in his class laughed, but Toby felt bad for the broken particles. They didn't deserve to be smashed. Maybe the hammer was the one the Communists used. His father had explained the Russian symbol to him – the hammer and the sickle and the violence of their image frightened Toby. The Russians wanted to smash Toby's world, and what they couldn't smash they would mow down with a sickle like the one road crews used to hack the wildflowers from the banks of roadside ditches.

The movie cut away to pictures of oval-shaped buildings standing on stilts as flying cars soared through the air. Toby knew someday he would own a flying car, and maybe he would roll back the plastic dome over the driver's seat and spread his arms and feel the wind through his fingertips just like he did when he rode his new bicycle. The future would be wonderful, and it would be made by breaking the smallest things his mind could imagine releasing their power to his bidding. Then Jesus would touch everyone. The Son of God would touch Toby's naked body so Toby could feel the joy of the Lord. Toby was afraid of burning in Hell or being burned to a cinder by the bomb, but he wasn't afraid of the burning hand of Jesus stroking him in places he couldn't talk about.

On Saturday mornings Toby and his siblings would rise early and watch static on the television and pretend they saw patterns in the black and white tweed of the empty signal until just after nine a.m. cartoons filled the major networks and they would jostle over who could turn the dial to their favorite station. There were only three stations, and each had its own programs though all of them began the morning broadcasts with either Popeye or Tom and Jerry.

Their mother didn't want them watching Popeye or The Three Stooges because she claimed the Stooges and the sailor who ate his spinach were too violent and Toby might end up in a schoolyard fight, or set a bad example for Dougie, though their father said it was good for boys to know how to defend themselves. Toby figured slapping someone in the forehead was better than poking their eyes out.

There was one cartoon they were permitted to watch, Tom and Jerry, where the cat always got the worst of it when the mouse handed the feline an exploding bomb and after he blew up, he played a harp all the way to cat heaven as he flew on tiny wings. There was never any tune. The cat just strummed. A boy down the block owned a cat and decided he could feed it firecrackers because he'd seen that on Tom and Jerry, and when he said his cat went missing Toby and his siblings knew what had really happened to the pet and that the boy was a liar who would burn in Hell.

Peace and violence were woven into the tangled tapestry of a life everyone told them they were lucky to live. Peace and violence were the reasons there was a bomb. The bomb kept the peace. No one ever dreamed it would be dropped on them, and violence was so innocent, so kind that it only happened to cartoon characters, though the cat that belonged to the boy down the block was the exception none of the other kids wanted to talk about. Peace and violence were the reason they were shown short movies in their classrooms, films not about oil or even nuclear energy where light bulbs could explode into mushroom clouds and wipe out entire cities, but instructional stories about how they could survive a nuclear attack.

Each day, without warning, Toby's teacher would shout "Duck and cover" and all the students would clamber under their four-legged desks and pull their chairs in front of the kneeholes to protect them from the blinding light. One child upset his chair during a drill when the principal came in to observe, and he was taken to the office and returned to the classroom with tears in his eyes and the palms of his hands tucked into his armpits. "Duck and cover" was a serious matter. The principal told them they had been timed on a stopwatch and Toby's class was slow.

"If this was a real nuclear attack, you would go up in flames before your teacher finished telling you to cover."

Toby asked his father if this was true. His father nodded without looking up from his evening paper and his pipe. The tobacco in the bowl of the briar glowed bright orange with every draw his father made before exhaling smoke out the other side of his tight lips. Toby wondered if that would be the way he and his family would die.

"I wouldn't worry about it, dear," his mother said. But when Toby brought her the Saturday paper with an aerial picture of an intersection in the downtown of the city, he read the bold headline above the front-page image on it: The Damage from a Nuclear Bomb. Circles emanated from the point of possible explosion. He sat down at the kitchen table and asked if the point in the middle of the photograph was where the bomb was actually going to fall. His mother shook her head.

"That's only speculation," she said.

On the following Tuesday morning in Toby's class, the teacher kept leaving the room and talking to other teachers as they paced up and down the hallways. Toby's teacher insisted the blinds be kept shut, and he surmised she was afraid the Russians would look in and ogle her. There was a problem coming to a head in the Atlantic, the teacher explained. The President had told the Russian leader to turn back the boatloads of missiles bound for Cuba because "They could kill every one of us if they got that close." The Russians were stalling for time, and a boy named Kevin who sat in the backroom made a joke as he repeated "No, the Russians are Stalin for time," and only Toby and a few others got it. Kevin was sent to the principal's office and hadn't returned when another teacher appeared at the classroom door, a young man who played the autoharp and sang folksongs at school assemblies. He pointed to the students and, looking at Toby's teacher, Miss March, said "It's time to go."

Miss March panicked. She stood up on her chair and shouted "Everyone run home! Now!" The girls in the class began to cry. The boys, who didn't grasp what was happening, looked shaken. Toby knew the score. The classrooms emptied. Students tripped on the stairs and others stampeded over them. Toby decided to take his time. It was a beautiful fall day. The air was clear, and the leaves were just beginning to turn red on the boughs of the maple trees. If the world was going to end, he decided, he was going to take it all in and try to remember it, not with sadness but with love. There were flocks of birds still straggling south – goldfinches, cardinals, a woodpecker high in an old tree who was hungry and kept knocking at the infested trunk for carpenter ants and small larvae.

He walked past the windows of a large room directly beneath the gymnasium. Behind the caged glass, he could see hundreds of students, some being ill to their stomachs, seated in rows with their heads between their knees. Some of the teachers were crying, others were shouting. Dougie might be down there, and he was worried for his little brother, but when he knocked at the door the janitor who answered told him to go home.

"Not without my brother," he said to the janitor.

The janitor hollered Dougie's name and his little brother appeared at the top of the stairs.

"You can't really leave," the janitor said. "Only Grades Four, Five, and Six can go. I guess they figure they'll survive the blast because you're older."

"You can't stop me," Toby said defiantly glaring at the sweating, bald man who was still holding a mop as if he expected to be able to clean up after the Russians dropped the big one. Clara should have left as well. She was a year behind Toby, but she was a fast runner and a scaredy-cat, and Toby figured she'd be home by now.

As the brothers made their way along the deserted streets, Toby remarked that it was as if the whole world had disappeared, and they were the only ones left. Ahead, on the sidewalk of the empty street, they saw another small boy. Dougie recognized him from his kindergarten class. Like Dougie, he didn't have a coat on. The boy turned down a side street.

"Maybe I should have stayed behind," Dougie said. "The kids in the basement were being ill. I wanted to help them but there was nothing I could do for them. I asked a teacher to give them water and he told me to shut up."

"That's typical," Toby said.

"I thought I saw Clara's legs running by the window," Dougie said. "Tobes, is the world going to blow up? That's what the teachers were saying."

"If it does, it does. Hey, maybe we'll get wings like Tom on the cartoons. Hate can't kill us." Toby paused for a moment. "I don't know why I said that last part. Maybe it's because Mom always says we're being killed by kindness."

For the first time in his life, Toby felt close to his little brother, protective yet not affectionate. He didn't want to hug him, not like he wanted to hug the naked Jesus in church. He wanted to be the big brother who would say everything is going to be alright, but no matter how hard he tried, it just wasn't in him.

When they arrived home, there was a note from their father addressed "Dear Kids" on the kitchen table. "Have taken your mom to hospital. The baby is coming sooner than we thought. Mrs. McGill said she will feed you supper if she hasn't already left for her cottage. Go down in the basement and stay there. Love, Dad."

"What are we going to do?" asked Clara with tears in her eyes. One white knee sock had drooped into her saddle shoe and her chin was covered with crumbs from the cookies she'd gotten into as soon as she arrived home.

"I'm going to ride my bike," said Toby.

"You can't. Dad told us to go down in the basement. If you go out, you'll be blown up," Clara pleaded. "You can't leave us here."

"If I get blown up," Toby said, "you're coming with me whether you like it or not.

Besides, the McGill's car is gone. I don't think they wanted to stick around if the bomb is coming. I'm going to ride my bike. There's not a car on the street. C'mon. It will be fun. Let's go out and enjoy the world while we still have it."

"That attitude," said Clara, "will be the death of you someday. Those are Mom's words. The death of you."

But Toby didn't wait. He was on his bike with Dougie peddling for his life after his big brother on his smaller bicycle with training wheels attached. Clara went to the basement with her Barbies.

That was the evening time stood still in the promised land.

On that October night when everything was on the verge of being lost and the only thing that was lost was innocence, the world began again but in a different way. Toby knew he and his brother and sister had been tapped on the shoulder by an angel and summoned to that moment, that place where everything was almost perfect and where all perfections were only brilliant and wonderful because they were doomed to fail, perhaps not as others imagined failure heaped among the cinders of a shattered world, but a place of defeat where dreams grow so large that they cannot endure for long. That night Toby imagined he could fly.

He got up a head of speed at the crest in the road where Oppenheimer Crescent flowed downhill toward Payne Way, a street of larger, posher homes that ran astride a dark ravine. Spreading his arms and closing his eyes, for the first time in his life, Toby took his hands off the handlebars and felt as if everything in his life had been foretold – the autumn sunset darkening around him, and that one, brief shining moment he felt what it was to be Jesus, naked on his cross, flying up to heaven or as close as anyone can come to it without being turned away.

Urineworts

WHEN WE WERE LIVING in the mining community, a place that is now a ghost town with nothing left to show for everyone's hard work except curb cuts for the long-lost driveways and a pine tree that has grown up between the arms of a carousel clothesline, I was told to stay away from the ditches.

The ditches had been cut out from the granite by the same jackhammer men who carved our basements from the rock. The ditches were meant to carry away snow and rain run-off. Farther down the block from our house, there was a patch of stone that resembled the pages of a book, a series of layers where the quartz butted up against the feldspar and the feldspar was overlaid with schist.

We used to stop our bikes in front of that patch of stone. On our street, the only street in town, there wasn't much else to notice except the mine-head at the end. Our fathers dug for uranium. They all died of lung cancer. They all smoked, and every man was radioactive to his dying day.

We begged our mothers to send us to summer camp. We'd seen kids on television paddling canoes and swimming in roped-off areas protected by floats. We tried to argue our case one Wednesday afternoon as the women gathered for their weekly bridge club. They were bored, too. One of the women, her lips over-pasted with bright red lipstick and her hair curlers covered in a kerchief, looked up from her hand as a cigarette dangled a long droopy pip of ash and said, "Kids, you live in summer camp. Go play in the woods and leave us alone."

One day a boy named Jerry whose father got crushed not long after that in a cave-in, hollered that he had a porcupine trapped on his front lawn. His chained dog was snarling at it.

Any other kid would have dragged his dog inside, but Jerry found it strategic. He stood waving his arms at the spiny creature, and between the dog and the gang of us who showed up, we tried to trap the poor quilled animal.

Instead of the thing just giving up, it ran straight for the ditch and dove in head-first. Just like that. It splashed about in the water, but porkies are supposed to float. Their quills contain air that buoys them up. They're meant to float. This one didn't. It may have gotten tangled in some brush beneath the surface. After a few minutes it grew still and floated with its face down in the green murk of street run-off.

Someone said something along the lines of "Now look what you've done," and we were all suddenly frightened and ashamed as if we'd killed someone's little brother. The animal just floated there. It wasn't pretending. We had trapped it and left it no way out.

Another guy suggested we get a shovel and haul it out because the quills were valuable and we could strip the bark off a birch in the bush and make baskets for our mothers, but no one wanted to touch the creature. We got on our bikes and rode away to the edge of a cedar clump and sat smoking some cigarettes we'd swiped.

Our fathers didn't know where the smell came from several days later. They talked on their front lawns, cigarettes dangling from the corners of their mouths and their hands in their pockets between puffs. They'd stand that way for hours, one saying something and the others listening and nodding then going silent until after a long pause someone would say something else. They looked defeated. But the smell. That gave them something to talk about until it, too, deserted them.

The next spring the melt lifted the water level in the connected ditches, so the run-off lapped at the lawn, and when the small flood subsided, in what was merely a foot of water rather than three or four, yellow flowers bloomed. They floated on the surface, bright and spring-like, and when one of our dads caught us pissing in the ditch because we didn't want to break our activity and go inside or go in the woods, he shouted that we were only adding to the problem, that we were making urineworts and they were a sign of putrid water. I'd seen them growing in the slug murk along the highway. But they weren't a sign of boys taking a leak or even of the tealeaf suspension of spring that had nowhere to go, but the porcupine speaking to us from the depths where his body settled, and he was saying he'd become a hundred wonderful small lives and each one was bright as the sun.

Warmth

You ask him how cold it was, and he replies by telling you how it sounded. Cold air makes a rushing sound. Even on clear November days when the leaves are off the trees and machinery from the farms shut down and there is nothing in particular to be heard, he says you can hear cold air.

You ask him what he heard during the three days he was lost in the woods, and he insists it was the sound of wind.

Wind howls as it shakes the trees.

No, he says. It is a different sound. It is the sound of someone shushing you to be quiet. Like a librarian, if you break the silence. It is a sound that tells you to listen. Cold air, he says with a certainty in his voice because he is a doctor now, is the same sound you hear if you put a stethoscope to your right arm and listen to the tide of your blood in the veins. He says it is the sound of loneliness. He says it is the sky trying to talk to anyone who will listen.

Ask him why he wandered off from the back forty of his family farm that autumn he was four. At first, he has a hard time remembering. He wants to say he doesn't know why now, but after a moment of thought the memory returns. He'd never been to the woods before. He guesses it was curiosity.

Then he turns his head and looks out his kitchen window. You can tell from the way his eyes stare into the field behind the farm that he is back in the woods. His body is shaking, his teeth are chattering. The temperature has dropped, and he feels the cold in his bones. He is about to go to sleep. He is frightened and calls out for his mother, then his father, but the wind rushes his words away. No one hears him.

The full moon is bright. He has just enough light to see by. That's when he sees it. Two eyes. Two moons. The outline of white teeth. He hears the growl of a coyote padding toward him, crouched in the hunt position. He'd seen the farm dogs almost kneeling in the same stance. Just before they leap and tear at something, their knees bend beneath the weight of their bodies to give more power to their attack.

He'd heard coyotes howl at the western edge of the farm. Their cries, he says, were haunting, painful. They wanted something badly. There's a lot of hunger in the woods, more inner ache in the bodies and limbs of coyotes than anyone can measure. But he had never seen one up close. Not until then. Long legs. A shaggy, grey-mottled coat. The tail up like a question mark. The hackles raised on the back of the creature's neck. Jim tells you he was frightened. You nod in agreement. You would be, too. The noises in the forest had bodies and a body is always hungry.

When the Provincial policeman found him, Jim was in a stupor from the cold. The constable asked him if he was all right. Jim nodded. Then the officer said the oddest thing, and Jim repeats it. He stood next to Jim and said, "God, kid, you stink. You stink of something I shot once."

Jim wakes up in his bed. He is wrapped in layers of blankets. His father pats his head and tells him he has to thaw out. The officer is standing at the foot of the bed. "Son," says the constable, "you are lucky to be alive. I'm not going to ask you why you wandered off. I just want to know: how did you manage to stay alive for three days? It's bitter cold out there."

Jim opens his eyes a little more. He says he wasn't alone. He had a friend.

"What kind of friend, son?" The policeman looks over at the child's parents. They are visibly concerned. The officer thinks Jim could have been molested. The smell on the boy's coat could be the stench of a vagrant's odor. That odor hangs on the vagabond.

It is the smell of rotting flesh, the scent of a person who has been outdoors in the cold too long. The smell of madness and depravity.

"A friend came and kept me warm," Jimmy tells the officer.

"Who exactly was this friend? Did he touch you?"

"Yes sir," Jimmy replies. "He came right up to me. He wrapped himself around me with his arms. He chased away a coyote that was about to attack me. He protected me."

"Can you describe what he looked like, Jimmy?"

"He was big. He had a big coat. He kept me warm with his body."

"What was the friend wearing?"

"Wearing? I don't remember. Maybe he had a hat. I lost mine in the woods."

The policeman closes his notebook and turns to Jim's mother and father.

"I'll come back when the boy's a bit more with us. I think he's hallucinating from the hypothermia. We need to investigate this. In the meantime, I'll put out a bulletin about indigents in the area. If the boy says anything about his 'friend', call me immediately. The doc says there's nothing wrong with the kid other than exposure from being out in the cold too long. But I'll come back tomorrow in any case. Let the boy thaw out for a while and get some shut-eye."

* * *

On October mornings just before dawn, a fog would hang over the mown stubble of the Davvy's cornfield. The earth looked like the head of a madman who'd cut his hair too short. The rows had been mown to their roots and the stalks had been carried away to be chucked in the silo as winter feed for the cattle.

You ask Jim about the woods. What were his first memories of them? What did he know about the bush before he wandered into it and went missing for three days? Did he remember being found? There'd been a manhunt for the boy.

Jim laughs at the word 'man-hunt.' He says it is a misnomer. Animals are hunted. People aren't or shouldn't be. He thinks of it as a search. Forty men walking up and down the dirt concessions on the last working days of the autumn before the snow fell. Days they could have been mending fences or trolling their fields for erratics that had surfaced during the growing season.

Then he pauses and tells you he would wake early on those autumn mornings and hear gunshots from the woods. The bursts of fire would crack and echo. Hunters. They were shooting deer. Jimmy's father wouldn't let the hunters set up a blind at the edge of the property. He was afraid a stray bullet might pick off one of his cattle or worse one of his family. Everyone had a story about a stray shot going through a window and lodging itself in a wall or a family portrait of a dead uncle.

The hunters would wait in the woods for a shadow to move among the trees. Then, they'd fire. Sometimes they weren't sure what they were shooting at. More than one story made the rounds about a lawyer from the city who shot his partner by mistake and made out it was an accident, then married the partner's widow.

The gunfire reminded Jimmy of someone snapping a branch over their knee, or the sound of ice giving way in the spring on the stream that ran fifty yards back of the barn and threaded its way to the woods.

The sun isn't up. There are gunshots in the October half-light. He thinks hunters are shooting cranes again. Jimmy had found a dead one lying in the field, one eye blown out or snatched away by a mouse or a mole. The bird lay motionless with one wing extended and pointing to the forest. Its feathers were disordered as if it had put up a fight for life when it died.

Cranes always stopped on their way south after the crop had been cut down. Their long necks and thin legs would be silhouetted in the fog. You ask him if he was haunted by the memory of the dead crane. He shakes his head. But then he adds that in the fog, as he saw them early in the morning from his bedroom window, they reminded him of Martians he'd seen in a comic book.

You are still curious why he wandered off into the woods. You need to establish this before you can get him to talk about what happened there in the rush of cold wind and the leafless fingers of the trees.

He was ashamed that the new ski jacket he'd gotten for his birthday had been fish-hooked by the barbed wire. He says that one of his greatest fears during those three days in the cold was the image of his mother scolding him and his father hitting him as punishment for tearing his clothes

Jim tells you that he'd been warned about the woods. He only learned the truth about them years later when he was trying to piece together his memories of those three days. Fact from fiction, people told him. A person can't go around telling lies or living in a dream world.

The trees are much larger now. The forest is denser. But when Jim was four, when he wandered into the bush, it was still a piece of land in transition. A place no one wanted. A haunted place. His great grandfather had known the man who once owned it. John Smith. Jim repeats "John Smith" as if it is the punchline for a joke. The name probably reminds him of a Nobody or an Everyman.

John Smith and Jim's great grandfather had gone to war together. John Smith, Everyman, soldier, and Cpl. Reported missing in action. Returned from being missing to active duty without proper explanation. Gone for three weeks. Claimed to his commanding officers that he had been trapped behind enemy lines in a shell hole. Lived rough in the cold. Commanding officers were about to issue a court-martial with the death penalty against Cpl. Smith. Shell lands on Battalion HQ. All officers killed. Records unavailable. Smith and Davvy, the last remaining members of their brigade, are promoted to help break in new arrivals. Reinforcements expected. Robert Davvy. Pvt. turned Cpl. Farmer and neighbor of John Smith Sgt. mentioned in dispatch for conspicuous gallantry. Details unaccounted. Location lost with company records.

Jim has the large, black but worn Bible on the table. He passes it to you. Pressed between the pages are yellowed newspaper clippings about Jim's disappearance. The pages are foxed. The spine is cracking. The covers are barely holding on.

Cpl. Davvy. Killed in action. 07/10/17. The notes are recorded in the back leaf of the Davvy family Bible. Birth and death dates of family members are listed in columns inside the front cover. The back cover is for family history or what anyone knows of it. The back material has a quality of editorial to it that facts simply cannot convey. That's what Jim's father would read to him. That was family history.

You ask Jim what happened to John Smith.

John Smith owned the lot that became the forest where Jim went missing. The Smith Parcel. Smith survived the war in body but not in spirit, Jim says. There were many men like Smith. He came back. In the middle of what is now that wood lot back there where his family's field ends, there used to be a house. Not a large one. A white, clapboard house with two windows either side of the front door. Single story. A saltbox sloping to a low-ceilinged rear kitchen. It burned down the night John Smith blew himself up. He probably blew the house up too, says Jim. The land some ancient Smith had cleared went back to weeds, then scrub growth, then low sapling trees, and then fledgling forest. That's how he knew it when he was in there, Jim says.

Were you looking for something in the forest, you ask?

Jim nods. It was haunted. He wanted to see a ghost. He'd never seen one. He thought he would meet one in the Smith Parcel.

Everyone said it was haunted. It was a place no one wanted to claim. When John Smith blew himself up, probably with dynamite but some said with a handful of German grenades he had smuggled home from the trenches, there wasn't much left of the man or his house. His left arm was missing. The place was blasted ground. No pun, he adds. Blasted ground, Jim explains, is land no one wants to farm because something bad happened there and could happen again. Everyone leaves it alone.

The fire that took the house and an outbuilding with an old horse in it lasted for three days. You mention it because you saw the write-up of the tragic event in the local newspaper when you were researching Jim's story.

Jim shakes his head. Is that what you call a tragedy? He's seen far worse in the emergency wards of the hospitals where he has worked. Tragedies are more than stories of people who go mad and then destroy themselves. They involve helpless victims. They involve people who cannot change the circumstances happening around them. Or the aftermath. The grieving. The terrible outpouring of emotions that compound suffering. Tragedies are about suffering that lingers.

John Smith cleaned up after himself. There wasn't much for anyone to find. He wanted to obliterate himself. He was thorough. The tragedy was in the land itself, in the forest, the crater where the house had stood, and in the low stone wall that had been the foundation of the outbuilding where the horse had perished because it was tethered by chains to a post. John Smith had strung coils of barbed wire around his house.

You ask Jim why he thinks Smith had to use the wire.

Jim shrugs. Maybe Smith saw life as a battle he could not stop fighting.

Maybe he was protecting himself. Fortifying his position. Waiting for the world to attack or counterattack. But who knows? Fear frightens a person more than danger, Jim says. Fear comes from what one doesn't see. Doctors aren't afraid when someone comes into the ER. They look at the situation. They triage the patient. They are prepared to do what needs to be done. They respond with training. Train long enough at something and it becomes instinct. Animals apply every bit of knowledge they learn. So do soldiers unless something goes wrong with them in their heads.

You ask about the woods the day his younger self went missing.

There was a coyote that was about to attack, Jim says. At first, the sound of the animal frightened him because he couldn't see where the creature was or what he was doing. When he finally saw the long-legged, mangy thing, he wasn't afraid. He was uncertain. He hadn't learned what to do or how to respond to what he saw, but he was trying to learn. At the age of four, a person is afraid of different things than those they fear when they are older. And they fear them in different ways.

The coyote was hungry. But even though the animal was about to leap, even though his teeth were bared and he was growling and drooling, and in the moonlight, the drool from the creature's mouth was visible and almost silver, that's terror but probably not fear.

So, you ask, what is fear?

Fear is when a person walks into the woods knowing that the ground is spooked, that no one goes there and shouldn't go there for a good reason – because the place is cursed. Taboos exist for a reason. And then when the wind begins to speak and listening takes over, the eye is drawn upward to a cleft in the branches of a larch or a young maple, and there, growing out of the bark of the tree as if it is part of the tree's flesh is a man's withered hand, amber-colored, shriveled, with the fingernails still pale as moons that once touched life and felt their way through the world. One finger is pointing toward the deeper part of the forest. There is something in the depth of the forest that is waiting. It wants to be found. That's fear. Fear is when there is no explanation for what happens next.

* * *

On the day four-year-old Jimmy Davvy disappeared, he'd been seen playing outside the yard where a fence separated the safe home life of his family from the cornfields. He tells you he never wanted to walk through the cornfields, especially in late summer when the corn was high. He was always afraid he'd meet a mad ghost in the straight, overgrown labyrinth of stalks, even though he wanted to know what a ghost looked like. He disliked the way the corn leaves reached out and scraped his face with rough undersides that wanted to grab and tear at his skin. The one time he set foot in the corn, his father almost ran him over with the harvester and told Jimmy what a fool kid he was for not listening harder for the sound of the motor. After that, Jim had listened to everything, even the smallest sounds. He never ventured into the field until the rows had been cut down to stubble.

No one sees him walk toward the crest of the field and disappear over the fence to the bush on the other side.

On the day he disappeared, his mother described him to the police. Jimmy Davvy is four years old. He is wearing a navy-blue ski jacket, a green woolen toque with a pompon, red mittens, brown corduroy pants, and black rubber boots with orange toes.

You read him the description. He nods. It seems right, though the memory of what he was wearing is something he knows only from the stories of his disappearance.

Jim looks into his coffee mug. He sighs and tells you his mother neglects to describe the color of his hair, the hue of his eyes, or how tall he was. Those things would be forensic details. Maybe, he says, she was avoiding her worst fears. She told him, later, she thought she'd never see him again.

You ask the question again of what made him go into the woods?

He remembers standing at the field's farthest fence. He is staring into the overgrowth. The leaves have fallen. Frost has traced its pattern on every leaf and dried pod. A carpet of fallen leaves shimmers. Poking up from the forest floor are naked stalks. The forest looks magical. The stalks remind him of a picture in a book his grandfather gave him. The book contains a photograph of a man in India who sleeps on a bed of nails. The cold air rushes overhead. He is being called into the bush. The air speaks with an emptiness that wants to be filled with his presence. He isn't afraid: he wants to know what emptiness is.

He walks into the bush, not very far, but far enough to lose sight of the fence between the bush and the edge of his father's field. Twigs snap beneath his steps. A rattling in the undergrowth follows him as he moves deeper among the trunks and branches. A leafless arm reaches out and grabs the green toque off his head. He runs. He is not looking where he is running. He has not yet been told the story of John Smith. He doesn't know about the crater where the house stood or the coils of barbed wire that are still strung across the overgrowth of Smith's Parcel. He trips. He is caught by something. He falls forward, but his coat snags on a twisted metal knot with needle-sharp ends. He fights to get free and another knot catches and holds his trousers. He unzips his jacket, but another barb has pierced his shirt and he screams in pain. He is ensnared by remnants of the past.

The harder he fights to free himself, the more he is trapped. He finds himself hanging, almost horizontal, on the rusty red lines that cut and wrap him. He cries but only the cold air hears him. The rattling in the undergrowth that followed him moments before is louder now. Something is nearby. But it waits. It is patient. Like cold air. It is just there. Waiting.

The sun sets. Jimmy can see it fall into his father's field. It digs into the corn stubble and buries itself. The air grows colder and louder, too. The night fills up with the sound of the wind. Other sounds talk to it. He hears an owl. It is in the trees above him, in front of him one minute, behind him the next. The owl is also waiting. Jimmy is not sure why it is being patient. The stars appear. He feels the cold working its way inside him. He cannot do up his jacket. The zipper is torn. His right sleeve is almost severed from the coat.

He hears the sound of something moving around him again. The thing that followed him earlier in the afternoon steps on dried leaves. The leaves crackle. The thing has a scent. It reminds Jimmy of when the farm dog, a Honey Lab, got wet in the rain. The metallic tang of water on fur, but stronger. More like blood. He can smell his own blood from the cuts torn in his chest by the wire. He learns that blood has a unique odor. The thing that followed him into the deep cluster of trees can smell it, too.

The cold makes Jimmy close his eyes. He is numb. The air, the rushing sound, fills his ears and eats its way into his body. His eyes are closing as he hears a growling from the thicket in front of him. Moonlight outlines the creature.

Jimmy has seen coyotes but none living, up close. Only dead ones. His father shot one in the barnyard one night and hung the carcass up by its hind legs from a chain draped over the barn door. This is a coyote. A live one. Jimmy can see its eyes, its teeth. He wants to cry, but because he sees it, he holds his voice inside him. A shout wants to well up from his throat. The coyote approaches slowly, hunched down, in the hunt position he has seen the Honey Lab take when it stalks a rat in the barn. The animal is about to leap. Jimmy holds his breath.

A shadow leaps for the wild dog.

The wild dog reels and howls because the shadow, large and black, has bitten into the coyote's neck, tossing it aside against a tree. The thud raises a startled cry in Jimmy's throat, the cry that only a second before he was fighting to hold in. The coyote yelps, picks itself up off the ground at the root of a tree, and runs. It runs so fast Jimmy can hear it thud against other trees. The animal is panicked. It is so frightened it isn't looking where it is going.

He stares at the shadow. It is reared up on its hind legs. The outline of a bear. He sees its claws draped from the ends of its arms. They hang, pads down as the bear roars, totters two steps toward Jimmy, and then falls forward on all fours. Jimmy holds his breath. He wants to say 'No' but nothing will come out after the startled gasp. He trembles, held horizontal on the wire. He cannot move.

The bear stares into the boy's eyes. Jimmy cannot blink. He cannot breathe. For the first time in his life, he cannot feel what it is to be in his own body.

Jimmy can smell the bear's breath. Rancid yet alive. Its nostrils pour damp clouds into the cold air. He can smell the dark fur. The bear sits down on its hind haunches and waits for Jimmy to move. The boy is numb. His arms, his legs, his head, even his mouth are dead to the moment. His heart pounds in his chest.

Then, as Jim tells it without you asking him, he says he knew what the bear was thinking and is certain the bear knew what was going on in his mind. For minutes that felt like hours, they looked at each other. Neither moved their eyes. Hypnotized. Jimmy says the bear and he were one being. They were thinking about the stars in the sky to the north.

You ask him if his response was fear.

No, says Jim. It was the same feeling he had the first time he made love to the woman he married. They stared into each other's eyes. They read each other. He tells you that it sounds stupid.

You say it isn't. He doesn't believe you.

There is a long pause. Jim's coffee is cold. He gets up and pours himself another cup, holds out the carafe without saying anything, and you point to your empty cup. He pours. The black coffee steams. It reminds you of your breath on a cold night.

You ask what happened next.

Jim leans back from the kitchen table. What happened next, he asks rhetorically? He says he shivered. He describes the sting of tears welling up in his eyes as he and the bear looked not only *at* each other but *into* each other. He says it is like when someone dies and is revived in the ER. They come back to consciousness. They say they have come back into the world. They were outside themselves. They were somebody else watching themselves. At that moment, Jim says he is the bear. The bear, maybe, is him. Whatever. The bear reaches out and puts its front limbs around him and pulls the boy close.

The tug on the wire digs the barbs deeper into the boy's flesh. The bear can feel his pain. The boy knows it. He isn't sure how he knows it, but the bear is feeling what he feels. He can see it in the large brown eyes. He can see its eyes in the moonlight. They are not mad moons like the ones he'd seen glaring from the coyote's head, but soft eyes, eyes that say, "I know. I care. I can feel your pain."

The bear pushes at the barbed wire, but it will not let go of Jimmy. The more he pushes, the more pain Jimmy feels.

The bear stops. He moves close to the boy. He presses his broad, furry chest against the child and takes the boy in his arms. He wants the boy to stay alive. Jimmy falls asleep and wakes. The bear is gone. A grey line of dawn is poking through the night in the eastern sky. Jimmy is warm.

An owl stares down at the boy. That is the end of the first day.

* * *

Mary Davvy recalls the day her son went missing. Her memory is detailed. She is ninety-two now, thin, stooped, but very alert. She lives in a small house in town, having given the farm to Jim. He doesn't work the land. He's too busy at the hospital. She supposes he could raise life from the soil, but she says he prefers to raise the living from the brink of death.

She insists, as you talk to her, that it is a crime for someone not to draw life from the fields, but, she says, her son is a doctor and that is what keeps him busy.

As the kettle steams to a boil for the tea she is about to make in a big Brown Betty pot, she says she wishes Jim had remarried after his wife's accident. You don't want to pursue that line of questioning. Grief is the subject of another story. She would have loved grandchildren but realizes he is probably too old for that now.

She asks if you have children.

You tell her you have one in college. Her friends, from time to time, also live in your house. The door is always open. You tell her you never know who you'll meet when you arrive home and need quiet to write up the story you've been researching. You say it is hard to make sure all the facts get into the piece with music playing somewhere in the house, just loud enough to be distracting and just far away enough not to be able to hear the words. But the friends are all right. No boyfriends overnight. You tell her you don't like meeting boys in the hallway on your way to the bathroom in the dark.

Mary Davvy laughs. She says children are a blessing, but no one can really understand them. She gathers that part of being human is to not understand someone else at all and understand oneself even less. The mysteries of life are beyond one mind or one lifetime to comprehend. She is anticipating your questions about the three days her son went missing.

You decide to break the ice on the topic of her son's disappearance while she's philosophical, laughing at the lives young people lead and shaking her head.

You ask the question. What does she think made him want to wander off? Had he been unhappy?

He was a good boy, then adds, a normal boy. He spent a lot of time in his room. She pours the boiling water into the pot to warm it and empties it into the sink. The kettle stays on the boil. She drops in the three tea bags, stares into the pot to make sure they are settled on the bottom, and then douses them. She says she isn't one for mugs, that she was born in a time that respected teacups. It is a foolish formality, she tells you, but she thinks the tea tastes better in china cups with saucers underneath.

You want to keep her on topic. You ask what went through her mind when she realized he was missing and at what point in the day that had been.

It was a day like today, she begins.

There are many days like today, you say.

It was cold. Clear maybe. She says she wasn't paying attention to the weather until she thought about her boy being out in it. All alone, she adds. After the first day, people began to wonder if he was dead. His father wondered. He didn't say so out loud to her, but she heard him talking to the constable. They had their heads down on the porch. Muttering. Muttering is what one does when someone shouldn't overhear a painful truth.

Her son was lucky, you say. Does she have any thoughts about how he survived?

She doesn't know. All she knows is what he told her afterward. Jimmy apologized. He said, at first, he'd been lured. That wasn't a word used around the house. He'd heard it somewhere and it set off a search for someone who could lure him away. Vagabonds, buggers. People around said they saw them, but they never came near the farms, and no one in his right mind would hide out in the Smith Parcel with the intent to lure a boy there. They wouldn't have lasted long on that ground.

You ask why.

The land was tainted. She qualifies the word tainted. It was poisoned, not merely with dangers the owner had left behind, but with a kind of wrath against the world. There are places that are taboo grounds, places that do not want to be inhabited by humans anymore. That is what she means by tainted.

You ask what Jim was like as a boy.

He never liked to help his father, she says. The two never really got along. He should have been doing chores, but his father let him sit up in his room and read.

What about? you ask.

Stories about wildlife. Not talking animals, she says, but real animals. He'd stare out his bedroom window even when he was four. He'd be watching the clouds. He'd be staring at the bush beyond the fence. One day he got lucky, and a flight of sand cranes landed in the stubbled field, but he came to me crying because some hunters on our side of the fence had brought one or two down. The rest of the time? Maybe he was watching his father, but when his father disappeared into the barn, Jim would get a faraway look in his eye. He'd be staring beyond the edge of the field, at the bush Smith had abandoned after he came back from the war.

Did she remember Smith?

No. All that had happened before she was born. Blew himself up. Her father had been one of the men who tried to free Smith's horse from the shed, but they'd been driven back by the barbed wire. Her father never got over the sound of the horse.

One of the men who had gone to see if they could save Smith or his horse sent his dog through the wire, but as the animal ran, a fine collie from the stories she'd heard, the creature exploded.

Smith had mined his ground. He hadn't intended to come out of his house, and he hadn't intended anyone to go in. She spins the saucer beneath the cup, her fingers holding the gold handle. Poor dog.

After that, the men decided to walk away. The police posted *no trespassing* signs. They didn't want anyone to suffer the fate of the collie. And who knew what was in there? Smith could have set canisters of poisoned gas for all they knew. So, the Smith farm became No Man's Land, a place no one dared to go. Trees, white pines that reach a good height in a hurry, scrub poplars, larches, the kind of overgrowth that can creep over a place in next to no time, that's what the land went back to. The land heals itself, she says as she sips at the gilded rim. The land doesn't want to be worked. It wants to be its old self. Maybe that's why Jim went in there.

Because? You have to ask. She may say something important.

Because he said he heard the air. Jimmy was a distant child. She tries to clarify. Distant isn't the right word. Dreamy maybe. But he had to dream in facts. That's what made him read constantly. He had to have facts. That's what made his story all the more strange. He was drawn into the bush by the wind. He said it made the sound of a train, though there aren't any trains in these parts. He told me when he was home and thawed out and his cuts had been stitched up that he could hear the cold air in the tops of the trees and that it was speaking to him. The doctor thought we should have his mind examined. Who had the money for that? The matter was dropped. Jim seemed normal enough for a boy. His mind liked to wander, but that's imagination.

She knows what you want to ask next. You want to ask if she believed his story about the bear, but you decide to wait, to put more information on the table before you get into the heart of the narrative.

You ask about whether the men who found Jim were afraid to look there first.

They should have looked there first, she says, with a note of anger in her voice. It might have spared Jim the agony of being pinned like that for three days. My father said the sight of the boy brought back bad memories. My father had served in the war. He'd watched his friends hanging on the wire until they bled to death or got caught in a crossfire. The wire cut into him very deep. His wounds were beginning to turn black. Infected. It was lucky they found him when they did.

You ask where the search began.

In the wrong place, she says. They could have looked at the Smith place first, but they were probably afraid of it. They knew the story. Instead, they took the easy way to search for him. They drove up and down the back roads with their truck windows opened. They hollered his name everywhere a person could hear it. Then nothing. No reply. They probably drove past the Smith Parcel umpteen times, but they didn't get out and look. The sound of their motors probably muffled Jim's response. Besides, Smith's Parcel was spooked, and it spooked them.

You ask what were they afraid they might find there?

The same barbed wire that snared Jim, the mined ground, the miasma of the place that drove Smith to madness. When a piece of land becomes haunted, people stay away from it. They won't say why. After a while, they can't explain why. Do you know why you are afraid of what you can't explain? Mary Davvy asks.

You pause for a moment and look at your notes. Mary Davvy rises from the table, goes to the counter, and brings the teapot with her. She tops it with boiling water. She brings the spout close to your cup as if asking if you want a warm-up and you nod, yes. Her answers are reserved up to this point.

You need to put an idea in her head that will enable her to talk in more depth about the day her son disappeared.

You ask how she felt as the day wore on?

Worried. When darkness fell, she says, she broke down in tears. She stared out her kitchen window at the field that was disappearing into the night. She felt in her heart that her son was still alive.

Somewhere, out there in the night, he was calling to her. Perhaps his voice had grown hoarse from shouting or crying.

You already know that Jimmy Davvy did not cry, that by the time his mother watched the world around her vanish into the ink of night, her son was being comforted by a bear. So you decided to ask her the question she has been waiting for you to ask. What about the bear?

What about it? she asks.

So how did Jim survive? All the facts say he should not have.

She replies that facts are a matter of perspective sometimes. Maybe a bear did keep her boy warm. Maybe it loved him the way a mother loves her child.

You ask if she thinks the bear was real or just a story of hope and kindness that Jimmy invented to help him survive the night, the cold, grey day of light snow that followed, and the night after that when, by reason, he should have frozen to death.

Love is real, she says. The doctor, she tells you, did not believe the story about being kept warm by a bear, the hairy creature wrapping its arms around her son and holding him to its breast as if he was a newborn cub. But it could have happened. She taps her finger on her saucer. She believes her son. The one fact she clings to is not whether the bear existed or not, but that she got her boy back.

The men of the area, she says, did not believe one speck of Jimmy's story. No one in those parts in those days trusted bears. They were vermin. If an animal came into the barnyard, broke down the wall of a hen house, devoured the chickens or the eggs, they'd shoot it. If someone left a pie to cool by a screen door during the summer, a bear might break down the door and eat the pie before ransacking the kitchen. They were vandals, those animals. But she says what was more troubling was the fact that no one had seen any bears in the area for at least ten years. Maybe longer. Then, she says, there was the problem of the bear even being in Smith's Parcel.

You ask what she means by the problem of the bear on the property.

The place, she says, was mined. The death of the collie years before had proven that. She says that before they passed, the men of the county who had gone off to war swore up and down that ordinance wouldn't last, that it would rot. It lay in the earth and rusted out.

To prove Jimmy wrong, she says with a note of sadness in her voice, a man named Ralph Butcher went to the edge of the bush with a bag of rocks after her boy was home. She says Butcher had a theory. He wanted to test it. They were good size rocks, and he had a strong arm. He'd been a ballplayer in his youth, she adds. Butcher started lobbing rocks into the Smith Parcel, and after about five or six rocks, one exploded. She heard it. Her husband heard it, and so did Jimmy. The child began to cry. He thought someone had killed the bear.

About half an hour later, there was a second explosion, and then a third, and then a knock at her kitchen door. Butcher was standing there with an empty burlap sack in his hand and stepped in, laying the sack on the back porch. He said to her husband there was no way anything as large as a bear could move around in that bush without blowing itself up. The ordinance hadn't rusted away. The place was live and booby-trapped and would probably always remain that way. He asked her husband how he could believe a boy's story about a bear when the fact was that the bear could not have moved through that patch of bush.

She looks in her teacup and begins to raise it to her lips for a sip, then puts the cup back. Do you know what my husband did, she says? He told Butcher to get out. He said no man would call his son a liar, not in his house, and not to his face.

You ask if Jim ever spoke of the bear again.

Mary shakes her head.

There are things, she says, he never talks about. His wife. The three days in the bush. If he's said anything to you, he has opened up, but most of the time he doesn't. Who could blame him? He'd survived three days on the wire. Most men from the war who'd been caught in the tangle of barbed strands didn't. They'd get caught in the crossfire of friend and foe alike. But Jimmy wasn't being shot at. He was a little boy alone in a forest. Maybe fears also help to invent the ways a person can face them to survive. He had a teddy bear that he slept with each night, but after the episode in Smith's Parcel, he set the bear on a shelf in the corner of his room. He asked for an extra pillow. An overstuffed large one that had been my mother's. The kind invalids used to prop themselves up on so they could appear to be part of life when they were ill and on their way out. And every night, Jimmy clutched it.

One night when he was about six, he was running a fever from chickenpox. She says she walked into his room. He was talking in his sleep, likely delirious, and he was talking to someone he kept calling Mr. Bear. She reached down to turn her son on his back, and when she tried to take away the pillow, he sat bolt upright, his eyes still asleep but wide and wild. And do you know what he said, she asks?

You shake your head.

He said, my Mr. Bear is protecting me.

* * *

There are problems with the bear story. Many problems.

You wonder if a child's fantasy life saved him from death in the cold.

You think Butcher may have been right, that something as large as a bear could not move around in the tainted ground of Smith's Parcel.

You wonder why the bear came to Jimmy Davvy's rescue. The animal could easily have killed the boy. The four-year-old's bones, shreds of his clothing, would be discovered by a curious hunter after the snow melted.

You wonder how Jimmy survived not one night but two alone and pinioned in the bush. There are too many questions for the story to be plausible. Does a person invent ways to save himself? Is it natural for a child to say he found warmth and kindness in his moment of fear?

You are reminded of the poet Rilke who says the monsters that haunt our childhoods are simply those things that need our love. Certainly, a child, a boy Jimmy's age, lives in that odd reality that comes before the solidity of facts that exist on the cusp of imagination to stifle our dreams. Call it the need for warmth, call it the sound of the cold wind rushing through the trees. The sound of loneliness and helplessness. Call it the imagining of death where death is something that has never been seen or experienced or even discussed. Call it what you may. You have one question now. Was the bear real? And was it something to fear or something to love?

No one likes to be helpless. You have a special place in your heart for those who can step into a helpless situation, who can take charge and make something right. That's the Jim Davvy who had been reticent across from you as you sat at his kitchen table. The man of few words, but great knowledge and action. The emergency room doctor at the county hospital. You decide you want to see him in action. You want to understand not merely what he does but why he does it. Maybe he can't explain it. Maybe his medical training has made him respond to situations instinctively. That's fair. But you want to see it for yourself. You phone him back and ask him if you can come to the hospital.

At first, he says no. He tells you that you won't see any bears in the emergency room. You will see people who are ill or injured, people who are clinging to life by a thread.

You reply that he clung to life by a steel thread, that over the course of three cold days and two nights, the second far colder and less comforting for its want of stars than the first, Jimmy hung on to life. Had he learned how tenuous life is when he was trapped in the barbed wire?

He laughs. There's a pause. Then he says you can come as long as you don't get in the way. No pictures. No notetaking. Patient privacy comes first. But you can observe.

* * *

Friday nights, late at night, Dr. Davvy tells you as he greets you at the nurse's station, are the worst. He is wearing scrubs. A stethoscope, the prerequisite symbol of a doctor at the ready, hangs around his neck.

He says you have been talking to his mother. Had she cast doubt on the bear story? You tell him that she had spoken of Ralph Butcher.

Jim nods then adds *that guy*. Sure. As the old man grew older and less able to control what he said he would drive past Jim in front of the high school and shout liar at him.

You ask if that upset him?

He says no. He says he knows what he knows. Then he looks you in the eye. The bear, he says, was real. His clothes smelled of it.

You realize you hadn't asked Mary Davvy about the smell the bear left on her son's clothes. Maybe she had too much on her mind at the time of her son's return. Maybe she attributed the smell to the bush, the stench of mud that soiled Jimmy's trousers, and the scent of feces. She had policemen coming and going, neighbors dropping by with covered casseroles. She had to worry not only about her son being missing and possibly dead but didn't have room in her head for community curiosity.

In those days, Jim tells you, people weren't just individuals. They were part of the hive-mind, the township consciousness. A person couldn't put a foot or a thought wrong. It just wasn't right.

A nurse rushes up to the station and announces she has a Code Blue in cubicle six. The heart of the old man who came in earlier in the evening is giving out. You follow Dr. Davvy as he runs to the cubicle and you would enter the scene of resuscitation, but a nurse raises her hand, stops you, and draws a privacy curtain across the entry. You return to a high stool at the nursing station and wait. Two paramedics are drinking coffee. They have replenished their gurney with sheets and their supply packs with i.v. bags and are about to go back out. They are waiting for the doctor's signature on some papers.

Half an hour goes by. Dr. Davvy returns. He pats you on the shoulder and says you should have a coffee with him. You ask about the man who coded out. Dr. Davvy smiles and nods, and with a flip of his head suggests the patient is upstairs in the cardiac unit.

Machine coffee is awful, but it has enough caffeine to see staff members through the long, often silent hours of the night. Jim pulls up another stool beside yours.

You ask him, again, if he invented the bear.

There are miracles everywhere, he says. There really was a bear, but it depends on what the bear is. He says his life in the ER should have made him a cynic, but he won't give in to that. He says life is something a person fights for. There is inspiration everywhere, not just in the idea that life is precious but that everything, the land, the fields, the bush, and the wind are alive. When he was trapped, he was afraid. Maybe, he says, the bear was not a bear as we know it but a presence in the night.

You add that bears are nocturnal.

Bears, he says, watch over us, especially in the northern sky on a winter night. He tells you a story about the night, a week, maybe two weeks before he went missing, when his father walked him out to the far edge of their field, the edge that abutted Smith's Parcel. His father kneeled beside him. It was cold. The rush of the air was loud, but high in the darkness, and his father pointed to the stars, following the tracing of a shape in the sky. That was when he learned of the Great Bear, Ursa Major, a pattern in the remote lights extending beyond the Big Dipper. That was real. His father told him there was a bear up in the sky, and that the bear watches over us.

You ask why his father told him that? What had the bear in the stars meant to the four-year-old Jimmy Davvy?

Bears are great spirits, he says. They walk on all fours. They sit on their haunches just like humans. They stand on two legs like a man. They are parents to their cubs. They never let anyone or any harm come to their young. They are protective. His father said he had once tracked a bear up in the north. He'd intended to go hunting, but the longer he pursued the black bear, he told his son, the more he realized he was beholding a creature of great dignity. It had humanity. He didn't shoot it.

You ask if that was why Jim's father had sent Ralph Butcher packing? Was there a connection between the bear that saved him and the bear his father had pointed out to him in the stars? Did the story of the bear his father had seen matter that much?

Jim says it kept him alive. He says the bear was real to him. As he looked up at the night sky that first night, he traced the bear in the stars. With his one free hand as the wire held him, he could hear the night sky, the rush of cold air talking to him, and it really was talking, Jim insists.

You ask what the air was saying?

He pauses for a moment. He says the air was telling me to look up, to look beyond it, to trace the outline of the bear and to call to it, not as one calls a dog, but as one summons a spirit or calls a soul back from the dead.

Like a Code Blue, you ask?

Maybe, Jim says. The longer he looked into the sky, the more he saw of the bear until he was staring into its eyes. He says a bear's eyes are both sorrowful and sympathetic, though one never knows what a bear is thinking and should never assume a bear is thinking the best. He pauses. He says he believes our lives, our spirits, call them souls if you wish, came from that darkness, and that the stars are not merely distant lights but flickers of a warmth that keeps us alive even when we are lost to the world. In that utter despair, the emptiness of space, we see stories, creatures, parables of life here on Earth.

You ask what those parables are.

Jim smiles. They are stories, he says, of how much we love life and believe in this world even when a person is utterly alone, in a forest, or their last labored breaths. Those stories are the ones a person tells themselves even when others say they are not true. It is that warmth that refuses to leave a person even when he or she thinks that death is approaching. Dying is lonely, but only if a person cuts themselves off from the life they have been part of. There is warmth even in the coldest things and on the coldest nights. A person fights to hold on to it, to find a source for it in even the most remote places, places that are almost beyond the power of the naked eye to see or a child's hand to touch. Everything around us is calling us to listen because somewhere, even in the wind, there is a voice telling us where to look for the warmth that animates us and reminds us how much we need to fight for life and why we need to hold on even as we are held by it.

Candlemas

HARV WAS ONE OF THE VETERANS of our station. He understood fire. He could look at a building in flames and say exactly what the cause was, and the fire marshal usually proved him right. Between calls, he would sit in the kitchen while I did the dishes. The newest firefighter always does the dishes for at least the first six months, a kind of initiation. He'd keep me company while I dipped my hands in and out of the suds.

Harv would sit at the table and just stare at a candle flame. The baseball player, Shoeless Joe Jackson, would cup a hand over one eye and stare at a candle flame because he claimed the focus helped him pick up on the ball's movement toward the strike zone. Harv's reason for watching the flame gently shape into praying hands was to let fire teach him about its life. He claimed it talked to him, explained itself to him, and revealed its holy mysteries in the glow and colors. I wasn't to tell the others on the shift. I had to promise. He would have been sent for a psychiatric examination.

Every fireman has a routine as well as personal rituals. Keeping the rig in tip-top order, checking, and rechecking the lengths of hose, laying the canvas snakes to dry in the racks, mopping the floor, and checking the pressure gauges on the pumper are all part of my routine. When I wasn't busy, I read history.

But when it came to personal rituals, Harv was the master. He claimed he was a hagiologist in his spare time, someone who studies saints. He would mark on the chalkboard in the upstairs lounge what saint's day it was. He believed in intercessors. I asked him why and he shrugged, but that didn't stop him from mumbling a prayer each day to a particular saint as he wrote the name on the chalkboard to begin the shift. A litany of the saints flowed from him. And always, as he set the brush and chalk on the ledge, he would add under his breath, 'Pray for us.'

I beat him to the punch one midwinter morning. It was Groundhog Day. I put that on the board before Harv arrived. I also added, in brackets, that if we didn't get it right, we could do it all over again tomorrow. Some of the guys laughed. Cap shook his head and pointed at the board.

'You're playing with fire, kid. There is no getting it wrong.'

Then Harv appeared. He was carrying three paper bags from an all-night grocery store and laid them on the adjacent kitchen counter. He looked at the board, said nothing, and turned to me. I could tell he wasn't happy. I was messing with his ritual even before the day's routine began.

Pointing at me like his finger was a gun, he said, 'The kid's cooking breakfast today,' then motioned me over to the bags. 'Unpack and fry up.'

There were about ten packages of bacon, five cartons of eggs.

'There are more eggs in the fridge. Did your mother teach you how to cook?' he asked.

'Sure,' I said. I wasn't a great cook. I'd watched. I'd seen it done. What could be involved? Put the bacon on the pan. Turned on the heat. Cracked the eggs into a bowl. Found the large skillet in the pot drawer beside the stove. Put some oil in the pan and mixed the eggs. Salted them a bit, too. Maybe I'd add a dash of pepper. Cap was always saying he liked pepper.

I had just laid out the bacon in three pans when Harv came over to me.

'You might want to cook the bacon on a rack in the oven,' he said. 'Don't burn the place down.'

One of the crew called out, 'I bet the kid forgets to turn off the oven and burns the station down. That's all we need – be a fire station that goes up in flames.'

Harv has erased my message on the chalkboard. It now read 'Candlemas Day.'

'What's that?' I asked.

'Candlemas is Groundhog Day, but instead of a rodent seeing his shadow it was the day Jesus was presented at the temple. Consider it his graduation day, his coming of age, the day everyone agreed he was prepared. So, in honor of the day, and because you messed with my board, you're my partner today, isn't he Cap?' he called to the chief.

'Sure is, Harv. He's got to go where you go.'

'Think you're ready?' Harv asked. 'And in the middle of a burning building, there are no do-overs.'

The bell rang on the oven. The stove was up to temperature, and I put the rack into the heat. I was about to start scrambling the eggs when the alarm rang. Cap went into his office and emerged shouting 'Four alarm on Lamb Street.'

Our station used to have a pole, but it was considered too dangerous when a guy named Zeke, an older fellow, leaped toward it and forgot to hold on. We ran down the stairs and jumped into our gear as the front doors of the firehouse opened and we pulled away to the wails of our sirens.

On Lamb Street, Harv grabbed my sleeve.

'Follow me everywhere except when it becomes too dangerous. Then, do what you can to save yourself.'

Flames shot from the windows of the building, an old relic from the last century. It had been a synagogue, but the worshippers had moved to the suburbs and sold the building. For a decade or more it was a nightclub called David's. Then a developer bought it and was in the midst of transforming it into condominiums. There was talk in the area that the renovator had gone bankrupt, that the bank had called in the loan. Now it was on fire.

'Grab the hose, kid. Cap wants us in there, up the stairs if they're safe, and to start working on the blaze from the inside.'

A ladder truck from the Tenth Brigade was pouring water over the roof and hosing the walls. The first thing they teach young firefighters is never to shoot water directly into the flames. There's a risk of the liquid turning instantly to steam as the flames grow hotter and hotter, and the steam can blowback, not backdraft, but blowback at the hose man and boil him where he stands.

Inside the building, all I could see was the outline of Harv's body, slightly hunched over the weight of the hose about two feet in front of me. He radioed that he'd found the third floor partially collapsed and that's where he'd start shooting. He turned to make sure I was still with him, and I nodded.

'Happy Candlemas, kid,' he said over his radio. 'Betcha didn't think the flames would be this big.'

The flames were bigger than anything I had seen. They weren't just ahead of us but suddenly were all around us. I began thinking that this is what the Temple in Jerusalem must have been like when Titus burned it down in 70 A.D. An ancient historian named Josephus describes it. I read a lot of history in my spare time between duties on my watch, and the guys kid me that the past is going to catch up with me.

As a panel on a wall fell away, I saw a niche with a small Menorah in it. I wanted to sink to my knees and pray, but the wall collapsed. Someone, perhaps the nightclub owner, had simply paneled over it. As the candelabra melted, I was certain that letters from the Hebrew alphabet curled in the dense black smoke, a smoke darker and blacker than what was curled around Harv and me. The flames, maybe the hand of God, were writing a message to us.

The hose fattened and came alive in our hands. Harv tucked it under his left arm and pointed the nozzle at the pit in the floor. As we poured and poured on the opening, the air exploded beneath us. The building shook. I felt the hose tug forward out of my hands. I couldn't hold on.

'Get out, kid,' I heard Harv say through the radio. 'Cap, it's coming down. Kid, get to the stairs. Now!'

"Harv!" I shouted, but he vanished into the smoke. The hose moved forward as if a snake was attempting to penetrate the fire, the holy fire. Then, through a parting of smoke, as if some invisible hand had pulled back a curtain drawn across a mystery, I saw Harv. He pointed to where the floor had been. He was on one side of a gaping hole and I on the other. He pointed up. He was going to find a way to the roof because maybe he knew the ladder team could reach him there.

'Hey, kid, I hope you learned a lot today, and it's not even dawn yet. I'm going up. You go down. Looks like you still have the stairs. Go, kid!'

I turned, half-stumbling, my hands pressed against the walls of the staircase. The runners were breaking beneath my steps. The building was burning from the ground floor up, a sure sign of arson, though that didn't cross my mind at the time. I just wanted to get out. The temple was alive with the fury of wrathful Cherubim. I could see its flaming sword leap out of the walls to try and cut me, and I fought it back with my gloved hands.

I was only ten steps from the door at the bottom of the staircase. I could see my station mates motioning me forward, waving me ahead, shouting at me to keep going, when a wall of flame shot straight upward between me and the portal. It grew wings, and the wings spread like an angel barring my way. I wanted to stop. I wanted to stand there and study the pillar of fire the way Harv stared at candles. The flame was beautiful and wonderful, yet I knew it was lethal. Nothing good comes of the moments when fire stands in the way of a man.

I could have died then and there. I probably wouldn't have suffered the burns that took months to heal and left me scarred but instead, I spread my arms and ran directly at the angel, and as I passed through it, trying to wrap it in my grasp and wrestle it away, I was certain it was wrapping itself around me and trying to hold on. I held it up and then threw it to the ground. And when I emerged from the building, I was burned but I had won.

My station mates doused me with water to extinguish my burning jacket and overalls. My boots had melted. That's how hot it was. The paramedics rushed in and removed my respirator and helmet. My gloves didn't want to come off. They had become part of my skin.

Cap stood over me. 'Where's Harv? His radio went dead about four minutes ago. I can't reach him.'

I was about to say Harv was still in there when the men of the Tenth pointed to the rooftop. There was Harv, walking the crest of the Temple. Some of his gear was burning as flames poked their fingers through the shingles to reach up and grab him. Harv was about to leap up for a ladder when the roof gave way underneath him and he fell into the building.

No one gasped. Every man from the four crews just stood there, silently, wordless. A final tongue of flame shot skyward, and the crews poured everything they had on the conflagration in retribution or tears, and some sat down and wept.

Inches

I HAD BEEN PLAYING by myself at the kindergarten table that my father had made, and my mother had shoved into a corner of our living room. It had a good view of the television, so when my mother was upstairs with a headache and the bottle of medicine she took for it, I could watch the set and draw what I saw. Sometimes, what I saw was unpleasant, especially around dinner time when a man at a desk would talk about what was new. I would see children my age, their eyes pleading for help and their bellies distended. They would raise their cupped hands to ask for someone to feed them, but no one ever did.

One evening, while I waited for my mother to wake and make dinner, an old man appeared in the living room. He was bald and wore a cardigan. I thought he might have been a neighbor or a friend of my late uncle who never came around anymore because I was certain the gold watch he kept in his pocket had broken. He was late because the watch no longer worked. The man who appeared sat down in the empty chair beside my table and asked me what I was coloring.

"This is food for the children I see on the television," I said, and he sat and studied my drawings for several minutes, commenting on how good they were, and asked my name when he got up to turn off the set.

"I wish you could feed them all," he said as he sat down again and sighed. "Perhaps I can stay for dinner. My name is Mr. Elmer. I have come a long, long way to see you."

"How did you get here?" I asked.

"I took a train. I think I left my umbrella on the train, but I shall see if I can find another one."

I asked him if he knew my uncle who was late and he said, "No," but that he knew many uncles who were late. He told me that there are places where there is no time, and as he spoke, he nodded, so I believed him.

I asked him what time was.

"Time is a television program. When the program begins, that's the beginning of a piece of time and when it ends, then that time is over. If there is no time," he said, "you are never late for anything unless you are watching television."

When my mother came downstairs, she began to set the dinner table and peel the vegetables for dinner.

"Please," I said, "can Mr. Elmer stay for dinner?"

She looked at me. "I don't know any Mr. Elmer."

"He came to visit me while you were asleep upstairs, and said he wants to stay for dinner."

"You're not allowed to have people in the house when I'm not awake."

"I know," I said, "I know the rule. He just showed up. We've had a very nice conversation. He told me that no matter how hard I tried I couldn't feed all the children on the television who are so hungry, but it was a good idea to try."

"Well," my mother said, "he got that right. The world's a bloody mess. I can't find enough ways to kill the pain it gives me, let alone worry about children on the other side of the world."

"So, can he stay?" I insisted until she gave in and I set a place for him at the table.

My father arrived home late. As he approached my mother at the kitchen sink to wash his hands, she drew back.

"It's on your breath," he said. "You might do something about your breath before you come downstairs. There's an empty place at the table. I told you I don't want company, not when you're like this, and not with the boy here and me exhausted."

"Ask the kid," my mother said.

"Who's coming for dinner?" he turned and spoke to me in a sharp voice.

"Mr. Elmer. He came to visit while Mommy was asleep this afternoon. You would like him, he is a very kindly old man." My father grabbed my mother by the arm and began to shake her, but all she did was laugh at him.

"Sit down and eat your dinner before your son's friend snaps it up," she snapped at my father.

My father said nothing. My mother said nothing. They ate their dinner in silence, and as he finished my father turned and looked at the empty place, not a speck of food on the plate, then stood up, threw down his fork which broke his empty plate in half, and walked out. My mother ran upstairs and slammed her bedroom door. I could imagine her lying on the bed, pouring herself another glass of her medicine. I went into the living room. Mr. Elmer had taken his seat at the kindergarten table.

"It is not my place to comment," he said as he brushed some breadcrumbs off the front of his cardigan and drew an index finger across the corners of his mouth, "but I do believe you need someone to talk to. Let's see if we can draw an airplane."

"Have you been on an airplane?" I asked. I hadn't.

"I have been many places, wonderful places. Places where everyone does everything and tells stories about what they have done."

"Have you ever seen an elephant?"

"Oh, yes, many of them. They should not be seen in circuses" he said. "Circus elephants may be fun to watch, but at the end of the show they are loaded into cages like prisoners in a jail and they are sad. I have seen them with their trunks down, their knees about to buckle under their tired bodies. But I have also seen them in Africa, in the wild, as they move in their parades through the grasslands, their tails swinging behind them, their heads nodding to the steady beat of their steps. They are happy. They are a family, and the family members care for one another. They never leave a young elephant behind. And I know how to ask elephants to dance, though not like they dance in a circus. That is cruel because someone is *making* them. When animals dance, whether they are elephants, or giraffes, or turtles, they dance because no one is making them. They do it because they have found what makes them happy."

"Are you happy?" I asked Mr. Elmer.

"Happiness is everything. I wouldn't want to leave anything out. What makes me especially happy is being here with you just to pass the time." He paused for a moment of thoughtful reflection. "Everything that casts a shadow makes me happy. There are happy shadows and sad shadows, but it is light that makes a shadow, never forget that. Every day, I step outside my house, look up at the sky, sometimes while walking to catch the train here, and I feel the sun on my face. That is the most beautiful feeling in the world because it makes me glad."

"I want to be happy, too," I said. "I think about what would make me happy. I want my mother to be well. I want my father to come home and play with me and be kind to us. I want us to move in a parade like elephants." With that, Mr. Elmer and I stood up together and swung our arms back and forth to pretend we were elephants with swaying trunks, and we both sat down again and laughed. That made me happy.

"I do believe," said Mr. Elmer, "what makes me happy is finding out how close people are to each other. Everything is close to something else. Right now, I am happy because I am sitting here beside you. You mustn't think that every shadow is a sad one. You might find sadness in one place, but within inches of it, you can find a bright spot, happiness, a treasure. Tomorrow I will tell you about the time I found buried treasure right where I was standing."

"Where was that?" I asked eagerly.

"I think I hear your mother moving about upstairs so it is time for me to go, but when I return I will tell you where to look as long as you promise to be a good boy and never forget that right where people stand is the last place they look for their own happiness, and if it is not right where you are, it is probably only inches away."

As Mr. Elmer turned to leave, I asked him what an inch was and he held up a gap between his thumb and his first finger. "Maybe less, though never more than that much."

In the morning, I got up and dressed myself. I had learned to do that because my father screamed at me one day when he was home that I had to stand on my own two feet, and that being four was no excuse for not being able to dress myself. In the kitchen, I sat down at the table, opened a loaf of bread, and buttered a slice, then spread a layer of strawberry jam on it from a jar my mother kept on the table. Mr. Elmer was seated at his spot. He wished me a pleasant good morning. I wished him a good day back. He smiled.

I asked him if he wanted any bread and jam, but he said he'd already eaten and brushed more crumbs off the front of his sweater. He suggested I have some milk to go with the bread and I went to the refrigerator, set the carton on the table, got a glass, and poured myself several good mouthfuls. My father came into the kitchen and looked around. He had been gone all night. My mother was still asleep upstairs.

"Who are you talking to?" he shouted.

I didn't want to tell him. Mr. Elmer was sitting very quietly and shook his head, "No," as if to say he didn't need to be introduced to my father. "No one," I said. "I am having my breakfast."

"I'm going out again. Don't make a mess. Put the milk away after you."

I cleaned up breakfast and Mr. Elmer joined me at the kindergarten table. "Yesterday," he said, "I told you where I found happiness." He pointed to his feet and, at first, I didn't understand what he meant. Then he lifted one shoe at a time and continued to point to the floor. "Happiness is always there but you have to know not only where to look for it but how."

"How does one look for it?"

"Come," he said and walked me over to the window. There were clouds racing across the sky but in between the clouds the sun broke through. "Sometimes it isn't there exactly when you want it or expect it, but eventually you can see it. You have to be patient."

"What is patience?" I asked.

He nodded and thought about an answer. "Patience is what you have when you when you wait for your mother to come downstairs from her room. It is the feeling you have when you are glad to see her, when you know you are going to see her, and she appears."

"So, patience is waiting?"

"More than that. Patience is waiting to find something that will make you happy."

We sat in silence for several minutes. Mr. Elmer asked what I was doing.

"I am waiting," I said. "I am being a patient."

He smiled, then he spoke again. "I promised to tell you about all the wonderful things I have seen in the world, but it occurs to me that you don't know their names because you don't know what is in a name. Names are made of letters. The letters are what we put on paper to remind us of sounds we make to describe things. Everything you and I say to each other is made of sounds, and each sound has a letter."

"Are they on the television?" I asked.

"Though I wouldn't think so, sometimes a voice comes on to tell you what channel you are watching, and they say the letters." He wrote down as many letters as he could remember on a piece of paper and pointed to each one and told me what sound he thought they made. We talked about letters for a long time.

Then he stood up, crossed the room, and came back with a magazine my mother had been reading. There were pictures on every page, and Mr. Elmer told me that there were letters all through the magazine and we looked at them and tried to imagine how the names for things sounded. He was very pleased when we looked at a picture of a cat and I said the word 'CAT.'

"I would like to have a cat, someday," I said. "I know its name now."

"Letters in the magazine – they are the shadows that make up words, little sounds that when put together form words just like we are speaking now." By the end of the morning, I was writing letters and giving them sounds.

"This magazine is called LIFE," Mr. Elmer noted. He pointed to the cover. "We all have a life of some kind."

"Do you have a patient life?" I asked.

"Of course. The best way to lead a life is to be patient and to like what you have. Having something is called a blessing."

"Yes, I saw that on television."

"Quite right. Everything that is close to you is a blessing. I like to count my blessings," Mr. Elmer whispered as he leaned over to me and told me how to count to ten. I repeated the words for the numbers, though I didn't tell him I had seen someone on television speaking the numbers and had repeated them all the way to ten. I think it was a game show and someone had to do something before everyone counted to ten.

When we finished the numbers, Mr. Elmer folded his arms and smiled. "I think life comes in all shapes and sizes, in all letters and all numbers, and that it leaves shadows all over the place, but everything counts."

"To ten?"

"No, not just to ten. To say something *counts* is what people say when they are trying to tell you that you matter to them. To matter means you are important to them, that you are a blessing for them."

"I'm not sure I matter to my father," I replied. Mr. Elmer could tell I was feeling sad.

"Oh, you don't know that for sure. He probably counts to ten for you."

"Shadows? Are shadows bad?" I asked him. "My mother says there's a shadow over our house."

"Shadows are what we make them to be." He held up his hands. Sunlight was streaming in the living room window and, when he played with his hands, he made a chicken appear on the wall, then a spider, an elephant, and then a locomotive engine that turned into a beautiful bird. He took me to the window. We looked out together. The mailman was making his way among the houses and his shadow trailed behind him. A delivery truck chased its shadow down the street, and the tree on the front lawn had a shadow that moved as the wind moved through its boughs. I almost began to love every shadow I could think of, but that night my father came home.

He was in a rage because there was no dinner on the table, and my mother appeared in her nightgown. Mr. Elmer's place was still set at the table. The dishes from the night before were where they had been left including my father's broken plate. He screamed at my mother that he expected dinner. My mother, in tears, ran to the refrigerator, grabbed a bunch of carrots, and took an enormous knife from the kitchen drawer, and began sobbing and chopping at the counter. Mr. Elmer stood with me in the doorway to the living room. I wanted to move into the kitchen to help my mother, but Mr. Elmer held me back.

My father grabbed my mother first by the hair and then by the arms and began to shake her like a rag doll. Then he struck her across the face, and she fell to the floor. The knife slid across the linoleum toward me. She yelled back at him. I didn't know the word she said but she was crying, and her eyes were red. Before she could stand up, my father was standing over her, hitting her again and again, and she kept screaming for him to stop. I bent down. I had the knife in my hand, and as my father hit my mother with fists so loud they went thump, thump on her head as she tried to cover herself with her arms, I told the doctors I just wanted to help her. She couldn't help herself. She had been in bed all day with her medicine and could not speak for herself, let alone stand up and make dinner. The doctors told me my father was not a bad man, that he was lucky to recover, and that if not for a matter of inches he would have been dead. I told them that most of the time happiness is only inches away. They looked very concerned when I said that.

The windows in the hospital were made of white glass that made a zoom, zoom sound when I ran my fingernails over them, but they did not cast shadows as much as clear windows. Between offices and examining rooms, I could see the outlines of people moving behind them as if they were puppets made by my friend when we sat together on one sunny afternoon, and he made pictures with his hands. Shadows in the white windows were only silhouettes. The light in the hospital made all the shadows dull.

At first, I could not find Mr. Elmer, in the colorless corridors of the hospital. I asked a nurse if she had seen him. The doctor, and other doctors that came to visit me, asked me who my friend was so I told them.

"He is kind," I said. "He tried to stop me from leaving the doorway and picking up the knife. But I couldn't help it. I wanted my father to stop hurting my mother." They wouldn't believe me.

They didn't understand me when I told them I was happy to be a patient. "Patients are people who are happy to wait," I said.

"Well," said Dr. Robinson, "you are certainly a patient now." That made me feel happy.

"That's what Mr. Elmer said."

At first, Dr. Robinson told me there was no Mr. Elmer. Mr. Elmer was only someone or something in my mind and that did not exist in the world. But even as the doctor spoke, I could see my friend sitting in an empty chair in the corner of the examining room, tossing his head from side to side and encouraging me to go along with whatever the doctor and the nurses said. They said only an evil, malicious boy would stab his father, that my father cared for me and my mother. I would ask why he hit her so hard that she fell to the floor. He kept hitting her. The knife lay at my feet. Mr. Elmer had tried to hold me back, but I had broken away. I had to save my mother.

"There *is* no Mr. Elmer," the doctors and nurses repeated. "You must forget he ever existed."

Over and over, I would describe my friend to the doctors and the nurses. I would tell them he had crumbs on the front of his cardigan, and then they would make me swallow pills and I would fall asleep. But when I woke, my friend was there, standing over me, looking concerned, telling me everything would be good again someday and that I just had to be a patient.

When a group of doctors sat at a long table and asked me questions, I told them the truth. They said they wanted the truth. I told them Mr. Elmer came to me every day, but the pills they gave me caused him to be delayed, to miss his trains, or for the rain to fall so heavily he could not leave his house to make the journey because he didn't know where he had left his umbrella. But despite their best attempts, Mr. Elmer always found a way into the hospital. He came and told me to look for my happiness and if I couldn't find it then maybe it was close by. He talked to me. He believed me. Why did the doctors and nurses not believe me, too?

The doctors told me I needed to send him away, but I wouldn't let him go. I could talk to him. I could tell him how I felt when my mother and father would not speak to me, and when the doctor would not listen the nurse would wrap me in a white coat with buckles and my arms tied up in a hug if I cried and kicked the wall and told them I wanted to go home.

"I'm here for you," Mr. Elmer would say. "I won't leave as long as you need me." And I did need him. My mother, I was told, had gone to live far away with someone I had never heard of, that if I wanted to see her, I should look up at the clouds and maybe I could catch a glimpse of her. I wondered if she had gone to live in the dark cloud that she said hung over our house.

My father never came to see me. A nurse told me he didn't want me anymore, that he had started a new family and would have a good little boy. But Mr. Elmer stood by me. He was always there, sometimes only inches away. We would write letters on pieces of paper and pass them to each other and sometimes I would hear him make the sound of what we had just drawn. The doctors did not like that, but they didn't know what to do. They let me have my paper and crayons.

One day Mr. Elmer and I were staring out the one window that did not have white glass in it. Below us, there were men in chairs seated in a circle in the garden. In another part of the yard, there were women who were tossing a ball to each other. They looked like they were having fun until one woman lost her temper and threw the ball at the window where I was watching. I watched it rise toward me and leave a spider web on the unbreakable glass that had wires woven into it. As it fell away, I watched its shadow growing larger on the ground.

I turned and looked at Mr. Elmer. We were both standing in the light, and I could see my shadow on the wall, so I waved to myself. Mr. Elmer turned to wave as well. He probably didn't know who or what I was waving at, and that's when I asked him. "Why don't you have a shadow?"

He smiled at me and sat down in an empty chair beside the window. He paused for a moment and looked out the window directly at the bright afternoon sun of a summer day.

"I don't have a shadow," he said, "because I am your shadow, and I will stay close to you as long as you live even if you think you don't need me anymore."

I stood up and looked beneath my feet and there he was. And he is always there, especially when I turn my face to the sun.

Toy Soldiers

After the car accident, he couldn't remember his name for a week. Another week would pass before he could read again. As he lay in his hospital bed for three days – a precaution against concussion complications – David had time to reflect on his life. As his memories came back to him, he was curious about what things he had loved best. What had they been?

"A marching band," he said out of the blue when I went to see him.

"As in the Changing of the Guard at Buckingham Palace?" I asked. When I was a child, I listened to a set of Christopher Robin records that had been my mother's. They were delicate and if I wasn't careful, I was warned, they would fly off the turntable because they needed to be played at 78 rpm.

"Exactly," David replied. "Toy soldiers. They were my world. I had a set of Grenadier Guards toy soldiers. They wore red tunics and tall, bearskin busbies. Some were marching soldiers carrying rifles. I had the bass drum player, a brass section complete with trombone players, and even the drum major who carried a long baton. What's the name for the thing he carries?"

"A baton?"

"No. It's a stick with an ornament on top. The drum major spins it." A nurse came in to check his pulse. "The thing they carry to begin governing," he said to her.

She looked at me as if I was the lifeline on a quiz show. "Public opinion? I know. It's a mace," the nurse muttered as she wrote notes on his chart.

"I keep thinking of my soldiers. I want to find that part of my life I feel I lost in the accident. Somewhere in the attic, they must be resting in the box where I put them when I was told I was too old to play with childish things."

David's nostalgia was slightly pathetic. I wanted to tell him he was a grown man, that he held an important job with an investment bank. People counted on him. They sent him get-well cards. They needed his keen mind to find its way back. His manager had told him to take a few weeks. After that, David was supposed to be fully recovered.

Concussions take longer to heal than a few weeks. The brain is bruised as it smacks on the inside of the skull. The neurons send the wrong signals. The patient is still inside his head. His life, his memories, his intelligence are right where they have always been. The problem is relearning how to access them.

David's phone was ringing the next time I saw him. The call went to voicemail. His manager said there had been a change of plans. They needed him back now.

He asked what he did for a living. I wanted to cry. In a few weeks, he had gone from being the man in the bespoke suit to being a little boy again. He had rummaged through his attic. The soldiers were lined up on the dining room table, all in neat files, all in the correct order for a march past.

"They don't have the right to call you back so soon," I said.

"It doesn't matter. I don't think I was happy doing whatever I did before the accident. The last time I recall being happy was the last time these chaps saw light," he said as he turned the drum major's head eyes right and tilted the mace as if he was saluting the Queen.

The soldiers had pale, featureless faces. David had given the boy next door some money to go to the local art supply store to purchase brushes, paints, and a white sharpie pen to detail the belts of the troops, but he had neglected to put a fine-tipped marker on the list. Surely the men should have mouths David said as he talked to himself.

"However will they breathe? And they need eyes and eyebrows so they can see where they are going. The only ones who don't need eyes are those in High Command and Britain's Ltd never made the High Command. They only made guardsmen and the marching band.

It was sad and dreadful to see my friend in that state. I patted him on the shoulder and let myself out. I returned a week later. I could tell he'd been ignoring his answering machine because the light was flashing madly and the call that came in during my visit was cut off before the message could be recorded. His company had fired him.

David wasn't bothered by what transpired. I was about to tell him he had cause for a wrongful termination suit and that there were lawyers who would only be too glad to handle such a matter, offering legal arrangements where, if they didn't win, David wouldn't have to pay. If David didn't win, the absence of a legal bill would be a moot point. David would not be able to pay his mortgage. The bank would foreclose his house, toy soldiers and all.

He grabbed me by the sleeve.

"You really must see! It is looking more splendid every day. Come! It's in the dining room."

Around the guard and bandsmen, David had constructed an intricate black fence topped with gold-colored lights. He had done a painstakingly careful job of working the filigree of the Buckingham Palace wrought iron. On the other side of the table, he had a scale façade of the monarch's residence, complete with a bunting-covered balcony and a miniature royal family, all proportional to the Grenadiers, waving to an imaginary crowd.

"You've been busy," I said. It was pitiable and impressive in the same breath. "How did you make the royal family?"

"Modelling clay that dries hard. The royal family must have a thick skin beneath the paint to take the abuse from the press."

I didn't have the heart to ask him if he was going to build an entire crowd to fill The Mall all the way down to Admiralty Arch.

"What has transpired at work?" I asked.

"This. This is my work. The doctor told me just before I was released from hospital that my injury would take time to heal and when I asked him how I would go about healing, he said I would have to rebuild my world slowly, piece by piece."

I wanted to cry. I remembered our games of racquetball when David cussed out the princes of finance who thought they were smarter than he was. Not only did David have the degree. He had the savvy. "Savvy is not just a quaint term for a street where fine suits are tailored," he said. "It's what goes on inside the suit that is savvy."

That night I turned away from my wife in bed and faced the window. Rain was pouring down the pane. The echoing light from the city spread a yellow glow across the glass. The expensive drapes that were hung at either side of the sash appeared pointless to me. We could have paid any price, not merely the most expensive price, for drapes that had the same effect. And what did they matter? Drapes all look the same in the dark. I was troubled. I had dreamed I saw David marching at the head of a parade. He was dressed as the drum major. He spun his mace around and around and tossed it in the air, as drum majors often do to show they are not just in command of their band or their guardsmen but jugglers able to perform incredible tricks while keeping in perfect step with their troops. Then David dropped it.

He bent down to feel the ground for the symbol of command, and I realized he didn't have eyes. His mouth was sealed shut. He had become the faceless miniature version of himself. The band kept marching. They parted around him as if they were the waves of the Red Sea, but when the musicians had passed, the guardsmen with silver bayonets mounted on the tips of their rifles began growling from behind their featureless masks and impaled David over and over until he was lying in the dust of the parade ground. The family on the balcony, not the present British royal family but figures of his own devising that included Queen Mary and King Edward VII and possibly George V, all raised their hands and gave him the thumbs down. I woke.

Even with my wife beside me in bed, I felt terribly alone. I wondered if David felt that lonely inside his head. Tomorrow, on my way home from work, I would drop by to see him. I had one question I wanted to ask him, though I had no business raising the matter: are you happy? Unhappiness has many expressions.

I am unhappy when I cannot communicate with my co-workers. I was unhappy before I met my wife. My mother said, "If you just meet a nice girl..." And yes, I am happy in a matrimonial way. My wife and I have a good relationship, but we don't communicate well. One can be closer to another than a knife to a spoon and still feel abandoned. Lucky David. He'd been given the shot in his head he needed to awake.

As I lay there in the dark, I remembered that I, too, had played with toy soldiers as a child. Mine were made of lead, which is one of the least desirable materials for a child's toys. My soldiers had been passed down through members of my family, from boy to boy, as enticements to loyalty, bravery, and service to a dying empire. They barely had a dot of paint left on them. One of the former owners was so inspired by his toy soldiers he signed up for service in the Second World War after lying about his age – he was a tall lad for fourteen – and was felled by a sniper's bullet three days after landing in Normandy at Sword.

There were two boxes of figures. In one box were Scotsmen who wore white pith helmets and green kilts. Someone told me my soldiers were Seaforth Highlanders. The ends of their rifles had gone missing long ago. Those with weapons looked as if they were fighting with folding umbrellas. The commander, who may have once held a pair of binoculars he raised to his eyes, was armless.

In the other box, the one I never played with, were Bedouins, men with long rifles, elegant winding keffiyehs, and sandaled feet. The two boxes had been purchased heaven-knows-how-long ago by some befuddled relative who fancied it would be fun to give a boy a starter kit for a colonial misadventure.

The longer I looked at the two forces side by side, the more I despaired. I had been told I was British and that the British never lost, yet there they were, my Seaforths, outgunned, out-painted, and waiting to die for some corner of a foreign field.

Thinking of my long-lost soldiers only made my loneliness and despair worse. The daily skirmishes I was fighting were battles I had been trained to lose, and I realized how lucky David had been not only to have been given a band, but the happiness of knowing his toy soldiers were a tourist attraction. I wanted to hum a march I had heard the Grenadiers play on television years ago, but I couldn't remember the name of the tune or even how it went, and I fell asleep certain in the knowledge that I, not David, was the faceless drum major trained to fall out of step without understanding how diverse and wonderous the world really is.

Sayings

I TOLD MY FATHER I'd devised a new saying about the old, rusting, red tractor, with its chuffing chimney and bobbing exhaust cap, he'd given me to learn on.

"Okay," he said, "let's hear it."

"An old tractor does as good a job as a new one that won't."

"Needs some work," he said. "More pith. Less explanation." He went back to tinkering with the motor on his new machine.

I thought my saying wasn't bad. I had grown up around sayings, and there is a saying for everything. My grandmother loved to stitch sayings in needlepoint and hang them around the house. A saying that was too long or convoluted confounded her. She'd look up from her threads and frame and ask, "Who thought this one up?"

There is a saying, "You cannot plow the same field three years in a row and expect a good crop." There's another saying, "When the soil turns grey so does a man's hair – even a young man." Inside the front door, there was "Bless this house." Behind the front door was "May the roads rise with you and the wind be always at your back." My father used to chuckle that she'd left the best part out, the part about "being half an hour in heaven before the devil knows you're dead." In the dining room she hung, "Bless these fruits," though the soil was so poor we couldn't even coax raspberries from the dust.

My childhood favorite was, "Early to Bed and Early to Rise Makes a Man Healthy, Wealthy, and Wise." She hung that bedtime sampler over my headboard the way some people put crucifixes on the wall or dangle dream catchers from the ceiling to catch the haunting replays of bad moments from the day. She said it was a reminder for me to go to sleep. I am a natural nighthawk. I'd lie awake and listen to hard rock from a distant FM station.

Opposite the foot of my bed, so it would be the first thing I saw each morning, was the prayer recited by alcoholics at AA meetings when they ask to be granted, "the serenity to accept the things they cannot change and the wisdom to know the difference." Mother was afraid I might hit the bottle if we had a bad season and the farm was seized. I wanted to tell her there has never been enough money leftover even in a good season for someone to imbibe.

Just about anything that sounded wise could make its way onto one of her samplers. Stitching the mottos was what farm women did after they had done everything else to keep domestic matters running in their households. She did all our laundry by hand, prepared every meal from scratch, and cleaned the rooms from top to bottom two times a week.

When she was young, my grandmother had won prizes at the county fair – when there was a county fair – for her needlework and the sayings that seemed to flow from her mind. She had been educated in a one-room schoolhouse. I doubt she ever read Shakespeare, though there was a Shakespearean twist to her maxims. She knew the Proverbs by heart as well as every line from Ecclesiastes and the other books of wisdom.

The Song of Solomon, however, was not to be quoted. "Those men got carried away with their talk of beloveds," she said. "The Bible is no place for the sort of language that gets talked behind the barn." Her explanation of The Song of Solomon was something I would have been proud to hang in my room.

My grandmother was so proficient at homespun philosophy and stitchery she was celebrated at meetings of the Ladies' Auxiliary. There was a time when her needlework was in demand. Even after mottos and samplers went out of fashion, she was still able to sell a few. The letters were decorative, oversized capitals adorned with enormous seraphs. One preacher declared that the tops of her letters were perches for angels.

In her lifetime, however, everything had changed. There had been two wars, and in between those conflicts, the soil had dried out and blown away into the eastern sky. The wars should have broken her spirit. The first war carried off her brothers. The second took her sons except for my father, her youngest. Her face became dry and lined. I thought of her when I touched our soil. The life was slowly fading from it. We could see it happening but could do nothing about it. "We can't even grow a gourd for God to smite," my father said.

An ancestor homesteaded our spread in the 1850s. He was lured by the vision of lush, rolling hills and fabled riches. There were minor stumps he had to pull, scrub growth that needed to be cleared away, but the topsoil was good to him. For six generations, life was bountiful.

Then the dry years hit.

The topsoil blew away.

But we survived, though what I saw in my grandmother's face was exhaustion from a long battle, a pity for the depleted dust as if it and the earth were holding a conversation. The deeper we asked the roots of our wheat to reach, the deeper we sank in debt to the banks and the government plans. She read the dire warnings in the almanacs but never believed them.

My father knew the truth in all its tangled complications but refused to believe it. In many ways, he was the worst kind of farmer -- an optimist who said the next good year was just around the corner. He said he could coax one more good season from the land, and when that passed and we had nothing to show for it, next year would be better. He would repeat his saying, "Where gold grows and ripens, gold lies hidden below."

I don't know where he got the money, but one day a flatbed arrived and unloaded a bright new harvester with an enclosed cab and a radio built into the dashboard.

"How did we come by that?" I asked.

His reply was that the new tractor meant I could work alongside him. Our old machine had been purchased by his father forty years before, and sooner or later it would give up the ghost, but my father believed it was still sturdy enough for me to learn how to handle. Besides, he said, "If you're going to find gold, you'd better be prepared to spend gold."

My father's new tractor had a glassed-in cab. The motor made a steady but soothing roar while the machine I inherited growled and ached as if it was shouting at the field. But the old tractor had been part of the land so long I knew it was trying to coax dead soil back to life.

Anyone could see the land was dying. Year by year, it paled and drew to death. I was determined to learn mechanics because I understood the new tractor would only last until the bank seized it. It was bought with money we'd borrowed and couldn't pay back. My father was going all in. "All or nothing," I'd heard him say when we played cards on the darkened porch and the beetles chewing at the first tufts filled me with a sense of foreboding. His excuse for buying the new machine was that now I could learn to plow.

My father had a saying, "A man has to feel his own soil before the soil will give him life from his labors," so I was proud on those late spring mornings when we set off together on our machines, the two of us abreast, he gliding over the landscape with his harvester's fine suspension and me on a ride as bumpy as a bull machine in a bar.

I wore ear coverings, orange cups that looked as if they could play music but didn't. To pass the hours of tedious straight plowing, I listened to Led Zeppelin in my head and sometimes bobbed to the beat of "Kashmir" or the throb of "Stairway to Heaven." Our farm was remote and far from everything I wanted to be part of. I got so used to wrapping myself in a world of my own devising I stopped paying attention.

In the sunlight of a spring morning, the rolling fields without a tree in sight are beautiful and hypnotic. The rising and falling horizon can lull a person into a false sense of tranquility. When I looked at our land, brown and holding the moisture from the final snows of winter and the measly spring rains that pursued the melting, I saw not only the land as it was but the land as it could be, as wind moved its hand over stalks of wheat, and I could see the imprint of its passing.

I thought I was good at plowing. When we reached the turn at the end of the field, I pulled away from my father and his machine and drifted off into a reverie. Every bump, every tug, and even the smell of the exhaust told me how the old red reliable was doing. For the first time in my life, I felt proud of who I was. I didn't want to run away from the farm or myself. I pictured my father, elderly and paunchy, sitting on the porch as I'd come in from plowing and hear him say, "You did good." He would raise his glass of lemonade and say, "Man's labor shows in his soul." My grandmother would not stitch that. Her time would have passed, but, just the same, I could feel his faith in me, and I was proud to be his son. That day, I'd have something to kid him about. I'd say how he fell behind and needed to keep up.

My father had halted his machine. He was wearing a brown barn coat because it was cool first thing in the day. Maybe he had bent down to inspect the soil or maybe he had hopped off his rig because he thought there was something wrong, something dry and dead about the land that he wanted to see for himself

I didn't see him.

I was gazing at the horizon. A flock of birds circled the hill on the east side of our farm.

I swear I didn't see him. Maybe I was distracted by the empty seat in his harvester.

I can't remember what happened next.

The coroner said I shouldn't blame myself.

The county investigator said my father put his machine on idle and jumped down from the cab to see what was wrong with the motor, perhaps a snag in the blades of the tiller. When he bent over for whatever reason, he suffered a fatal stroke. One of the inspectors hinted my father had been conscious in the end, but immediately took back what he said. "Not knowing the truth is a gift of angels," he said, phrasing his words as a saying.

I live with the hope my father was dead before my tiller tore into him, and even if he had been alert enough to see me coming when I didn't see him sprawled on the ground, we were too far from the house to get help, and even if I had not run him over, there was nothing I could have done to save him. And I live with the truth he may still have been alive. His blood mingled with the soil, and that year, our final good one, the farm had a bumper crop. It was like he always said, "Land doesn't mean anything unless you give your life to it."

Macarons

Before I grew up and became a man, I was a happy little girl. My parents were victims of a car accident on a remote country road in Gloucestershire. I have vague memories of sitting in a car seat in the back of their Vauxhall, the windshield shattered, and their heads slumped forward. I cried out for my mother and my father. Neither answered. Life could have become and probably should have become tragic, but that kind of tragedy is a cliché predicated on the expectations of society. The way to overcome tragedy is to adapt.

I was rescued from being a ward of the state by my Grand-mère, who, someone told me, was my father's grandmother, though I was never certain. I don't think she was elderly: she was, to put it politely, uniquely antique. I have no idea what happened to my own grandparents who would, at least, have understood the changes happening in the world of the 1960s. My guardian was a relic of the age of Proust. She spoke in maxims in the manner of Proust. Her conversation was beautifully crafted so that, when she said anything, *bon mots* fell from her lips like Van Gogh's paintings of rain.

She conducted her life as if everything that touched her was a work of art. When we were in London rather than Paris, she would lock herself in a cupboard she claimed was her boudoir. Gilded and ornate with putti fluttering among starry ribbons of gold, the armoire took up most of her Paddington bedroom. She would close the mirrored door behind her. Her parting words each day that she shut herself away were, "Be good now, and learn the beauty of life. Go see what you can notice by staring out the lounge window." She wrote in the dim, cramped space with her dresses hanging about her head and shoulders. If she shifted for comfort, the wooden hangers would clack together. She had outfitted her "room" with an antique Georgian lap desk of the kind Keats carried during his Italian sojourn and asserted her desire for sessions of sweet silent thought by lining the cupboard with cork. When she opened the door, a fox stole hung its head next to hers as if it were about to bite her ear. In her own little world of the wardrobe, nothing disturbed her but the past. I have no idea what she wrote. The solicitor took it away for posterity the evening she passed, though she told me more than once that little boys were a rare delight, but little girls were works of art that came to life like Pygmalion's statue: companions of beauty and grace. I think she was lonely, and I was her girl.

When she came out of the closet, she would proclaim with a sweeping gesture that she had embraced a moment of profound sadness and knew it intimately. She would say that in the course of a single, well-crafted sentence she had found a way in which love and suffering could not only be "the mistress she could not deny" (her words, not mine) but a language unto itself, conversant with her heart and soul. Then, she would tell me to put on one of the pretty frocks she liked to see me in, and off we would go to Paris, via a Charing Cross express to Dover, the Channel Ferry, and a mail train to Paris that stopped in every possible hamlet in Normandy. She would sit in the dining car, sip Dom Perignon, and explain to me the delicacies of a fine aspic, the intricacies of a well-performed sorbet, and the beauty of a bottle of Chateau Cheval-Blanc. I was not permitted to drink. I asked her what it tasted like. "Like crème caramel at the Ritz," she would answer.

She spent lavishly on food when we were not home. Food at home consisted of smoked salmon or prawns for me and a bottle of freezer-chilled vodka for her. Every time we went to Paris, we dined at Maxim's. The maître d' hôtel did not, as a rule, permit children in the hallowed home of fine cuisine, but he said, and my aunt translated, that having known her for what seemed like a century, and possibly was a hundred years, that a polite, well-behaved, pretty little girl such as me would always be welcome. I knew what badly behaved children were like. I'd seen them throwing tantrums on the streets of Paddington, their mothers dragging them by the arm, their faces attempting to turn blue, and their legs kicking. I understood at an early age that little beasts who knew nothing of manners behaved like a truck shattering the front window of a four-star restaurant.

And I was pretty. My hair was never cut, and every morning she would brush it out and tie it with a blue ribbon. The dresses in which she attired me were from the nineteenth century and beautifully preserved. They had been hers, she said, and she relished the thought of seeing me in them. I stood one morning in front of a full-length mirror, and I saw myself as Renoir's "Girl with a Watering Can." My navy dress was trimmed in white lace. All I needed was the *arrosoir* and the picture would be complete. I was darling. I had no idea that I was any different from any of the other little girls.

And because I was the perfect child, the image of pulchritude and refined delicacy, not to mention politeness, I was served my first macaron at Maxim's. I closed my eyes as the flavor of rosewater, riding on its shell of almond with a playful crème de la rose between the sweet layers of meringue melted in my mouth. Yes, I was the perfect little girl and macarons were Grand-mère's way of telling me how much she adored me.

After lunch one day, during which I fell in love with steak tartare, Grand-mère and I walked the length of the Jardin de Tuileries but passed over the Louvre. We would go and appreciate the spiritual perfection and enlightenment of the old masters another day. Instead, we arrived at a *salon de crème glacée* where I discovered pistachio ice cream served on a chestnut-flavored meringue. When Fortnum and Masons still made ice cream their forte in the Fountain Room, I pleaded with the waitress, Irene, to replicate what I had tasted during my trips to Paris. They came close, but it was missing that *je ne sais quoi.* The *salon de crème glacée* disappeared years ago – replaced by a bistro of moderate but not memorable fare, a steak frites tourist eatery – and I have never been able to relive the taste of that moment. Some things are meant to vanish. That is why we are given memories, inexact as they are. Reconstructing an experience, unraveling the mystery of a first taste, is part of the art of living.

What I have not lost is my love for macarons. I believe the best macarons are made in London and that is one of the reasons I make the city my home. There are other considerations, of course – a vocation in finance, the proximity to the English countryside, especially Gloucestershire, where I go on weekends to walk the lanes and try to remember what my mother and father were like and where I lost them.

Along the way, there are always good pubs that serve wonderful English fare. English fare is demanding, as opposed to French cuisine. The French can do so much with so little. To be a good Englishman and eat like an Englishman requires a strong fork and a sharp knife. There is a quality of the English spirit that is inherent in a main course of roast beef, potatoes or turnips, baked parsnips, a perfect Yorkshire pudding, and the hint of Lea and Perrins rather than a reduced burgundy in a *sauce au jus*. And even in that iconic English meal, the French have a specific vocabulary for everything on a plate. They eat words the way other cultures eat chicken.

When we were in London at Christmas – Grand-mère was now well beyond antique and appeared to be dying of eternity – we dined at a carvery. It may have been Simpsons-in-the-Strand. In those days, the mid-Seventies, Simpsons was one the good spots for a slice or two of Christmas goose and a helping of roast beef. I was ten or eleven at the time. The heights of culinary adventure I had scaled with Grand-mère had made me, how shall we say, a solid child, on whose bones what would have been excess on a girlish frame was becoming sinew on mine.

Grand-mère was telling me a story about Camille Saint-Saëns who she had known around the time he composed his famous Symphony No. 3, the one for organ where the great pipes of Saint Sulpice must have exploded in the ears of the composition's first audience. I was telling her how I thrilled when the great chord announced itself in the final movement as if heaven was opening, and how, that morning, I had listened to her recording of the composer's Christmas Oratorio. I was telling her what a fine piece of music the oratorio is when my voice dropped. It did not merely drop. It sank as if it was a flat, heavy stone tossed and sinking in a millpond. It hit the floor. Foolishly, I tried to project more sound, and my voice became deeper and deeper. She dropped her fork and stared at me.

"Please do not be impossible at a time such as this, among all these people," and she gave "*impossible*" the French pronunciation. An appalled look appeared on her face. I think she suddenly felt betrayed. People will feel betrayed if one of their most precious illusions is suddenly shattered. She motioned to the waiter and instructed him to pour me a glass of burgundy.

"But Madame," he said, "the young lady is too…young."

I made the mistake of saying, "Please," and out of my throat came the sound of good English beef, the deep, well-roasted sound of a barrel of porter. I had given him my order not half an hour earlier and larks had ascended from my lips. He looked shocked.

"You appear to have something in your throat, Miss. Perhaps I can…"

Grand-mère pointed assertively at my empty glass, from which I had been drinking Perrier, and began to choke. The waiter filled my glass, but immediately put down the bottle and bent down close to Grand-mère. She reached for her throat, coughing as if a piece of goose had gone down the wrong way. Then she stood up, holding her neck, looked up to the stained-glass ceiling and, pointing at something I could not see, exclaimed, "*Formidable*," and collapsed on the floor.

Her solicitor, Mr. Gerdings of Gerdings and Strapp of Lincoln's Inn, arrived at our flat the afternoon before Grand-mère's funeral. I sat in a Louis XV armchair she loved, my face turned toward the lounge window. I remembered the hours I had spent in that chair, studying the street, and waiting to see what would happen. I wondered if my life had been observation without comprehension. I could not recall a single thing I had seen. My dress, a white pinafore, circa 1910, was pulling at my shoulders. The solicitor, knowing I would likely be incapable of feeding myself, let alone eating according to Grand-mère's meticulous standards, opened a take-out box.

"Fish and chips," he said. "This is what the world eats when your Grand-mère's not about. Got it up on Marylebone Road. There's a good fish shop there. Have it. You need to keep up your strength."

He stared at me as I tore into the battered cod and the greasy chips. The box came with little plastic packets of dark vinegar, and I was even more ravenously hungry when the fish had been christened.

"Tell me," said the solicitor, "I realize from your Grand-mère's will that you are *not* a young lady but a young man. "Didn't anyone notice you were a boy when you went to school?"

"I never attended school. Grand-mère told me my education should be in the graceful arts, in the galleries, restaurants, *salons de crème glacée*, and it should all be, as she put it, *exempli gratia*. I'm not sure what that means. I guess it means I didn't go to school. I learned how to read. Proust, especially Proust, but also Voltaire and Saint-Exupéry. I wasn't permitted Baudelaire or Rimbaud. Grand-mère said there'd be time enough for that later,"

"So, how did you learn?"

"I learned to read the menu at Maxim's. *Fois canard confit. Lotte a la Dieppoise, Légume de Saison.*"

"You recite that like some children recite A.A. Milne."

"Who was?"

The solicitor leaned over and slapped my knee. I didn't think that was proper behavior, but he smiled and then said, "Let's take you out. Get you a haircut, a suit, tie, some proper Oxfords, a sturdy belt, and a wallet you can stick in your back pocket. You'll be well-off for quite a while. Your gran left things in good order, despite her extravagance in food."

"Grand-mère," I said. "She was always Grand-mère."

"Before we go, when you finish your fish and chips – they're good, right? Before we go, there's something I need to tell you. I don't want you to be shocked." He drew a deep breath. "Your Grand-mère was, and I don't know any delicate way to put this, was a man. She was your Uncle Henri. Do you know how old he was when he passed away?"

I shook my head.

"He was one hundred and seven. He enjoyed every inch of life. The story about your Uncle Henri is that he began dressing as a woman around the turn of the century. He told me, she told me, they told me, they were terrified of war, of the carnage, of mangled bodies, but more so of the terrible food that soldiers must eat. His father had been horribly disfigured at the Battle of Sedan in 1870. Maybe you haven't heard of that. Your uncle hid his fear of dying in a gruesome war in couturier and sapphire brooches so she could feel the way she wanted to feel. She wanted to be herself. I dare say she was trying to do the same for you.

I had heard about my ancestor. Grand-mère kept a book of French military history in her glass-doored Second Empire book-case. A bottle of absinthe sat beside it and an empty glass that never seemed to be put to use. I know now that it was a memorial to her father, to Uncle Henri's father, to a man my guardian must have thought frightening with his disfigured face hidden behind a white silk scarf.

So, the day they buried my guardian was the day I began to grow into manhood. I eventually went to a public school – that had been left in her will – and I played rugby. I was rather good at it. I was a sturdy lad, and I had never suffered for want of good food during the years I was a little girl.

Dream Lover

There was a time when I had an old Bakelite radio my parents were given for their first apartment, and the best songs I heard through the crackle of static late at night were about dreams. The radio would grow red hot and it only carried the AM band where voices crowded to be heard and the blurred sounds of Top 40 songs scrambled and bounced over miles of cities and towns and farm fields. The songs about dreams were the best because the dreams were about girls.

The dreams I dreamed reminded me of the home movies my father made of my life when I was a child. Christmas morning in footed sleepers. Birthday parties when we were permitted to drink Coca-Cola in the dining room and my best friend showed off by holding his nose and shooting a stream of brown liquid out his tear ducts. The sprockets appear in the final scenes. The movie runs out and I am blinded by the light. And even though dreams are hard to remember, I'd dream of girls, especially the ones I knew or who I wished would know me. They were always distant. They could stand next to me and be as far away as salvation from my worst fears.

I'd dream of being on a tropical island with the girls in my class who I wanted to be alone with. I'd wake up and they'd be gone. I'd think about them all day. I'd stare at them.

Of course, those girls ignored me. I don't blame them one bit. Even though they were each my version of a dream lover, I was not exactly their version of a dream come true.

My first pimples were appearing, and my voice was still trying to climb down from its perch, and it broke whenever I tried to talk to them.

One of the girls even went so far as to tell me to my face that she would never go out with me because my cheeks looked like a pizza, my voice sounded like a canary, and I was nothing but a dreamer.

I wasn't deterred. I looked up her number in the telephone book. My luck was that her last name was Smith. I called about twenty households before I got the one where her mother answered. Her mother frightened me. She wanted to know what I wanted. I tried to explain before her daughter took the receiver and asked herself, "What do you want?"

When I asked if she would go on a date with me, she said, "You dreamer! No way in like forever. I've got bigger dreams than you."

The last time I saw her was in a grocery store. She was nineteen and had two kids, one in the shopping cart basket banging two cans of soup together and the other in the flip seat teething on the handle grip. She looked as if she had a third one on the way. When we were in school, she told the class her dream was to become an actuary.

There was one girl I knew who gave me hope. She spoke to me. I met her coming out of her piano lessons as I was going in. When I learned she was going to the piano teacher, I asked my parents for lessons. We didn't own a piano, but a neighbor said I could practice on their old hymnary upright that was gathering dust in the corner of their living room. It had belonged to the neighbor's mother. I was privileged to play it, though Rock and Roll was off-limits. My pieces had to be Beginner's Level Conservatory songs or nothing. I was terrible at piano, but I asked for the lesson time on Wednesday afternoons when my dream girl would be going in just as I was coming out.

The girl going into the lesson went to the same junior high school as I did. I made the mistake of telling my best friend, Mark, all about her, how wonderful she was, how she was a superstar at music and would write a big hit someday.

Mark and I had been friends since we were five. We played road hockey and tennis together and hung out in the early autumn with a gang of boys from school who played touch football. We dreamed of becoming professional athletes. The ones on television made it look easy. We'd watch a game and Mark would point to the television set and say, "Yep, that's a dream job."

The piano teacher hadn't been my choice, nor was the piano for an instrument. I wanted to learn guitar from someone who had long hair and was cool and could teach me the chords for Roy Orbison's "Sweet Dreams Baby." My cousin let me try her guitar and offered to show me how to play the song "Dream a Little Dream of Me," that Cass Elliot sang.

The elderly piano teacher was old and had a bad temper. She'd been a friend of my mother, who used to be in the same bridge club. My mother left the bridge club along with Mark's mother because she couldn't stand the piano teacher's bickering about how terrible the youth of the day had become, yet on the subject of music the woman had brainwashed my mother into believing I had to learn proper, classical piano first or there was no point to learning any music at all. Anything else was just a wild dream. The piano teacher was down on her luck. She needed the work. Her husband had left her in a yellow convertible, waving with the top down, and driving up and down the street with a young woman in the passenger seat before disappearing forever. He was cool. Cool was something the piano teacher did not understand or accept.

Her son was cool.

He angered her during one of my lessons by riding his Harley to Niagara Falls and back just to see how fast he could do a round trip. He stood in the doorway of the lesson room and smirked at her.

I know she wanted to whack him across the face. I know she wanted to pick up his motorcycle and toss it through the garage door if she'd had the strength. Her temper burst into open flames that day. I got in the way.

She couldn't hit him, so she hit me across my right knuckles with a metal-edged ruler because she said I played a sixteenth note instead of an eighth while trying to jazz up a version of "I'm a Little Teapot." I was way too old for that kind of baby song. I wanted to play something by The Beatles. They weren't allowed. The blow stung.

While she was embroiled with her son, she threw the ruler down on the high notes and laid her hand on the raised edge of the piano above the farthest right-hand keys.

I picked up the ruler and hit her back.

She screamed.

Her son laughed at her and walked away.

That was my last lesson.

I was cut off and couldn't meet the girl of my dreams, even if we'd only passed in the stairway to the piano teacher's basement studio. In my dreams I had danced with the girl of my dreams on those stairs, imagining I was Fred Astaire and she was Ginger Rogers just like in the old movies that played on television late at night.

The teacher told my mother I was a failure, perhaps the biggest failure she had ever encountered, a failure beyond my mother's wildest dreams. I was a terrible boy who would never amount to anything. A no-good. A criminal waiting to commit a crime. She showed my mother the red marks on the fingers of her left hand.

"I use my hands to make my living!" she told my mother with venom in every one of her words.

Just to rub it in and show me what I was missing because I was a criminal waiting to develop, the piano teacher invited me to her students' recital at the Heliconian Club, an old church in the midst of the downtown student ghetto where long-haired youths gathered in Haight-Ashbury North to live life their way and according to a new set of social norms.

When my father parked the car, turning to me and saying, "Look at those long-haired creeps!" I knew the invitation was a set-up. I was supposed to throw myself on the mercy of the cranky piano teacher. I was to beg for salvation from a life of long hair and wild music. I decided to have none of it.

Two weeks before the recital, I had asked the girl of my dreams to a tea dance in the gymnasium of our school. It was guaranteed to be a dark event where a blues band, later to become a famous blues band, was playing, and tiny adolescents tottered at arms-length with each other, laying sweaty palm upon sweaty palm, and straining to be polite.

She said, "No," and hung up the phone.

I was glad she hung up on me as I listened to the dial tone. I was dying a thousand deaths inside just by having to talk to her. I could not have gone through with the dance. But I worked up the courage to call her again several days later and ask her to our piano teacher's recital after I learned I had been invited though I couldn't understand why. I knew the girl of my dreams couldn't say no because she was going to be there. She was playing something called a *gavotte.* I had no idea what it was, though I told her I wanted her to play it for me. She asked me why I had hit the teacher.

"She isn't awful, and she didn't deserve to be hit."

I replied she'd hit me first.

"You're a big baby," she said and hung up on me again.

When I entered the women's club – it had that church smell of Gestetner machine paper and worn-out dusty carpet – there she was, the girl of my dreams.

She was with Mark. The girl of my dreams was with my best friend.

She opened the show.

She was a showstopper.

Everyone applauded.

Mark stood up and shouted her name and yelled "Encore."

Then everyone in the audience stood up and shouted "Encore." I wasn't sure what an encore was, but the girl of my dreams sat down and played the piece again. The second time she tripped over a few notes and the reprise drew only polite applause. I wanted to feel sorry for her, but I couldn't. Mark looked at her consolingly.

Was it a good *gavotte* or a bad one? I'm not sure. I'm no judge of these things.

There was an intermission in the middle of the show before some of the more senior pupils and friends of the piano teacher were to close the evening with performances of difficult compositions. My parents were talking to other parents. I popped into the back room where the piano teacher's pupils were waiting.

One boy who I knew was throwing up from nerves into a wastepaper basket.

I said, "It will be all right, you'll see," and he shook his head. He had bitten the nails on four of his fingers down to bleeding wounds. I offered him a tissue from my jacket pocket, but the tissue wasn't clean, and he shook his head as if he were a condemned man waiting to be led to his execution.

"She will kill me," he said, unable to stop the bleeding with the lining of his trouser pockets. "I thought this would be my moment," he said. "It won't be. I am a failure."

"Hey," I said, lowering my voice in case the girl protégé was in the room, "Welcome to the club. It could be worse. The girl of your dreams could have shown up with your former best friend."

I nodded in the direction of Mark and the girl of my dreams, but I'm not sure he understood me.

When I returned to my seat from the green room that had begun to smell very green, there was Mark in the front row. He was holding hands with her.

The first pianist in the second half was a Chinese girl about my age who had first smiled and then winked at me backstage. The smile was okay. The wink frightened me.

She curtsied to the audience and then announced, "I have composed my own piece. It is called 'My Dream.'"

I looked over at the piano teacher. The woman was shaking her head vehemently at the student and began wagging her finger to say "No!" but the young composer was unruffled by the negative response. She sat down at the keyboard and began to play.

The tune was a cross between Debussy's "Claire de Lune" and Saint Saens' "The Swan." It was lilting, pleasant, very poetic, and didn't seem to have any specific melody. Her fingers ran up and down the keyboard in soft trills. It reminded me of a bird trapped in a cage, flitting from perch to perch, frightened and anxious but unable to escape.

She paused and lifted her hands from the keyboard. The audience, having never heard the piece, began to clap. But the pianist stared at the keys then continued playing. The piano teacher was now shaking a fist at the pianist.

The girl glanced into the audience and saw the look on the teacher's face, then stood up with one foot on the loud pedal, and broke into "Great Balls of Fire," kicking the piano stool out from behind her with the other foot and sending the bench tumbling down the platform steps.

I stood up.

I don't know why I stood up, but I stood up, whistled, and hollered "Ya!"

My mother tugged at my sleeve for me to sit down, but I put my fingers into the corner of my lips and whistled even louder.

"Sit down," the teacher said, running to my seat on the aisle and shaking me by the sleeve. "You're a disgrace!"

And I looked her square in the eye and said, "Just living the dream!"

When she finished, the Chinese girl turned to the audience, bowed to stunned silence, and then skipped to the green room behind the stage.

Later, I saw her father shaking her like a rag doll outside the club.

Her mother was weeping.

The girl was smiling, and it was a beautiful smile. She caught my eye as she smiled. It was a smile that said, "I am no longer going to tolerate what I have to endure."

And now, the scene in my head freezes in its frame, just like in those home movies my father shot on Christmas morning or during birthday parties in our dining room when Mark blew a stream of Coca-Cola out his eyes.

The moment is motionless as if someone has stopped a Super 8 projector, mid-frame, and I am in the Heliconian Club, an old ladies social club surrounded by hippies like an island in a sea of the counter-culture revolution, and I am bent over and whispering in the ear of my childhood self and telling that thin, pimply little boy that life twists things. What is one day's nightmare becomes the next day's dream, until everything changes and becomes serious and I try to tell my own son what is right and what is wrong despite what he wants or thinks he wants.

When the pimply kid from the Super 8 movies, the one who in the final reel turns his back on his father and walks away finally grows up – and all through it, he thinks it takes forever -- he will wonder how he survived it and recall the night he discovered how to dream his way through the world, and how dreams are worth the pain of dreaming regardless of how they turn out. But the kid isn't listening. He's not interested. I could tell him anything. I am just another grown-up going blah, blah, blah in his ear and he's learned to tune them out.

He's home and sent to his room after the recital. The house is dark and silent. Everyone but him is asleep. He's listening for distant voices of a now that ceased to exist the moment it happened and lasted no longer than the light of a falling star or an image flashing through his head in a dream or the blinding glare at the end of a home movie. He is dialing around on the AM band of an old Bakelite radio in the darkness and wondering if anyone out there in the vast static of star land is speaking to him or trying to explain in song or words or even in silence just how he feels. After being reprimanded for wild, shameful behavior, he realizes what he's done was so wrong and yet so important to the beginning of his new life.

He's got the sound low, and his ear to the overheated clock radio in the boxy maple headboard of his single bed. Slowly moving the dial with his hand, he picks up a faint signal from somewhere hundreds of miles away in the Midwest. The electric clock buzzes in his ear with the sound of Time.

Through the overlay of voices on a warm June night, he hears a song about someone dreaming a little dream. He begins to drift off to sleep, and as he does one of his last thoughts is of a tune he learned in nursery school about a boat drifting gently down a stream. And in the morning when he wakes, he will have come ashore in a strange, uncharted land that is enchanting and frightening in one breath, and he won't understand what he encountered until it is too late to dream.

Mack the Knife

CHEESE EXPLAINS SO MUCH about the type of person who ought to be murdered. A true *affineur* knows the correct knife to use for each cheese and each victim. Harder cheeses such as a crystaled, buttery *Parmigiano-Reggiano*, describe someone who is resistant, lapidarian, and inscrutable, whose life must be grated away shred by fine shred or skewered on the end of a long, thin, and very sharp blade. Softer cheese personalities, the runny kind, suggest sentimental characters who are harder to render lifeless because they are physically and emotionally oozy. They are the *brie* of humanity who become softer and softer the longer they are left at room temperature or endured over hours of pointless conversation. Imagine a sweet old auntie or a gran who really must go but has been left out on a marble palette too long, malleable as *chevre* lingering in direct sunlight. Some individuals of this ilk, the cloying girlfriend, or the bow-tied beau, require spoons and scoops if they are to be consumed properly, and everyone knows spoons and scoops are next to useless for homicidal purposes unless poison is in play. A spade for *Danish Blue* won't do the job either. A true *turophile* trusts that everyone, beneath outward appearances, is resistant to being murdered and is a hard curd at heart.

My friend Benny's Uncle Thomas was a rank old round, a character of pique, whose sharpness and pungency of character reminded me of stale *limburger.* Benny had been orphaned as a child after his parents had a food mishap in Austria, and the old uncle, his only living relative, had grudgingly taken him in. One of the things Uncle Thomas denied Benny was cheese. The old man insisted it was rancid milk and a complete waste of money. But that was not the reason why Uncle Thomas became Benny's target.

There were deeper, more profound reasons that worked like rennet in my friend's resolve. The old man represented everything Benny detested – a resistance bordering on fear that made the world ugly and made life grey, narrow, and damp. Benny hated his uncle not only for what the man had taken from him, but for everything Old Tom had taken from British life.

If asked about what he had done with his long life, Uncle Thomas would tell people he had worked at the BBC. He would cock his ear toward whoever was speaking, making them uneasy, as if he were hanging on every word and waiting for someone to say something that was not to his liking. In a tiny office squirreled away in Portland Place, with a glass listening booth taking up most of the space, Uncle Thomas had been the BBC censor. Uncle Thomas's job was to listen to every new recording as it arrived at Broadcast House and determine whether it was fit for the sensitive and soft-headed listener.

The tawdry, the lewd, the lurid, or the merely suggestive lyrics from American songs crossed the Atlantic to find Uncle Thomas lying in wait for them with his rubber stamp and his keen ear for innuendo. The raw innocence of jazz sexuality was easy to reject. When it came to religious or theological matters, Uncle Thomas also drew a strict line as to what was permissible and what was not. Billie Holiday's "God Bless the Child," was rejected because the BBC did not take God lightly. The same fate met Louis Armstrong's "Mack the Knife" in March of 1951, but for entirely different reasons.

"It was a damnable, bloody, incitement to homicide," Benny's uncle ranted over dinner one night. Benny called the old censor a crackpot.

"Nonsense!" Uncle Thomas shouted back. He banned the song about "pearly whites" because "it might trigger another outbreak of Jack the Ripper." Meanwhile, Kurt Weill's *Three Penny Opera*, from which Armstrong borrowed the song for his New Orleans cover version, received an evening airing courtesy of the English National Opera on the Third Program. To get the Weill opera to air someone sent a memo to Uncle Thomas to tell him the *Three Penny Opera* by a composer whose name was pronounced 'while" rather than 'veil' was the "German anti-Nazi version of John Gay's *The Beggar's Opera* – a fine piece of traditional eighteenth-century English stagecraft and a pastiche of several noteworthy Francois Villon poems." Anti-Nazi? Enlightenment drama? French poetry? What could possibly be wrong with all that?

Even as a young boy, Benny was aware his Uncle Thomas had a skewed perception of what cut it and what should be cut. When McDonald's opened its first franchises in London in 1975, the chain was promoted on television with Ray Charles, disguised as a crescent moon, singing a version of "Mack the Knife," rewritten for the Big Mac.

Benny frequented the franchises despite Uncle Thomas's protestation that American cuisine was invading England and would eventually trigger the downfall of British culture. The Quarter Pounder with Cheese had piqued my friend's teenage tastes. Benny told me that when he tasted the orange square on the Quarter Pounder with Cheese, he knew there had to be something better in the world than what lurked beneath ketchup and a toasted bun.

What a person is denied eventually expresses itself as an obsession. As I mentioned, the forbidden fruit in Benny's house was cheese. Uncle Thomas could not abide its taste, smell, or texture. He owned a fine, monogrammed, sterling silver Stilton scoop that had been passed down from the early Nineteenth century and bore the maker's mark from Garrard's. "Silversmiths be damned when it comes to cheese," Uncle Thomas roared when Benny set a jar of Leicester on the table and produced the polished scoop. "I'll not have any rotten dairy goods near my food." Benny put the scoop away but kept his uncle's mean-spirited reaction in his emotional larder. If and when the opportunity presented itself, he would find a way to put an end to Uncle Thomas.

When Benny took a year off after his first term at Birkbeck to backpack across Europe, he began his sojourn in Athens where he discovered flaming *saganaki.* In a market in the north end of Athens, an uninteresting suburb of narrow streets, Benny was certain he had met, face to face, the Greek herald of cheese, Aristaios, son of Apollo, who was sent to Earth to bring mankind the gift of cheese. In the shadows of the cramped market, cheese sellers sat in their stalls as Benny browsed rounds of *graviera* and *manoypi* and fell in love with the aroma, sweet curd and sour, the soft and the hard. He professed he experienced a moment in which he felt he understood the world, and that life was about cheese. When I questioned him, he explained that cheese was the foundation of Western philosophy.

"Think of it," he said. "We are born milky and fresh from the underbelly of a warm being. Then, we are mixed with the ingredients that will determine who and what we are, what we become, and how we are known. And, in the end, if we are not consumed by the hunger that drives all things to sustain themselves on other things – a nod to the Roman philosopher Propertius he had read in a Penguin edition when he came to visit me during the Christmas break one year because Uncle Thomas was ranting about the degenerative aspects of carols – we grow old, become rank, and either mummify or express ourselves in furry mold."

"That's a rather original way to think about life and Western philosophy."

"Yes," said Benny, "and as I was walking among all those crowded market stalls cast in the shadows, the dark *affinage* of our mortal experience, an old man leaned out with a pointed knife, and on its tip was a wedge of *mizithra*, a soft, white cheese, dipped in honey, and I understood that nothing so wonderful could be born of this world. It was ambrosia. And when I took it from the knife, the point caught the one thread of sunlight that seemed to enter the market, and the blade tip glowed like a star. I went back the next day and the old man was gone. In fact, no one had ever heard of him, and I ached, longing for just one more taste of the food of the gods."

Benny had been so transformed by the experience that he had shipped a box of selected cheeses from the Aristaiopolis to his Uncle Thomas in the hope that the change would be contagious. Uncle Thomas was called to the Post Office and asked to explain the rancid package. "Toss it out," he told the clerk. "That boy's up to no good."

And when Benny gave up his studies to apprentice at cheesemonger Paxton and Whitfield on Jermyn Street, Uncle Thomas had been the first to condemn the act. "That's a street full of tailors, and you, lad, can't keep a secret like a tailor."

That is when Benny became a collector of cheese knives. His favorite, he would tell me as he balanced the handle in his hand, was a thin, razor-sharp blade with a lethal point he had acquired in that cheese market on the outskirts of Athens. It was a copy of the knife on which the vendor had held out the ambrosial wedge of *mizithra.* And though I had never known Benny to be a violent person, I knew he had little respect for his uncle.

"Please don't tell me what you are going to do with that blade," I told him emphatically. "I think I know, but I do not want to be an accessory to whatever inevitable conclusion you are about to enact."

Benny looked at me hard and then winked.

"I want you to come to dinner tomorrow evening," he said. "Uncle Thomas is celebrating his ninetieth birthday. I am going to surprise him with some of the hard stuff."

For a moment, I thought he was speaking of a good single malt, but it dawned on me that Benny rarely drank. His knife of choice was going to serve the hard stuff as dessert, after which Uncle Thomas would get his just desserts.

Dinner began civilly.

Benny had prepared a very fine leg of lamb and served it *au jus*. Uncle Thomas questioned why there was no wine on the table, so to please the old man he produced a bottle of Retsina. Uncle Thomas frowned.

"That's that piney stuff. Dirty bathwater to me," he snarled.

"It is the Greek choice for a rosemary lamb main dish, and for the sweets at the end of the meal, I have a wonderful bottle of pink Zamos. If you close your eyes and think your way through the essence of garlic, basil, and tzatziki, you will feel a cool breeze blowing across the Aegean and imagine that breeze once danced around Helen of Troy and lingered at the foundation of the Acropolis where it circled the seat of Ares, the Areopagitica, where men could speak freely without fear of being censored by some old bastard."

As Uncle Thomas began to shake his head in protest, Benny produced from a silver-covered serving dish a copy of Milton's *Areopagitica* and began to read aloud. He reached the passage where Milton presents the argument for freedom of thought and speech, a passage of prose so essential to the life of nations that it is carved on walls. When Benny finished his taunt, he shoved the platter of lamb aside, stood up, and uncovered a serving dish that held a chunk of *mizithra* and the thin, pointed knife he had purchased in Athens, the blade Benny kept for hard cheeses.

Uncle Thomas, sensing what was about to unfold, beat Benny to the knife and snatched the blade away from his nephew's outstretched hand. Benny laid his palm on the table in front of his uncle to lean over and yell more of the Areopagitica into the censor's face. He exclaimed, "What do you think of that, you nasty old slug?"

"Take that, you laggard," the old man shouted and drove the knife through Benny's hand. Benny dropped the book and the most terrifying, ghostly sound rose like someone enduring Hades from deep within my friend.

I was still carving my morsels of the lamb, but I watched in stunned silence as Thomas stood up, pulled the knife from the table and Benny's hand, leaving a red stain of blood on the white cloth, and plunged it theatrically into his nephew's chest. Benny staggered back in pain and shock.

"Do you know what killed your parents in Austria?" Uncle Thomas hollered. "*Der faulig Käse*! The stinky cheese! And to think I raised you and gave you everything I could possibly give you – a good school, time to bum around Europe until you found yourself – I even let you pursue your *turophilia* much against my better judgment when we both know *affineurs* are a dime a dozen in a world that has gone rancid with poisonous mold! And you thank me by plotting my murder with that idiot friend of yours there. Look! He hasn't even moved a twitch to help you."

(I have to admit that what unfolded before me, with its Aristotelian unity of time and place in the most Aeschylean fashion imaginable, was stunning and catastrophic – something that evoked the shock and awe of an unspeakable tragic catharsis. I felt both pity and pain for Benny). I spontaneously overflowed my powerful emotion all over the table.

Uncle Thomas continued his rant.

"Look! Your fool's just dyspepticising himself," he said, gesturing at me with the Greek knife, "cutting his lamb! You think you're clever, Benny, that you could put one by me and then one in me, but I found the knife while you and your friend were busy uncorking that coniferous swill and chilling your pink little sweet drink for afterward to toast my demise! I hear everything. That's always been my job. I catch nuances. You hear nothing. I'm not deaf or blind."

Uncle Thomas was standing at the head of the table, glowing as if he had been the winner in a Greek tragedy, but everyone knows there are no winners in such plots. My chief concern was whether I could get out of the house, get Benny help in time, and if the old man were going to pursue me, hack me down, and roll my body in a carpet. The knifepoint in Uncle Thomas' hand dripped with my friend's blood in small red tears on the tablecloth. As Benny collapsed, he tore at the edge of the cloth to try and hold on not only to the dinner plates and serving pieces that followed him to the floor but to the silver dish of *mizithra*, sighing as he fell and saying something about hearing the old goat sing.

Confused, Uncle Thomas stared at Benny. "A goat singing? What on earth do you mean?" Now I was terrified and ready to break down in tears. Uncle Thomas stood there laughing at us and pointing the blade of the knife, first at me then at Benny.

"The old guy finally got my goat. My words will soon rattle in my throat, and my pain will bleat at you. *Tragoidos*," Benny choked. "But the goat song, the tragedy, will be mine, not his."

Badlands

WHEN THE WAR ENDED, Myrtle greeted me on the dock in Frisco. The homecoming should have been a picture out of *Life* magazine – sailor kissing a girl – but my right hand got burned bad that day in Leyte Gulf. I don't know why our ship got picked on. We were one of the smaller carriers the Navy had tossed together to say they had superior numbers. And there were bigger targets that the enemy could have chosen to go for when they attacked. Maybe they thought a little one would be easier to sink. Others, bigger carriers, had taken hits, too, and they made the newsreels. We didn't.

One of the big boats took so many hits and was so horribly mangled no one could tell if it was a ship or a piece of scrap metal. Her captain made the decision not to take the easy route home to the West Coast but to limp all the way around the globe to New York. It was a brilliant idea. It showed resolve and defiance in the face of all odds. My friend, Sparky, was on that ship. He told me keeping his ship afloat was pure hell, but the brass loved it. A chance to show the grand old flag. A chance to brag about glory and courage and being indefatigable.

Sparky's ship made *Life* magazine's cover.

My carrier, just like my life, was part of history but easily forgotten. So, instead of doing something heroic, we took the direct route home. As we sailed under the Golden Gate Bridge, even though we didn't need to go under the bridge because we just had to turn around and come back out again, there weren't any folks standing at the rails and cheering, there were only cars headed to and from Oakland. The whole homecoming thing was a flop. A crappy tin can all banged up. I stood on the flight deck and waved like an idiot until I was told I was an idiot. I don't think anyone saw us. Not even the inmates at Alcatraz.

Myrtle keeps saying I'm a sucker for a flop.

"Why weren't you on a battleship?" she'd ask, and I'd answer that the Navy trained me as an aircraft mechanic, and I'd still be one except for my hand injury. I didn't mind being on my pint-sized carrier. It wasn't glamorous but we were doing the same job as everyone else in the Pacific Fleet. Besides, I'm a romantic. I believe in small, noble gestures.

As soon as I had Myrtle in my arms, I said, "Baby, let's head east."

I think she thought I was talking about a little cottage on Cape Cod, maybe an inn for lovers from Boston or an illicit weekend rendezvous from New York. Maybe Myrtle pictured herself making small talk with advertising execs and their secretaries while I sent up smoke signals in the kitchen, slopping scrambled eggs and bacon well into the mornings.

But my idea of east was a new gaming town rising in the desert. Some wise guys from New York figured they could make a lot of money off servicemen who needed somewhere to stop and blow off steam. Somewhere they could carry on and not get noticed. The idea was a mirage.

Sparky sent me a telegram and told me he couldn't believe the action there, and if Sparky couldn't believe something then I had to be part of it. I cabled him back: "Count me in." I arrived with no prospects. Sparky never showed. He'd moved on and for the longest time I didn't know where. I felt suckered because I'd built the whole thing up to Myrtle and it was a letdown when we arrived.

We were on the bus heading east from California. Myrtle started whining about why we couldn't have stayed on the coast, perhaps gone south to LA. She said she could have been a Hollywood success story and why didn't I appreciate her movie star good looks?

I tried to ignore her. I said, "Geez, I just fought a war. I just crossed an enormous ocean red with the blood of my fellow Americans (I was being dramatic for emphasis). Can't you leave me alone to enjoy some peace?" and I pointed out the window to the desert that spread before us.

Then she said she was thirsty, so we got off the bus in Las Vegas and I told her I'd buy her more drinks than she'd ever had, and she was good with that because Myrtle never turned down a drink. But the Vegas everyone knows now hadn't happened yet. What it became was thirty years down the road. That's a long time to wait, especially for Myrtle. As the bus pulled away in a cloud of dust, she hit me on the shoulder with her handbag.

"It's hot and dusty and there's nothing here," she scolded me.

"It's the desert," I said. "That's why they serve drinks here. People get thirsty in the desert, and when they can't quench their thirst, they have more and more drinks until they don't care about the heat and dust, and they start feeling lucky and gamble the rest of their money away. That's the whole point of what is starting to happen here. Just wait until they build it. You'll see. Sparky says that's how it's going to work. Drunk people feel lucky. That's a fact of life."

Luck didn't have anything to do with it. There is no such thing as luck, though I believe in providence, divine intervention, the sort of thing that gives a person hope. I think of providence as a narrow shred of possibility that defies logic and circumstance despite the way we deserve what we get. Sister Bernardine and the nuns drilled that into me. And for the first several years in Vegas, I felt as if I had done something good, something worthy. Maybe not in this life. Not just in the Navy where I'd run through flames to rescue guys trapped below deck, but something I couldn't recall, possibly something I did in a past life where my heavenly reward followed me into this version of my soul. And even if I couldn't remember what I'd done, I was happy to take the payoff that life was offering me. Who am I to refuse a gift or a miracle especially when an entirely new town was rising out of the badlands like a pillar of fire in the desert?

There wasn't much to Vegas when we arrived.

I pictured myself as a dealer at a casino, but the schmuck in charge took one look at my hand and said "No." At the time I was hurt. But that no led to other things. Things I couldn't have imagined.

I finally got a job in a smallish, poorly lit lounge – back east they'd call it a seedy low-life joint or a bar that didn't pay its electric bills but in Vegas it was the new concept in watering holes. I learned to mix drinks, mostly martinis. No one could see my hand in the low light and even if they did the clientele was too drunk to care. Within five years, the owner got tired of running the place and I bought it for a song. The day the deed was signed over to me, I stepped out the front door of my newly acquired establishment to greet the dawn, and as I spread my arms and looked up at the sun there was a huge fire about three or four blocks away and a pillar of smoke was rising from it.

"Lead me on!" I hollered. "I'm ready to follow."

I bought Myrtle a house, so she'd have a nest to call her own. She wanted what every woman of the day was supposed to want if the magazines and television commercials were true: a kitchen with bright new, appliances that did everything from keeping food cold to dicing the cat. Were we happy? Myrtle stopped complaining for a while and she stayed out of my hair.

My hours were long because a lounge in Vegas never closes. Not like New York. There is no beginning and no end to a day in the desert. There is no time. There is only the heat during the day when the light is so bright a reflection off the chrome of a car's bumper could fry an egg behind your eyes and the cold at nights that make me feel lonely when the moon looks like it's chasing me as I drive home. Vegas was a place that existed in a state of amnesia, a perpetual nowhere between reality and illusion. It is even more like that now, only glitzy. Back then the town was just learning how to be everything and nothing at the same time. Nobody knows your name unless you're a member of the local business community. Soon, everyone knew mine.

I have never been afraid of my own name, so I put it up in a big neon sign out front of the lounge: Kaufmann's. I haven't had much to live up to or much to live down when it comes to my name because I've never been sure of who I am.

What little I know came from a nun in the house of charity where I grew up. Sister Bernardine was elderly and was never sure of her facts. Her story was that my father intended to join my pregnant mother in Philadelphia, but his ship caught fire during the Atlantic crossing.

"Aren't you lucky your parents weren't on the same ship?" the nun asked with her face poking out the porthole of her wimple.

The only evidence of my identity was a newspaper clipping of the tragedy at sea. My mother must have folded it into my blanket before she turned me over to the Sisters. Sister Bernardine shoved it across her desk to me as I was instructed to leave the foundling's home when I turned sixteen. I read the clipping, then lost it somewhere.

The clipping described how ships had attempted to rescue the passengers from my father's vessel, the S.S. Hoxie Gorge, and were in sight of the burning ship's column of smoke when the vessel exploded and took everyone to the bottom. I am not even sure if I was Kaufmann's son. He was one of seven passengers who were listed as dead. Maybe that's why I joined the Navy. I'd spend hours of my free time at the rail, staring into the waves as if the waters were going to part and the truth would pop up and greet me. Maybe the clipping was just something my mother tore from the newspaper because it was a roaring story. And as for my mother? Who knows? I wasn't broken-hearted when I lost the yellowing scrap of paper because of something Sister Bernardine told me.

"There are two things a person is permitted to carry with them throughout their lives and should never compromise under any circumstances: their dignity and their name."

I wasn't sure about my name and, as Myrtle kept reminding me, my dignity was a matter for speculation with Billy in the house. I can't recall how Myrtle came by her horizontal friend. Billy thought he was a country singer. He wasn't. His straggly blond hair began at least an inch above his forehead. He performed in my bar, but even with only two patrons in the place, Billy got booed off the stage. He moved in with us and I was glad he was there to keep her company. I had a bar to run, and the bar had my name on it.

I told Myrtle that my character was a paragon. I think I used that word correctly. Paragon. The guys at the lounge liked the word, too. When we discussed it, everyone sitting on their stools repeated it together as if they were singing a litany. Ten guys in suits on bar stools, waiting for the phone to ring: Paragon. Paragon.

"How can you sit there, in your smoky little dive, with all those shady characters and their illegal businesses and know that I'm at home carrying on with a lousy singer?" Myrtle shouted at me as I stood outside the bathroom and waited for Billy to finish showering and shaving. "Don't you have any dignity? What do you do all day?"

"We read poetry to each other," I said.

That was the truth. The guys love anthologies. They love discussing, "the proclivities and the intricacies of the English mother tongue in the expressions of its most renowned wits and rhapsodes." We all agreed we'd explain what we were doing there exactly in those words if the cops got suspicious and started asking questions. The cops never did, but an extensive vocabulary *is* the hallmark of a gentleman. That's what I told Myrtle.

She scoffed and thought I was lying to her. "You're running hookers, aren't you?"

"Not I. Oh, no, not I."

I didn't care. I was busy. I had to earn a living. I had to make sure that she and I, and yes, Billy, were fed and had a roof over our heads.

By then, I'd gotten used to Billy. He was like a son to me, and because my wife was ten years older than me, he was young enough to have been her kid. If he started up with his playing and his stupid lyrics, I'd just get in the car and go to work. I didn't mind that the guy had it good. He kept Myrtle happy. The lounge kept me happy. It was a tidy arrangement.

I love a 'tidy arrangement.' Everyone does everyone a favor. The Gaming Commission took their cut from the fruit machines I kept in a room at the back because the ding-ding sound from them gave me a headache. If someone wanted to come to an arrangement with someone else, they'd rise from their barstool or table and tell me they were going 'fruit shopping,' and slip into the slots room. The liquor came courtesy of these arrangements and at rock-bottom prices from a distributor who owed a favor to the Gaming Commission. All I had to do was keep my mouth shut as a favor to everyone and I did, to the point I earned the nickname "Clammy," Clammy Kaufmann. Getting nicknamed in my line of work is very important. It denotes standing. It adds to one's dignity.

Sparky, who had run craps with me in Philly before the war, had disappeared from my life. I had no idea what he'd gotten up to. My guess was that he'd probably gotten booked. But out of the blue, he called me. He called me at the lounge. I don't know how he got the number or how he tracked me down, but there he was on the other end of the call. The regulars on their stools who were waiting for their daily business opportunities all looked up from the Grecian poem by Keats that we were discussing. Sparky said he wanted to come for a visit.

When he showed up, he was wearing a white dog collar. He'd become a preacher. He said he'd gone to university, found the Good Lord after trying to save a family from a burning tenement. He got all the kids out but not the mother. And the pillar of smoke from the event reminded him of me because he always told me I'd end up wandering in the desert with only a pillar of smoke by day or a pillar of fire by night to guide me. I never disagreed with him when he said stuff like that. He made me feel Biblical.

Sparky was teaching at what I call a 'holy' university, one of those places where people go to ask questions about what God is, and when they can't find answers, they spend the rest of their lives instructing others how to ask questions for which there are no answers. Education is about knowing less when you are finished with it than when you began. When he arrived, I asked him if he had found any answers.

"Not enough," he said. "I'm still searching. I don't know if there are answers, yet I know there are a million questions"

"Let me know the minute you find any answers," I said.

"You're not taking me seriously, are you. You've thrown yourself into this den of iniquity, into this Sodom and Gomorrah of low life behavior, and you have lost yourself."

"Hey," I said, "I built this joint up from a second-rate lounge into a really excellent second-rate lounge."

That got a laugh from the guys on the stools as they'd paused in their daily business matters to discuss whether the 'Tempe' mentioned by Keats was Tempe, Arizona.

Sparky hollered at them.

He called them heathens. He told them they were sinners.

They agreed enthusiastically.

He told the guys on the stools they would be damned.

They all nodded. Sounded about right to them.

Then they asked him, "What's your point?"

That's when Sparky stormed out. I never saw him again.

If circumstances had been different, I would have made my peace with my friend, and we would have gone on as we were – me being the idolator to his prophet. I tried to get to the airport, where I thought I could head him off before his flight out, to apologize and make amends with the guy who had been my best buddy growing up.

But the traffic was snarled. There was a car on fire up the highway. I could see a column of smoke climbing into the air. When I reached the airport, I was trying to park my car, but I didn't have exact change and the guy in the booth had to go and get a roll of quarters.

Sparky's plane was on the runway. It taxied down the tarmac, revved up, and as it was lifting off one wing dipped suddenly and the plane cartwheeled down the white lines, like an acrobat on a desert highway, then burst into flames.

I saw a plume of smoke rising in the distance, though this time it meant something different to me. It wasn't a sign of blessing as it reached into the empty sky but a hand stooping down from above, trying to hold the earth from rising up and making a grab at heaven.

I sat down and wept.

I wept all the way home.

I drove along the main drag.

The old hotels were being knocked down. Skyscrapers were rising in their place.

And I thought, "I'm living in Babel…these towers will be knocked down in my lifetime."

Sparky's death was a gut punch. It tore at my stomach. I'd sit at the bar and drop two tablets of Alka-Seltzer into glasses of water. The guys on the stools told me all that fizz would eventually kill me. The lounge became my obsession. I set up a cot in my office so I could sleep there instead of going home to Myrtle and Billy. I was afraid of myself. I was afraid that I had sinned because I knew that somewhere in my past I had done something wrong, and I was destined to wander in the badlands all the days of my life.

That's when the nightmares started. I kept having dreams where I was back on my carrier, in the hell of that long day in Leyte Gulf, on the flight deck strewn with the dying, the screams of men in agony, the sounds of incoming suicide planes, then being ordered below to the hangar to help fight the fire and running into the flames and pulling guys out, and not knowing what I should do. I wanted to run, and I didn't know where. In circles, circling back upon the way I'd come? I looked up and amid the screams of the injured a pall of acrid smoke was climbing skyward as if the ship was sending up a distress signal or a call for mercy in the wilderness of the sea.

The night my carrier burned, after a beautiful Pacific sunset that would have made a lovely postcard except for the destruction all around me, I came topside and looked at the sky to see if the stars were still there and they were.

One guy on his stool explained to me how, after Dante went to Hell, the Italian poet crawled out a vent on the bottom side of the world where the smoke of damnation ascended into the foothills of Purgatory.

"You know what Purgatory is, right?"

"What's your version?" I asked him.

"It's like the way into town, the desert, the place where you have to look hard to see signs of life but they're all around. It's like a waiting room when you go to pay someone's bail. There's life, but the chairs are hard, and you've got to think about what you're going to part with if the guy skips out."

"But Dante got lucky," I said. "He saw the stars through the exhaust."

"Yeah. Kind of like a car in a garage when someone needs to make an exit."

I asked, "Why were you reading Dante?" and the guy on the stool replied he was Italian, and his wife left it lying around the house and he slipped it in his pocket for a little light reading. Made sense to me. But what he said about Dante climbing through the vent of Hell and seeing the stars brought back all sorts of things I thought I'd buried in me, memories of my day in the inferno and how I emerged from it.

The flight deck was hissing with steam. My boots were melting beneath me. Fires raged in the bridge and the conning tower. The anti-aircraft bays were barbecue pits.

The pillar of smoke had been replaced in the night sky by a pillar of fire. I saw what the Israelites saw when they wandered for forty years in the desert, clinging to the one shred of hope that remained to them after a hard life of servitude. They thought they were heading to the Promised Land. None of those wanderers in the desert ever got where they wanted to go, but the pillar of fire by night was a sign just the same that they were going somewhere as they walked in circles.

That's when the pain in my right hand grabbed me and I tried to pull my arm off. When I'd been busy in the hangar trying to quench the fires of Hell as our gas tanks and oil drums exploded, I had no idea how badly I'd been burned. Topside, in the light from that pillar of fire, I looked at my right hand. It was charred, and what was left of it was loose and peeling skin. I couldn't move my fingers. I couldn't make a fist. My first thought was, "I'll never fight again because I can't make a fist." And then I stared into the open palm of my left and for reasons I can't explain, I looked into my hand to read my lifeline in case it had been lying to me.

Sparky and I once dropped into a palm reader in Boston when we'd taken the train so we could see the Phillies play the Braves. The palm reader showed me how long my lifeline was. She'd never seen one so long. She stroked my hand as if I held a blessing.

"You will spend a long life trying to find your way," she said.

When Sparky presented his left to be read, she shook her head and muttered, "I hope it will be quick." His lifeline was half the length of mine.

When I'd wake, drenched in sweat on that cot in my office at the back of the lounge, I'd think "Why now, why after all these years am I being visited by memories I thought I'd never have to live with," and the answer came to me. I needed to find my way out of the badlands I'd bottled up inside.

So that's why I was puzzled when I found myself bleeding from my side in the middle of the desert with Billy and Myrtle standing between me and the setting sun, their bodies casting shadows on my face in the afterglow, so they looked like specters or demons.

She'd said, "This is going to be bad for our marriage, but…" And then she shot me. Myrtle wasn't a good shot. If she had been, I wouldn't be alive.

When they turned to walk away – her gun had jammed, and Billy said they had to go and get another and Myrtle argued with him that getting a new gun was good money after bad and that they ought to find someone to fix the broken one – and I was left looking up at where they had been. I felt more alone than I had ever felt. They got in Myrtle's car and drove away, leaving me lying there, dusty, wounded, bleeding all over an expensive suit, but still alive.

I looked around at the stillness. The sun was setting. I listened and couldn't hear a word. Maybe the world was saying 'No.'

A no is a word that changes everything.

A no changes the course of a life.

A no decides things will be different from that moment on, sometimes for the good and sometimes for the bad.

Moses came down from Sinai and found his people worshipping a golden calf and let out a loud 'NO!' That little word changed everything. His followers wandered in the desert for the next forty years trailing after pillars of combustion.

"May we go to the Promised Land today, please, oh pretty please?"

Moses pulls on his long, shaggy beard and says, "No."

I dusted myself off, crawled out of the hole I'd found myself in, and began walking, with the silence of the darkening desert spreading around me, and the stars shining brighter and brighter with each step. I was feeling a terrible thirst. I thought I saw Sparky standing at the side of the highway. I wanted to ask him if he'd found any answers. He smiled, but true to form he just disappeared.

"Lord?" I asked, "Now would be a good time for a sign. Show me a little smoke or a little fire, that's all I ask."

And I heard a voice inside me, a voice crying out from the wilderness, saying:

"Put one foot in front of the other. Keep going."

I walked the shoulder of the straight and narrow road and could see ahead a couple of miles where I knew the highway bent around a curve before it veered off toward Vegas.

That's when I heard a boom, and then a horn, a faint blare in the distance like an angel's trumpet, sounding a single blue note. Maybe that's how the day of judgment arrives. A single blast from Gabriel atop a mountain. But the longer I walked, the louder and clearer that note rang out. I could see a pillar of fire rising into the sky and thought I recognized the sound because it reminded me of the horn from Myrtle's car, a full, rich middle C she insisted on having installed as a customization for the convertible I bought her. Long, powerful, and heavenly it blew.

I wondered if maybe Billy and Myrtle had hit a truck while they were arguing about the gun and having taken their eyes off the road were distracted by each other, or if they had driven away without their headlights on and slammed into a hillside or an oncoming tanker truck.

Perhaps I was being wishful. I shouldn't wish for bad for others nor should I wish for good for myself, as Sister Bernardine drummed into me. I shouldn't wish for the world to change because the world is God's work and little boys in houses of charity have no business arguing with providence because whatever happens is all in "the plan." I should only ask for guidance, a way to pass through the darkness and follow a sign from the Lord without asking where it will lead me. Take the straight and narrow as far as it will take you. Then, hang a left.

No. She didn't say that.

That's me being an idiot again. Not taking things seriously. That's my head talking to me. The loss of blood messing with my brain. I thirst. I thirst.

I keep sticking out my thumb out for a lift but even when a driver slows down, he immediately speeds up because he sees me bleeding. He thinks I'm on the wrong end of a business deal and doesn't want to have any part of me.

Or maybe the driver sees me bleeding and decides "Not in my car, Bub."

So, I'll just keep walking.

That's it.

Left foot, right foot. The way I learned it in basic training. The way we were drilled in the house of charity when Sister Bernardine got the idea that physical fitness involved marching up and down in tidy ranks. Straight and narrow.

I want to know what's burning. I want to know where the fire comes from when it rises into the starry sky and there's nothing there to burn – no ship, no shipmates, no plane wreck, no childhood friend. That fire is a sign. I follow its pillar of smoke by day and pillar of fire by night as it rises from the mystery beyond the bend in the road. And I leave it to the grace of a higher power to determine if it will lead me out of the badlands.

Hopeless

NONNINO HADN'T WOKEN as Frank lifted the yellowing snapshot from his grandfather's hand. The woman, little more than a girl, was smiling. She had beautiful round eyes and curly dark hair resting on the shoulders of a flowered dress. A long, stony street wound downhill behind her as if she were emerging from the nether regions of shadows behind her and the camera had just turned to catch a blinking glimpse of her radiance, her slender figure, and her butterfly smile. She was not Nonnina. Frank's *nonna* had come later in his grandfather's life after Nonnino had made the long journey to Canada. Years must have gone by as his grandfather wished he could write to the woman he once loved but was afraid any sign of life from him in his new identity might imperil his beloved. The problem of contacting the love of his life was further complicated. Nonnino could only write his own name.

The old man woke. He pointed to the photograph in Frank's hand.

"*Lei bellissima, no?*" he said as he reached to take the snapshot back.

"Is it Nonnina?" Frank asked.

At first, the old man shook his head back and forth as if trying to decide what his answer would be. Frank's *nonna* had been shorter, her eyes narrow, and her cheekbones high. She could cook like no one else, which is why the meals Frank sometimes brought for his *nonno* would go uneaten and sit for days in the refrigerator, until Frank tossed them out thinking that the effort had been wasted on a man who was shrinking into himself, withdrawing into his own world, and taking with him the old consumables he thought necessary, his tomatoes and his homemade wine he cellared in a cinderblock room off the lower kitchen where the real business of food happened for special family dinners. The old man would explain there was no point in eating the food his grandson brought in for him. Nothing could compare to Nonnina's manicotti and tortellini.

Nonnino took the photograph from Frank and slipped it into his shirt pocket.

"L'amore è senza speranza," Nonnino said through his raspy voice.

The only things Frank had ever seen go into that plaid work shirt pocket where the braces from the old man's trousers cut deeply into his shoulders were his unfiltered cigarettes. After the old man beat a bout of pneumonia and relinquished his cigarettes on the orders of his doctor and his daughter, Frank assumed that the shirt pocket would remain empty forever. He was wrong. The pocket was now for keeping something close to his heart.

Nonnino repeated the phrase, adding *"e ti può anche uccidere facilmente."*

Frank sat with his grandfather silently in the living room as the afternoon sunlight filled the space between them, and the longer he stared in silence at the old man the more Frank wondered what his *nonno's* life had once been, what his reasons were for leaving Italy so quickly, vanishing into the world without a trace of who he had once been or what he left behind. Here was a man of mystery, whose years showed on his hands and face and whose silence held experiences that only Nonnino knew.

Everyone in the family said, "He's just quiet. That's his nature." But there was more to the quiet than just the language gap that separated the old man from his family. Those who could understand Italian knew what the old man said but they were not capable of asking him for me. They were part of this country and Nonnino belonged to another place and another time. Was the old man suffering from a broken heart? When he drank a glass of wine, he would stare into it as if he had lost something important in its tint. Had the woman in the photograph deserted him or had he abandoned her? She wasn't family, a sister, or a cousin. She bore no resemblance to anyone Frank had ever met. He wanted to pat his grandfather on the knee to say goodbye, but the old man was asleep again, so Frank quietly pulled the front door shut behind him.

"He's not doing very well, Mamma," Frank said into the receiver in a low voice so as not to startle his wife or his children. His kids loved their great-grandfather. They weren't sure who he was exactly. He was an old man they visited now and then. The kids would climb into Nonnino's lap, but they were puzzled by the surprised look on Nonnino's face when they spoke only English to the old man.

"He was holding the picture of the woman again today when I slipped in to see him," Frank told his mother on the phone. "He really must learn to lock his door."

"That wouldn't let the angels in," Frank's mother replied, "besides, at his age, he says a murderer might do him some good."

"He didn't say that, did he? That's awful."

"He said it in Italian, so it sounded wise and beautiful." His mother paused and Frank broke the silence.

"What did Nonnino do back home?"

Home could be anywhere. Toronto was Frank's home. He never thought of any other place as his. On his honeymoon, Frank had taken Bridget to see her distant relations in Dublin before they went looking for Nonnino and Nonnina's families in Lazio where Nonnina's family was from, and Basilicata where Nonnino claimed he was born.

In a small town about a hundred miles south of Roma, Frank and his bride came across an old woman in a bakery who thought she knew his grandmother, but added, with a sigh, that the entire family had been killed one night during an American bombing raid, and Nonnina's poor brother, so handsome and just recently reassigned to fight the Germans, had died with them. He was found holding his mother in his arms in the rubble of the butcher's shop that the family ran from a storefront below their flat. The irony, the old woman said, was there hadn't been any meat for months. They could have fled but they kept the shop open on the hopeless pretense that it was their duty to serve their community, "*mucche immaginarie.*"

When Frank and Bridget traveled south to Basilicata, all they could do was stare at the dusty, sand-colored hills. The weather was boiling. Bridget's fair skin burned in the hard sunlight. She insisted they go to the coast, and Frank abandoned his search. There was nothing to look for and nowhere to look. But despite their failure to connect with Nonnino's roots or to break the stony silence he maintained about his past, his family, and his former life in Italy, Frank's mother was able to elicit a small bit of information from her father. He had been a train engineer.

"Mussolini shot train engineers who ran late," Frank said after clearing his throat.

"There may be something to that," his mother replied before saying that her favorite television show, a medical drama, was about to begin and rang off.

Frank understood that when people flee from their pasts, they often hide in the last place anyone would look for them. Canada was such a place. The last place anyone would look for him would be in the depths of solid rock. He knew his grandfather had spent time in Sudbury working in the mines, then three years in the smelter's acid vats where splashes burned through his work shirt and scarred his arms. Frank's mother had been born in Sudbury. She was proud that her father was one of the first Italians that the Irish and Scots permitted in their tunnel crews. There was a framed photograph that Frank kept on his dresser of his mother standing with a landscape of treeless rocky outcrops rising behind her. When he was a child, he asked her if she had grown up on the moon.

"No," she answered, "and then we landed in Toronto where your grandfather worked construction. The city needed strong men. They were building the Gardiner Expressway. It was heavy, dangerous work. He would come home, his work boots coated in concrete so that every step was more labored than it had to be. He loved to fix things. When my car broke down, do you know your *nonno* fixed it? He said he knew how to fix any engine. I asked him where he had learned to be a mechanic. I thought I could make myself popular with the boys, which I did, by having them come around and get their cars tuned by Papà. He tuned the cars and the boys alright."

But for all he could glean from his mother about who and what his grandfather had been in Italy, the answer always ended in silence. The young woman with the large, round eyes, a Renaissance beauty who could have been painted by an Old Master, remained a mystery woman. Frank was amazed that her photograph survived Nonnina's editorial eye. The attributes for 'l'arte culinaria' Nonnina inherited from her butcher family made her a superb cook, a commander in the downstairs kitchen (the upstairs kitchen was kept only for show) where the real cooking took place. She, too, was a Eurydice but in her own way. Frank could still picture his grandmother emerging from the depths with steaming pots of marinara sauce.

The next day, Frank left work early to go by Nonnino's and make sure the old man had shaved and hadn't spent the whole night in his chair. His worst fear was that Nonnino would lose track of time or bodily functions. His grandfather deserved dignity and cleanliness, and even though their relationship was separated by the language barrier, with Frank grasping the odd phrase and memorizing it and attempting to remember the intonations, he and his grandfather had never been close. And again, without Nonnino noticing he was there, Frank had let himself in.

The old man had washed, shaved, and changed his shirt. He looked as if he was expecting company. He had abandoned his house slippers and donned scuffed black Oxfords, and Frank was impressed that the old man had been able to bend over and tie the laces himself. No one else could have done it for him. There were no visible signs of visitors, no plates on the kitchen counter, no flowers or candy.

Nonnino was, again, holding the picture of the girl. He opened his eyes and looked up as Frank entered the room, and he was about to slip the photograph back into his shirt pocket when Frank pointed to it and asked, "Who is she?"

When his grandfather suddenly spoke English, Frank was startled. He'd never heard him speak in any language other than Italian, but from his lips issued the answer to his grandson's question.

"She's Rosetta. My rose. We met when sold me a glass of chianti."

"You speak English!"

"Enough to…" and Nonnino raised his fingers as if he were shuffling money between his thumb and his index finger. "You know. I had mouths to feed. We earn to eat and eat for love."

After a moment of silence, the old man smiled at his grandson. "You want to hear about my broken heart? I loved your *nonna*. She, God rest her soul, was a good woman. A saint. But when I was young, I had an angel. Rosetta. Her father owned a *taverna*." The old man stared at the photograph. Tears were welling in his eyes.

"I was a train engineer. It was not a good time to be a train engineer. If a train ran late, for this or that or whatever, the driver would be pulled from his cab and shot. Mussolini's orders. The trains had to run on time. One day, just outside of Naples, rocks, you know mountains...they fell on the track. I had just left Rosetta in Frosinone. They called her '*Il fiore di Frosinone.*' My flower. I could go back for her, but I was afraid, and the *fascisti* were shooting engineers. They were shooting their families. We were all supposed to be afraid. If I had written for her to come to me in Marseilles where I went to work on a ship, *sarebbe stata uccisa*...they kill her. So, I run here. New York. New York...okay, but too poor for working. Everyone in New York already had a job. I heard about the mine, so I head to Sudbury. Sudbury was good. I meet your Nonnina there. But I never forgot my *fiore,* my flower."

"Where were you from? Mamma says it was Basilicata. What town?"

"It doesn't matter. It had a name. I had a name. Not my name now. Everything is past. I left everything behind. The town? It was destroyed. My *mamma* and *papà*, my Nonnetto. All killed. I don't know who killed them. Maybe, I think, I should write them a letter, but I never learned how. I learn engines. I make things run. I am an engineer."

"So, you never found Rosetta," Frank said.

The old man shrugged. "Only in wine.

"Someone I knew, the conductor on my train, he ran away the same day. He ran in the other direction. That's smart. If we ran in the same direction, who knows? Maybe they kill us both. I walk down a street when I arrive in Toronto, and he calls to me. He calls my name. Marco! Marco! Some wise guy answers Polo because it is a game or something. I turn. There is Carlo. We stop. *Ci abbracciamo*...we hug. I ask what he hears about Rosetta. He shakes his head at first. Then, he says, she looks for you. She looks in New York and Boston. Then she goes home. The war came to Basilicata. Then nothing."

"That's sad, Nonnino."

"Everything is sad, but nothing is hopeless. Maybe she lives. Maybe she has children. Maybe she is a *nonna* now. Nothing is hopeless. If she is dead, she is an angel. If she is alive, she has beautiful grandchildren. I should not have turned when she followed up the dark, narrow street, but I hear her footsteps behind me, so I turn. She smiles.

She," he says, tapping his index finger on the snapshot. "I turn. I take her picture. I look. She fades into shadows, so I sit in this chair, in the sun, at this window, and I wait to see if she appears. I tell my *mamma*, 'Someday I marry Rosetta.' My *mamma* tell me when I look at this picture, 'Marco, you are hopeless.' "Yes," I tell her. "I am hopeless. I never stop being hopeless."

The Ghosts

"EVERYWHERE THEY GO, the ghosts leave their footprints on the earth," Tan said, as he dug around a land mine while Kwon and Tsin stood by and watched. Gently moving the edge of a bayonet around the device, he removed a layer of mud. "This one has been here a while," he said, looking up and smiling, then wiped his forehead with the arm that held the weapon.

The bayonet was not his – the Labour Units were only issued shovels and without rifles there was absolutely no reason why they should have something to attach to the end of a weapon, Major Jolliffe explained. Jolliffe didn't last long. He'd been followed by Hobart, then Carruthers, then Miller, and now the young Bingsley who wanted to be home and rid of his "Asians," as he called them.

The truth behind the Labour Battalion's lack of rifles was that their officers simply didn't trust them, at least that's what Kwon said when the Chinese diggers – in uniforms but not entitled to call themselves soldiers – had moved through the trenches and collected bodies of the fallen. They were unable to defend themselves against the enemy. They made pikes and used their shovels as weapons, but such things were useless against munitions.

Kwon kept count of how many Chinese he had buried in the Canadian cemeteries. The Chinese dead were kept to one corner of the memorial grounds, "their own place," as Major Jolliffe said. At least their headstones were of the same white marble as the others. Their names were known only unto God or to those who could read Mandarin. Most of the laborers were Cantonese.

Tsin took the mine from Tan's hands and carried it over to a length of lumber where other mines lined the board like pies cooling in an afternoon breeze. Someone else from their battalion would come and detonate them later.

"Where is the next one?" Tsin asked.

Kwon shrugged.

Tsin was not good at finding them, only at unburying them. During the course of the day, as they worked their way across a shell-pocked field half a mile outside Ypres, they uncovered three tons of salvage metal, mostly steel, some brass, a dozen unexploded ten-inch shells that were probably German because, as the war lingered, the munitions workers lost heart and fewer shells exploded. They had uncovered an entire tank but were told by their CO, Bingsley, that unless they could smell bodies inside it wasn't worth the effort to dig it out.

"Well?" asked Bingsley.

Kwon shrugged as if to say, "Well, what?"

He pretended he had trouble with English when it suited him, although he knew exactly what was being said whenever one of the ghosts opened their mouth.

Kwon had been a cook in Vancouver for sixteen years, arriving in Canada too late for the hard work of railway construction, or the suicidal missions of explosives handlers. Both the Pacific and the National routes were complete, but the mystique of the trains drew him to the rails. He was good at cooking. The Canadian Pacific gave him a job in the kitchen car of a passenger train and then, for the usual reasons of someone resenting the Chinese taking jobs that whites could do, he ended up on a maintenance caboose and found himself kicked and beaten daily by the navvies on the Cariboo run.

When the war came, Kwon worked in the laundry at a training camp in Penticton, and after sweating himself to dehydration, volunteered for the Ghost Patrol, the brigade that did the heavy labor that was considered beneath the dignity of the average Canadian soldier.

His war had not been without its glories. A photographer had snapped a picture of a burial detail he'd been part of – mainly soldiers who fired a salute – for a fallen German airman. When the assembly of dignitaries, flyers, and ministers dispersed, he'd asked the photographer why this body was more important than the thousands of others he and his battalion had buried.

"Blimey," said the cameraman. "That there's the bloody Red Baron. You're part of history now, lad. You're the one who's putting the scourge to the ground." The Baron had been buried in an elegant black coffin with brass handles. Both the wood and the metal caught the sun.

Kwon looked up at the sky and set to work shoveling with Tan and Tsin and Charlie. Charlie didn't last long. He got careless with his spade and exploded into a million parts. Kwon retrieved his mate's right hand, put it in a small wooden cartridge box, and mailed it home to China.

"The sky," Kwon thought, "that's the place to be. Not here. Not in all this shit. Nothing will ever grow in this place again. This is not night soil. Tan was right. This is the soil of hell, what the ghosts leave behind."

There had been days when hell was only an inch or two beneath them. Tsin had stuck his spade in the ground just after sunrise one morning, and by noon, they had unearthed a trench with one hundred and sixty bodies twisted in a forty-foot channel.

Tan shook his head as they attempted to disentangle the corpses from each other. Some would not part with those they held in their grasp, either because one dead man held someone who had been his friend or because two lives that opposed each other had been vanquished in each other's grip. Bingsley told them to put the Brits in one pile, maybe they were Australians – the buttons would decide – and the Germans in another. If the bodies had numbered collars, they could be French.

Bingsley insisted the French never held that sector, but sure enough they found beneath the top layer of the dead a second trench with over seventy Frenchmen. There were no Germans on that layer. An officer from the command center arrived, inspected the situation, and told them to put on gas masks. The earth was still sweet with the sickly smell of mustard gas. Tan pointed to a patch of earth he'd tossed up where the parados once ran. It was still steaming, and the steam was green as rice shoots he'd picked as a boy in his grandfather's flooded field.

After that, after witnessing beauty in its most absurd expression, they told each other what they saw and the way they saw it as a way to mitigate the horror.

Kwon usually saw something first. In a collapsed dugout on what had been the German side of the Vimy sector, he uncovered the broken shards of a tall blue and white jar. The writing on the bottom said it had come from the village of Ch'in Shin Ga that was only two rivers from where he had been born. That night, as they boiled their ration of rice and added chunks of tinned beef to it, Tan and Kwon studied the porcelain puzzle.

"Did you get all the pieces?" Tan asked.

"They appear to be there, perhaps lacking a sliver, but they are mostly there."

Tsin appeared out of the darkness.

"I found most of a house. The woman was terrified. She held a pitchfork to keep me away. She must have thought I was the devil or something. I spoke to her in French, told her I was part of the clean-up detail, and I convinced her to give me this!"

He held out a tin pot with a small wooden ladle protruding from the lid.

"My friends, we have glue."

"There's nothing around for miles. How far did you go?" Kwon questioned.

"Three or four miles. It had been a command post, from the looks of it. They had glue and not just any glue, but glue, the woman said, that will work on porcelain."

"Are you sure they didn't just hand you a jar of congealed honey? You can get congealed anything these days," Tan said, doubting that Tsin had returned with anything but useless muck.

"No, really. It is glue. Glue, she said, is very popular these days, especially around here. People are putting their lives back together as they return. When she found out that we're the ones who are clearing the fields and making them more or less safe for people to walk in, she said she was very happy to meet me. And she was very impressed that I knew French. I told her I'd learned French in a logging camp in Northern Quebec. She, of course, didn't believe me at first and told me that if I wanted the glue, I had to prove I was a real lumberjack and not just some strange foreigner marauding through the night in search of something to repair a jar. So, I obliged her. She'd gathered some lumber. Likely gotten it from the walls of a trench – it was damp and muddy on one side and bloody on the other – and asked me to chop it into firewood. I lit into it and in no time she had her wood and I had our glue. So, now we can put this jar back together."

Kwon held up each piece and using the edge of the tiny ladle gently coated the edges of the shards, handing them to Tan who blew on them to hasten the glue's drying. When the adhesive appeared to be setting, Tan handed the fragment back to Kwon, careful not to let his fingers touch anything but the center of the piece, and Kwon attached it. They worked throughout the night. Tan said they'd be tired in the morning, that Bingsley would say they were being slow again, but the process of reconstruction was too engrossing for them to leave off.

The overcast departed and the stars grew bright and clear above them. The flickering of the fire made Tsin think of how the jar had been made.

"Someone," he said, "shaped it out of river clay mixed with powdered bone and ash, had fired it in a kiln after lifting it off the wheel, and delicately with a cats-hair brush had painted the fine blue lines of butterflies around the vessel's girth, repeating a pattern of marigolds in bands at the top and bottom of the work. Then, as a lasting gift of dawn to the future, a glint that reflected the wavering light off the surface of the jar, applied the glaze and set it one last time in the kiln."

When the vessel was reassembled, Kwon placed it on the brass base of a ten-inch shell he had retrieved from a field earlier that day. The explosive tip was long gone, blown into the sky like Charlie or fallen from the sky like the Red Baron. It made the perfect jar stand. The three men knelt in front of it and stared at it in awe.

"How do you suppose it got here?" Tan asked.

"Maybe they didn't know that these jars were for the ashes and bones of our forefathers. Maybe they did, and the ghosts have set upon them and made them pay a horrible price for what they did to the dead. Maybe they just didn't know. The people here once treasured such things because they understood that a jar such as this had undertaken a long and difficult journey much like the ones we have known. Those who travel take the world inside them and are vast beneath their skin. Maybe, long before the war, people valued jars such as this because they came from far away, from the place where those who made such things lived in the center of the world. We are from that place. We have come from the navel that keeps the world in balance."

"But, Kwon, we aren't without our own history of hardship and bloodshed," Tan sighed.

"No, we aren't. But despite the floods, the famines, the wars we have known that have torn our Middle Earth to shreds of tattered silk until we thought we had no past worthy of civilized beings, our ways are as fine as any you will ever know. We certainly never did anything this vile," Kwon said, as he pointed beyond them into the darkness.

"Here," he said returning his gaze to the jar, is proof we are not merely animals who toil in the stench and rot the ghosts have left to mark their path but men worthy of walking upon the earth and learning as much of it as one life can contain. Each of us is a jar. Look at what we hold. Life and death. Not all the Jolliffes or the Bingsleys who order us to our work can say they have seen the butterfly the maker painted on the porcelain when it opened its wings and it rose with the sun. And when we are done, either here or somewhere where toil shall end our days, we know we will return to Middle Earth, to the center of the world that balances all life. That's a better fate than those we find in these fields who will never go home."

Tan fashioned a casket the size of the jar from belt boxes and biscuit tins, and Tsin wrapped it in a lambswool vest they found among the Canadian bodies.

"We must be gentle with this," Kwon said. "It is the doorway to our path home. I have a suggestion. If we all last long enough to go home, not just back to Canada but home to China, the last one's bones should be buried in this jar." Tan and Tsin agreed. It seemed right. The vessel would carry them on the waters of eternity.

They dug a small grave at the base of a blasted oak, the only remaining vestige of a tree for miles, and buried the jar on its eastern side.

As their battalion moved farther and farther away from the buried jar, Kwon wondered if one of them should go back for it and make sure it was safe. The three agreed that when they were out on rest, they would retrieve what they had restored.

The next morning, Tan woke first as the dawn was beginning to brighten from grey to orange. He poked Tsin and Kwon and pointed to the eastern sky.

"Isn't it amazing," he said. As he spoke the ruin around them became alive with butterflies, blue and yellow, broad-winged, fluttering against the dampness of the September morning.

Each man held up a hand and each found an insect on the tip of his index finger. The small creatures took wing, and, perhaps foolishly, Tan, Kwon, and Tsin began to chase the butterflies like fascinated boys, laughing and running recklessly into a field they had not yet cleared. They vanished in the first full breath of sunlight the way ghosts fade to shadows when a day begins.

A Narrow Space

My mother never said much about my father. He was someone I had to imagine from scant details. My parents had met,-certainly, but they had come from different backgrounds – he from Hungary and she from Poland. They had been brought together by a bread line in a Displaced Persons camp after the war. He was sixteen and she may only have been about fourteen. I quizzed her many times about how old she was when she fell in love, and she refused to speak about it. I think she looked at my father as a protector, as someone who understood her fragility. Even though neither of them spoke the same language, there was a bond between them.

I won't call it an unspoken bond, but a relationship that was based on an antiquated code of kindness. He would arrive home after work each day and bow and kiss her hand. They were no Ozzie and Harriet. They were more like a Duke and Duchess, quaint, antique, and mannered. Both were out of their depth in Canada. People didn't behave like that here. We said grace at the start of each meal, crossing ourselves though we didn't go to church. I don't think they understood what the priest was saying. They felt their belief in their hearts, but the language barrier was a wall between my parents and God. Neighbors, shopkeepers, gas station attendants were all frank to the point of being harsh. I was the product of the fresh start, the new beginning in a new country and they both spoke to me in broken English with a helping of their mother tongues thrown in.

I don't blame them for avoiding church. Maybe they had their reasons. God had not been kind to them. They had grown up in an age of glowing ambition that hid a terrible spirit of brutality beneath its neck-tie bandanas and tidy uniforms, its celebration of national flowers, and its do-or-die beliefs. I am certain that God had stood by and watched as the war devastated not only their lives but their identities. In losing their homes and their families, they lost themselves, and God did nothing to help them find what lay beneath the rubble of familiar landmarks.

They were DPs. They carried that pejorative term the rest of their lives. In Canada, DP was an acronym for someone who was less of a human being than others. Maybe it wasn't meant to convey that, but if I explained how my parents met, I could sense people looking down their noses at me, and still more so at my parents. My mother and father had had to invent themselves all over again once they arrived here. I'm not sure either of them succeeded. There were awkward moments at parent-teacher evenings and public gatherings when they didn't understand or fit in, stammering to find the English word that came so easily to others.

They tried to help each other but both were working from the same icy isolation, one in Polish and the other in Hungarian. Who were they? Even now, years after the war, and years after I buried my mother, I am not sure. I credit the Red Cross. There's that old question about 'where was God?' and the answer someone gave about 'where was Man?'. The answer was that Man destroyed their worlds, and Man fed them bread when they had nothing left.

My father got a job working construction when they arrived in Canada. He didn't have the hands for it, at least as I remember them. His hands were graceful, slender, and almost delicate in their transparency. I often wondered what he had been before someone in some colored shirt – it was an age of shirts and the color defined one's political belief and even one's fate – called him into the ranks of young men his age who disappeared without a trace as Europe burned and bled.

I often thought he might have been a musician. He didn't see me watching him, but I saw him once when the radio was on. The

CBC was playing a melancholy violin piece by Brahms, or maybe it was Kreisler. In any case, he didn't know I was standing in the room. He had his eyes closed. He was enveloped in the melody. It broke my heart to watch him holding an imaginary violin, tears welling in his eyes, as his right arm drew an imaginary bow over the invisible strings and his left hand fluttered to play the notes.

Wanting to know about one's parents is part of growing up, but just when I was old enough to ask the right questions of my father – who are you, where did you come from when you had a home, and what did you love, what did you read, what were your parents like – a police officer and a man in a long coat and a fedora arrived on our front porch. As soon as she opened the door, my mother knew. Neither of the men on the porch had said a word to her, but she knew. The men took off their hats and held them in their hands as if they were ashamed that they owned them. My mother wept. I stood in the doorway to our living room and did not know what to say. Had I known my father, I might have had something to grieve for. He'd fallen six stories to his death. Last week I stood on the spot where he had fallen and watched a demolition crane knock down the medical building where he had not been properly tied off. The past vanishes just like that. There is a café that now has a sidewalk table on his spot. I think I am the only person left who knows what happened there.

My mother was a stoic. I think that's the best word for her. I wouldn't call it bravery. It wasn't courage, but a kind of determination, a resistance to the world that would not back down from the challenges it threw at her. The day after my father's funeral, I saw her out the window of my schoolroom. I looked up from my notebook and fat lower-grade pencil, as she moved from door to door, offering herself as a cleaning woman. I was taunted about her work by the schoolyard bullies. Some even beat me up. Their parents had been Canadians during the war. Some of their fathers had been in the service. Mine was called a kraut, a collaborator, and my mother was no better. Her nation had surrendered.

Before the war, I am almost certain that my mother had come from a well-to-do family. Once when we were downtown, she paused in front of an antique store window and started naming the various types of figurines and candelabras that were displayed in the window. Some people who had been DPs brought their precious belongings with them, had carried them in their hands, had held on to them even when they needed bread. They had fled with them when the Russians came from the east and pushed the Germans out. It was this country that made them part with their heirlooms. What they were left with was a silence in which they had no words to express themselves. Here, ill-equipped for arrival and distrusted by those who had arrived long before them, they had parted with their relics of nineteenth-century gentility.

The Russians, I learned later, had raped every girl and woman in their path. It was their custom, their way of exacting revenge on those who had invaded their motherland or who had let invaders cross their country to lay waste to their steppes of wheat. I asked my mother what my grandparents did. She said they had owned a business. I asked if they were alive, perhaps waiting for me on the other side of the ocean, beaming with joy at seeing their grandson and spreading a table in our welcome. No, she said. They had been murdered. By whom? She wouldn't answer. I left the kitchen where we had been talking, but when I looked back at her, standing at the sink with the tap running, she was weeping.

How did you meet Papa? I asked her one summer morning as she was getting ready to go to her day of back-breaking work. Day after day she would come home reeking of her own sweat, the onion smell of hard work and pain. Her feet swelled and she was still a young woman. Was he handsome?

We met in the camp, she said. It was run by the Red Cross. He was wearing a checked shirt, a shirt that said he had no political affiliation, that he wasn't going to be fooled again like all the others before him. He would line up behind no one, she said, except me.

A line-up?

Yes, she said. Bread. You have no idea what thousands of starving people are like. They will do anything for a chunk of bread. They will push and shove, and if they have other mouths to feed, children or parents or elderly friends, they will press into a narrow space and force themselves on the bread givers.

But your father was different. He was tired of the world being a hostile place – that much he told me through an old man who acted as our interpreter until the fellow died of sorrow when he learned that his entire family had perished. Everyone was hungry. Your father received his share, but just as the bread ran out and people had to be turned away – angry people, frightened people – he turned and looked me in the eye and said, here, this is for you.

You must understand, she said, we were crowded together in the long line-up for bread. There were many things we could live without – sanitation, privacy, even a roof over our heads in a heavy downpour – but we could not live without bread. You had to have long arms, and his hand reached the bread giver first, but when he saw me, he leaned around and gave me his share.

I picture them walking hand-in-hand on a long road west.

The sun is setting. It is in their eyes.

They look like Adam and Eve, who are setting out into the world at the end of that Milton poem I read in university. Hand-in-hand, making their solitary way.

She stumbles, turns her ankle, and is limping. She is carrying a blanket and there is something precious in it, something more than bread, and my father takes her arm and raises her up. She smiles. He tosses his blanket aside to help her.

Someone behind them shouts to move along. They are slowing the march.

But my father won't leave her. The crowd of travelers moves around them, crowds them in, so they have but a narrow space to stand.

And when someone tries to push her on, he stands his ground and holds her in his arms and she asks him never to let go, not today, not tomorrow, not forever.

His Polish is terrible, but she thinks he has asked to help her along, and as a gentleman, perhaps an accomplished violinist, he is true to his word.

The Apples of Her Eyes

"You smell like rotting fruit, and you have only hours to live. Right now, your sugars are at thirty-six point five. Just lie back and let it happen. Dying will only be harder if you fight it," the doctor told Henri.

Henri could smell apples. Not ripe ones, but windfalls rotting in the weeds at the roots of a tree. He remembered the cider bin at a great uncle's farm. He could never forget the sweet yet bitter tang of that corner of the barn where the aroma of beauty and death sickened and fascinated him until he began to gag. He did as he was told and closed his eyes.

He was standing in an orchard. Between the leaves and the boughs heavy with a crop of apples almost ready to be picked. Henri saw a balding, bearded man emerging among the coins of light. A russet-dappled red and yellow fruit dangled above him like a jewel. He craved the apple, desired its sweet juice on his tongue, the crisp sound of his front teeth sinking through the skin, but the fruit was beyond his reach, and he did not have the strength to stand and pick one.

The man reached up and with a gentle, twisting tug, the apple let go of its branch. The man handed Henri a perfect, red apple as bees hovered above the orchard- keeper's pate.

"It is sweet and good, is it not?" said the man. *"Dulce et decorum est?"*

Henri took the apple and began to rub it against his chest. Polishing an apple so its skin could sparkle in the sunlight had always been a ritual. He stared at the gift in his hands and felt its girth as if it were the equator of a small, perfect yet forgotten world.

"If I show you what is inside an apple, Henri, do you believe you will find the paradise you lost? You have been eating your apples the wrong way. You have failed to understand what they are trying to tell you."

Henri woke and called for the nurse.

"I need an apple," he said. She did not listen to him. The nurse raised his hospital gown and stuck a needle in Henri's stomach. He winced at the pinch.

"I didn't think I'd see you this morning," said the doctor. "We were able to bring your sugars down to eleven. You are lucky to be alive. Even eleven is dangerous, but it will do for the time being."

"May I eat apples?" Henri asked.

"An apple every now and then, if not in excess, is the one sweet you can have now that you're diabetic. The goal for you will be to balance sugar intake with fiber. An apple has enough roughage, if you eat it with the skin on, to cancel out the carbohydrates. We are starting you on oral insulin. You'll lose a lot of weight very quickly. No carbs. High protein, low salt. Lots of veggies."

Henri was certain he had seen the man in his dream before. He searched through thousands of images of apples on his laptop, scrolling through pictures of farms, markets on early autumn mornings, rows of trees against blue skies, and children biting into Granny Smiths. Then he found what he was looking for.

The apple that the orchardist held out to him was not a real fruit but a gem from a painting. The painter had created dozens of canvases of apples: apples in bowls; apples resting on their sides next to loaves of bread; apples beside knives.

He needed to see for himself what the man in his dream had shown him: the apple seen not from the side but from its base, the apple as an eye staring back at him as he looked up at it on the bough. With his strength returning, Henri informed the law firm where he worked that he was taking an extended leave and booked a one-way airfare to London.

In the Courtauld, Henri stood for half an hour in front of Lucas Cranach's "Adam and Eve," before a guard took pity on him and brought him a wicker chair where he sat down at arms-length from the work. The wooden panel on which it had been painted had warped over time, and the curve reminded Henri of the surface of a tree trunk or a globe. The animals were glancing at each other, some with a sense of impending hunger and others wary of a change in the world that was to come. Eve was handing Adam the apple of the Tree of Knowledge. A unicorn poked its head around a shrub in the background as if to say goodbye.

By early afternoon, Henri had closed his eyes and fallen asleep in the chair. When he opened them, the first thing he saw was the argus-eyed tree. The fruits frightened him. On his way back to the hotel from the Courtauld, Henri could see apples everywhere. The face of Big Ben became the bottom of an apple. Round windows, manhole covers, cannonballs atop balustrades and monuments – London was growing apples everywhere.

Milton, in *Paradise Lost,* believed that the apple had been a necessary dark gift, a means of tempting mankind from ignorance to find for himself an understanding of the divine. Humans had to suffer, whether from Type 2 Diabetes or lethal heart attacks, or loss of spouses, in order to learn what God knew but could not teach unless mankind possessed a curiosity to understand not only the world but the divinity in and beyond all mortal things. Human beings, as was the case with Dorothy in the *Wizard of Oz,* had to discover the truth for themselves.

That night, Henri met the orchardist again. The man was opening the gate to a lush garden, an Eden of lavender and lilies, the perfume of which was a breath of Heaven to Henri. He watched as larks and swallows threaded the boughs of the trees. Light through the branches dappled both him and the bearded man as they walked among the heavy boughs that bent beneath the richness of their fruit.

"There is a purpose to everything, and a time for everything, and to know an apple is to celebrate the constancy of change that life gives us because it contains the paradise we have always sought and that we thought, mistakenly, we had lost. We need to know not only where to look for our happiness but how to recognize it if we see it."

Henri woke in the darkness. His heart was pounding, and he was weeping. In the morning, he took a taxi to a square off Marylebone Road. The Wallace Collection was the final museum on Henri's itinerary. After the floors of Medieval miniatures and Old Masters, Henri arrived at what had been the servant's quarters on the top floor, and a sign on the doorframe stated that the rooms were dedicated to the works of Paul Cézanne.

The description beside the first painting explained that Cézanne studied apples because he was a diabetic. They were the one sweet that the painter was permitted. Red and gold russets were, among other things, one of Cézanne's temptations. *Dulce et decorum*, thought Henri. In apple painting after apple painting, Cézanne held out the gift of a fruit, and each was the image Henri had been offered in his dream at the hospital. Observed from what most people consider the underside where the delicate yet withered brown remains of its blossom with five tiny brown points like a star remind the viewer that seasons pass, an apple was a portrait of a time where spring-times faded to shriveled flowers, and nothing lasts except the eyes that stared into Henri's soul.

"I am not the only one with an absurd obsession," Henri thought as he returned the gaze of the canvases. But the longer he stood studying each image, the more Henri thought, "There is no way to describe what the apples mean other than to say these are portraits of desire."

Henri felt a profound disappointment. Desire seizes a person. When it is gone, when one is unhappy in life because that longing cannot be answered, the fear of death rushes in to fill the vacuum of denied want, and a soul searches for fulfillment. Language has no words for that emptiness, yet when he closed his eyes, he saw apples. He saw an answer in their eyes, and in each eye he recognized a look, not of judgment or fear, but of love. He had seen it before, but he could not remember where.

Painter after painter had captured that look in the eyes of their subjects or in something as simple as an apple. Cranach had an entire tree of apples rising from the soil of Eden between Adam and Eve as if to suggest that what binds men and women to each other, while separating them eternally, is desire. He felt he had failed to grasp the answer to the question he was asking now: why did all the great painters depict the apple from underneath, from the eye that stares back at the beholder?

After the Wallace Collection closed for the day, Henri walked to Marylebone Road. He stopped at a fruit stand and bought a bag of golden apples before going to a café up the road for a coffee, white with sweetener, and a plate of smoked salmon. After he ordered, he took one of the apples from the bag and set it on a plate. He reached for a knife. Rather than cut it the way he had been taught, in long wedges like time zones on a map or the ones his wife baked into pies, he turned the apple on its side and cut it through its equator. That is when he saw what he had been seeking.

The heart of an apple is a star surrounded by points of seeds. To cut the fruit as he had been taught was to miss the reminder of the little heaven in an apple's heart. As he stared at the star, he was smiling. He caught a glimpse of the happiness that he thought he had lost.

The night Henri met his wife at a party in a crowded High Park apartment, he offered to walk her home. They were talking enthusiastically about what they wanted to do with their lives. His wife said her dream was to own a farm with an orchard, to grow her own apples and make pies, perhaps sell them from a stand at the end of the farm's lane.

"I can see it," she said, "I can see an Eden to call my own, a chance to start the world afresh and live life as if no one had lived it before."

Henri had forgotten that moment. It was not an invitation to design their lives, but a simple wish for what life could be – a garden, an orchard without labor, a place where one did not have to strike an accord with the past to enter the future without the failures of those who came before to weigh them down.

Lights from the stores on Bloor Street illuminated her features, and he paused for a moment. He looked at her and he saw how beautiful she was. She, too, stopped, and they saw each other as if they knew the world around them could be different and new if they made it so. And as they drew apart after their first kiss, and they began their solitary walk, hand-in-hand, he looked up and saw an electric sign above the entrance of a Vietnamese Restaurant, the Phō Stella, and the bright star of its neon sign was glowing and buzzing in the damp air. The sound reminded him of honeybees busy in an orchard, and Henri was certain he could see the star reflected in her eyes.

Skating

I LOOKED FROM THE LIVING ROOM WINDOW in the early grey light of a December morning and saw my father standing in our garden. New snow had fallen in the night and covered the trees and grass with a smooth, even blanket of decoration. And in that first light I saw his grey-blue shadow and his breath curling in tiny clouds from his mouth. The first rumble and muttering of the city's morning traffic could be heard through the glass. He looked lonely as he stood there with the garden hose in hand. A trickle of water drizzled onto the snow. A silver drop of liquid sat on the end of his nose like an acrobat balancing over a precipice.

By the time I washed and dressed and made my way into the kitchen where my mother was cooking breakfast, my father had already left for work. I asked her what he was doing in the garden on such a cold morning.

"You're up awfully early," was her only reply. I simply shrugged off the episode as another unexplained eccentricity of my parents' adult lives, another odd ritual or behavior that in time I would come to understand.

That night, after my father and I had finished my arithmetic homework and the endless columns of long division and carryings of sixes and sevens which left me just that, I heard the back door close quietly, and I made my way again to the living room window. Beneath the starlight, my father's figure seemed to grow against the white snow. His shadow was cast in a deep navy blue by the glow from the kitchen window. His thumb pressed against the nozzle and the spray caught in the wind and flew back in his face, covering his toque with a myriad of tiny stars that glistened in an icy constellation. I grew tired and went to bed.

This ritual kept up for several more mornings and nights. "Dad is building a rink in the garden, isn't he?" I said matter-of-factly to my mother after the third morning of spraying. "Does this mean I can learn to skate?"

"Your father is quite the skater himself," she replied. "Before I met him, he cut quite a figure on the blades. When we were courting, he'd take me down to Grenadier Pond and we'd skate round and round beneath the moon to the most beautiful music you ever heard. There's nothing like the cold wind in your face and the feel of speed as your edges cut into the ice. If you ask him nicely during the holidays, he'll teach you how."

When I woke or just before I went to bed, my father would be out in the garden hosing down the backyard in the silence of the winter stillness. The yard grew slick with the sheet of ice that gradually hardened into a greyish-white slab that shone as smooth as a mirror.

On the morning after a heavy snowfall, I heard the scraping of a shovel and watched him piling banks of drift at the edge of the rink. I realized it was the first morning of the holidays and I went back to bed to dream of skating.

I dreamed that I was the fastest skater in the world and that the entire Toronto Maple Leaf team appeared over the rim of our garden fence to ask me to skate for them in the final game of the playoffs. I had seen the games on television when the Saturday night babysitters let me stay up that late. The players moved over the white surface of the ice like beautiful swift eagles through a clear blue sky, gracefully swooping in on goal and lifting their sticks in triumph. I longed to skate like those players, like jets, like hawks, like lightning.

That morning, after I had washed and dressed and eaten breakfast to my mother's satisfaction, I went outside to the garden and stood before the rink. The sun had just broken through the tarnished clouds that arched over the city, and the small halo of yellow light around the glow filled the garden with a delicate splendor. The ice spread from fence to fence in a silver carpet, and I stepped aboard the surface and carefully slid across it in my boots. For an instant, I was at Maple Leaf Gardens and the crowd was chanting my name.

Christmas morning started early at our house. As the first light crept over the backyard fence, I tiptoed bleary-eyed into the living room and stood in front of the tree. Beneath the spreading green boughs and red and silver ornaments was a large box in candy-cane paper with a bow on top and my name on the card.

"Go ahead and open it," my father said as he stood quietly in the doorway and tied the sashes of his bathrobe. My mother followed him into the room and sat down on the couch. I tore at the paper. The blue and black and red cardboard box beneath shone with the words "Bauer Deluxe Figures. Boys Size." Figures! Figure skates? The Leafs didn't wear figure skates. My face fell.

"Now you can learn to skate like your dad," my mother said proudly. I could tell that my father had seen the look of utter defeat on my face during the instant that the true nature of the blades registered in my mind.

After the Queen's message and the official greetings from members of the government, my father took me out to the garden, sat me down at the picnic table, and helped me into the new skates. He crouched and tugged as the laces fed first through the eyelets and then through the rows of black metal tongues that gripped and tightened above my ankles. Then he bent over and put on his own skates. I stood, and my ankles bent beneath me.

"Mine are made of kangaroo leather to help me jump better. They don't make them like that anymore," he announced proudly, the words clouding from his lips with every vowel. His boots were soft and supple whereas mine were stiff and bit like clamps into my lower shins.

He stepped over the banked snow and sailed across the garden. I stepped over the mounded edge and landed on my face. My feet suddenly felt very strange. They refused to hold me up no matter how hard I tried to balance on the thin strips of metal that glimmered beneath me.

My father floated over and grabbed me under the arms and pulled me up. "A couple of times around just to get your balance and soon you'll be flying." He held me up like a rag doll as my blades and feet dragged along beneath me. Within an hour I had managed to stand upright in my own painful little evolution. I took an uneasy step forward and started to move. I think I was skating.

"Let's see you do your edges," my father called from the other side of the garden. "Get the edge and it will be easy." He demonstrated by turning effortlessly in a neat circle like a falcon hovering in a summer sky.

Edges? Every time I leaned even the slightest bit sideways, over I went. My arms and legs were covered in white. My rear was becoming damp and cold. The legs of my pants stiffened and turned solid. When I did manage to move forward, I often caught my picks and went face-first onto the ice. The situation was soon hopeless. My thoughts of becoming a Maple Leaf rapidly dimmed before my eyes.

As my mother set the Christmas turkey before us with all the pomp and ceremony we accorded the bird in our house, and as my father gripped the carving knife and drew it several times against the sharpener, my mother asked how the skating was going. How on earth could I tell her that I was terrible. "Always try to do your best," she would tell me. A terrible feeling of disappointment welled up from my stomach. Over dinner, I thought I could gradually approach the core of the problem.

"I'm not sure I'm made for figure skates," abruptly came out, although that wasn't quite the way I had meant to say it. My parents looked at each other silently. I hadn't really meant to say it that way. I wanted to say that I would keep trying, that I would be a great figure skater like my father, but at that age one of the problems with life is that statements seldom leave the mouth as they are intended. "I really want to be a hockey player. Like the Maple Leaf guys on tv." My father simply smiled at my mother and asked me if I wanted more turkey.

The next day I did not take to the rink. The skates sat in the corner of my room with their tongues hanging out, taunting me. By the middle of the week, they had become part of the landscape of my own little space, hardly noticeable amid the jetsam of clothes and toys. One morning I discovered they were gone.

"Where are the skates?" I asked my mother.

She shrugged. "You didn't seem to be cut out for them. I guess your father has taken them back to the store." I felt awful. I realized just how much my father had wanted me to be a figure skater. "Keep trying, you'll find your edge," I heard him saying in my mind over and over again. I stared out the living room window at the rink. It lay gray and dejected beneath the overcast sky. A soft wind blew a tiny snow devil across its emptiness.

But when my father came home from work that night, tired after a long day caused by the time off for Christmas, he carried under his arm a cardboard box, without any wrapping except for a simple paper bag. This time a black and white box read "Bauer Hockey Skates -- Boys Size."

I immediately laced them on all by myself and wobbled out the backdoor to the garden with my hockey stick and a puck. My rubbery little ankles splayed sideways, and I grunted and strained to move forward with no more grace of motion than a landslide. But I was, at last, a hockey player, and I chased the puck around the rink until my mother called me into bed. As I took off the boots, the burning sensation of blisters shot through my feet, but I didn't care. The Maple Leafs would find me yet.

The years have passed. I have suffered and suffered again with my favorite team. I keep dreaming that they will find me. I also dream of a winter night long ago when I saw my own life spread before me. Although I did not know it at the time, it was a foreshadowing of my own chosen path of painful grinding because I did not have the patience or perhaps the foresight to follow the ways and dreams my parents laid before me in their gifts of love and caring. Doing things the hard way has become my way of life. And my parents? I realize that all they ever wanted for me was to be happy.

And in the small hours of that night when my father came home with the hockey skates, I thought I was dreaming when I woke to the sound of the shovel gently moving across the rink in our backyard. I rose from my bed and tip-toed silently downstairs to the living room window where I parted the curtains and peered into the moonlit shadows that hovered about our house.

In the blue and somber tones of the snowy midnight vista, I saw the outline of my father gliding quietly around the garden, easing effortlessly from one foot to the other. His body was graceful and streamlined, soaring elegantly among the stars that reached down to lift him into their splendor, his silver blades passing through the solid surface of the ice and trailing immaculate thin lines behind him like a draftsman crafting a beautiful and intricate design. He mohawked and danced with his arms extended from his body and leaped almost weightlessly into the cold and silent air.

"Keep trying," I hear him saying still in my mind, as if it was only seconds ago. "Keep trying and you'll find your edge."

The Star-Maker Machinery

HEAVEN HAS ALWAYS TERRIFIED ME. The thought of endless eternity scared me more than all the little bars we played in up and down the Talbot highway. They were mostly joints where migrant workers came to get a taste of home on the nights they were permitted to stay out late. I couldn't blame them. Their quarters were terrible, mostly ramshackle sheds no longer fit to store planting and plowing machinery in. We sometimes played salsa, although badly. I'd been to the country south of Monterrey and had picked up a few tunes from Los Hombres de Linares. The pickers liked that. It was their small echo of home. The locals didn't and told us pickers can't be choosers, especially when it comes to calling the tunes. Our gigs never lasted long, and our money lasted less time.

There were some dry towns as well, places where the window blinds never went up on towns where the dead were more awake than the living. Our drummer got us a good gig in one of those. We played a bit of country at a plowing event. The mosquitoes got bad around sundown, and we had to stop playing at ten because we were eaten alive. The organizers docked us an hour's pay. They treated us like migrant workers.

We'd made it down to Windsor where two piers of the bridge shook hands over the Detroit River, and when I looked closely at the bridge as the trucks passed over in the darkness and the skyscrapers from the other side lit up the river as if it were a wound in the earth that bled gem stones, I couldn't help but feel that everything wants a piece of eternity.

What was terrifying, as I helped haul the rented sound system into the broken-down van that we used for getting around – the cliché down-on-our-luck quartet – was the way the moths fluttered around the fluorescent lights of the rickety bandshell in the middle of what the town called a park. I stopped for a moment and stared at the insects. They adored the light. They were drawn to it, hundreds of them, like souls to heaven. They beat their wings to dust trying to get a piece of what they thought was eternity, and that frightened me.

Our last gig was at a tavern near the empty factories where cars used to be assembled. In the good days, when the factories first shut down, the rusty area was a safe haven, but it had gotten rustier. No one came into the bar. No one wanted to hear us. We'd burned through our cash. I was broken and stranded in clear sight of Motor City.

The tavern owner at our final gig told me not to pawn my bass. He said he'd spring for a room at a local motel and my bus fare back north the next day. He liked me. I was respectful to him. The other band members, especially our drummer, weren't. The guys ran up a huge tab, and when the gig ended, they couldn't pay. I don't blame the owner. I thanked him for his kindness. He said I could come back anytime as long as I brought a different group.

The Cloverleaf Motel had a good location long ago. People would stop there. Now they didn't. It was situated right next to a highway cloverleaf. Someone thought the name would be lucky. When I asked the clerk at the front desk if the owner chose the name because he was superstitious, the guy just shrugged and said, "Look where you are."

The place didn't look all that bad from the outside but inside it was a chemistry experiment gone wrong. The bathroom had black mold. There was one channel on the tv where I could binge-watch a snowstorm. The hot water handle in the bathroom sink was missing. An old, purple brocade couch covered in stains I didn't want to think about sprawled in front of the window like an unwelcome guest. Some of the stains were pale, some were dark. I didn't sit on it. It had been a crime scene. I moved the couch to barricade the door. Being in the dark made me afraid.

Around midnight when I was still up reading and trying to think if I should compose another song or just give up, a man two doors down was taken away by the police. I could see the flashing lights through the edge of the drapes. I didn't want to look.

I had a long journey the next day, and after that, the flag-stop bus north of Toronto would let me off at a logging road, and from there I'd walk the long way in to our cabin, and hope when I get there you'll still be there. I wasn't expecting to find you. I figured you'd be gone, tired of waiting for a bass player who kept losing his bands.

I never stopped thinking of you or our cabin in the woods. I pictured you looking out the dining room window onto the small lake that doesn't have a name, and because the lake was deep and the brush was cut back away from the shore, we didn't have the plague of mosquitoes that ruined summers elsewhere. We'd lie on a flat slab of grey rock beside the lake on summer nights and you'd ask me to name the stars and I'd turn to you and say, "How should I know?"

You'd reply, "God knows their names because they live next door."

I think you expected more from me than I delivered, and I had a feeling you wouldn't be there when I got back. When I called you on the road, after you'd stopped yelling at me, you'd tell me how the silence, especially the silence at night, was driving you mad. You were alone in the bush. "No one," you said, "deserved to be alone." I'd tell you to go out and look at the stars.

"They terrify me," you'd reply and begin to weep. I'd try to comfort you by telling you that I'd written a new song about you, and I would sing it until you calmed down.

When I worked up the courage to turn off the light, I tossed back the bedspread and decided to sleep in my clothes with my boots off. I had no idea who or what had been on those sheets, but I was dog-tired and turned off the bedside lamp.

That's when the ceiling lit up.

It was like coming out of the house on a summer night and lying down on my rock slab beside the lake, and suddenly I felt very small.

The longer I stared, the more I realized the stars were not random. Someone had painted a moment of the sky on a summer night, capturing a vision of July, perhaps from memory. Was it the position of the stars at the instant of their birth? Was it their way of saying they were cursing their life, and that the heavens moved by the force of their own indifference, and we were mere observers?

For the smaller stars, they had daubed with their fingertips, and for the larger ones, perhaps the planets, they had used self-adhesive glow-in-the-dark stickers like the ones my nieces stuck randomly to the walls of their bedrooms.

Whoever had created the astronomical map had worked around the spackle with incredible accuracy. With my scant knowledge of astronomy and memories of my grandfather pointing out the stars when we lay down on the hill behind his farmhouse, I could see the dipper. I could make out Sagittarius and Capricorn.

I thought of the opening passages of Genesis, how in the beginning God created the heavens and the earth, and that the heavens were a sign. But this was not the work of someone who was a casual observer. This artist knew his or her stars and, to get each one in its correct place, must have worked in the darkness, standing on the same bed where I was lying, and reaching up while saying "Let there be light."

There was a sadness to them, a sense of ending that spoke to me of someone who had reached a point of despair and wanted to reach back to a time or place when everything in the universe was in its correct place, when the music of the spheres – not the junk played by a band of drunken rowdies in a broken down van – sounded through eternity to announce a moment of great importance, whether good or bad.

Was it someone's act of sanity or insanity? Was it the last gasp of a mind losing its footing here on Earth and drifting off among the stars, trying desperately to seize what this tiny planet could not give them? Had it been the night someone first made love? Had it been the position of the stars in the sky when they had committed a wrong that cast them into the eternal darkness between stars, the void or chaos where a scream or a shout in the vacuum of deep space might as well be a call for help in a dream where not a sound comes out of the throat? Or perhaps the artist knew that he or she had little time remaining in this life and wanted to be remembered for having looked into the sky on a summer night and found their moment in the vastness of eternity.

The dome of eternal darkness said, "This instant was important to me, but who I was is not important to you."

I felt as if I had invaded a universe that was not rightfully mine. Whoever made the heavens above me possessed a profound knowledge of the night sky, the kind of detailed understanding that knows even where undiscovered stars exist at the far end of the Milky Way. Their light died years ago, but the mark of their maker was still there, arriving to touch those who looked up from the darkness of a horrible place and understood that something miraculous yet far away had burst into existence.

And as I moved my eyes from one side of the cosmos to the other, I swore I saw a shooting star, a fragment of a world that had traveled longer than time on Earth and was disappearing into the atmosphere before my eyes. I wanted so very much for you to be there beside me, for you to witness what I was seeing before the first light of dawn would cast it all back into its oblivion of crude plaster spackle and the easy sky of the day.

That's when I wept. I wept because someone knew that the rock or chunk of ice would arrive in this time and this place and that as it disappeared it would startle the beholder, make him or her fear insignificance, leave him or her wondering if they'd ever get out of a place that contains all life, all light, and all time, and maybe write that one perfect song about the stars in a woman's eyes who was probably gone by now and would not be waiting for anyone to come home, the way a meteor feels when it vanishes alone in the sky.

Eternity

GURPREET NEVER FORGOT the loss of his brother. He felt Harpreet's absence deeply when spring was in full bloom and his mother laid a feast for Vaisakhi to celebrate the return of light to the world. Harpreet had died on the fourteenth of April. As his life ebbed away, he bled into the cold earth of the mountainside, and in the morning, after his remains had been borne away by the medical evacuation team, each drop of blood flowered to assure Gurpreet that his brother had died so that life would return to the world. Every splendid blossom on every rain tree and every mauve petal on a Pride of India tree between the killing ground and home summoned life to open its eyes.

Their troop was dug in on the eastern slope of the narrow valley. Their regiment had been sent to the frontier to die for Mother India as a form of atonement for having played a part in the death of Indira Gandhi in the Safdarjung Garden. Mrs. Gandhi had thought she was on her way to meet a television crew from Ireland's RTE. Her Sikh bodyguards had been her assassins.

And although he could never say so in public for fear of repercussions to his family, in Gurpreet's mind Gandhi's killers were martyrs. They were avenging the horrors that the Prime Minister wrought upon his people when Hindu troops overran the Golden Temple in Amritsar. The Punjab was no more a part of the spirit of India than Brazil or Tahiti. The unspoken code among his brethren was that of loyalty to power until power finally recognized the independence of the Punjabi State. For generations, Gurpreet's family had harbored the dream of a free Punjab, and his service to India was a paradox he constantly wrestled with in his mind. He and his fellows were caged tigers.

To Gurpreet, every man in his regiment was a tiger; but tigers in the Sikh tradition are soldiers, and soldiers obey orders. They die because they are told they must die. No matter what they were asked to defend or fight for, they would do it with ferocity and determination. Some of his ancestors had been unlucky when they chose to challenge the power of the Raj, yet that tiger strength had always been the spirit of Gurpreet's family. In the grand scheme of things, they were footnotes to history. The story of his brother's death was such a notation. It was yet another moment in his family's legacy that was either shrouded in mystery or that remained hidden forever in the darkness of a meaningless border clash.

The brothers had agreed that they were more afraid of silence and darkness than of the din of pitched battle. Facing them on the opposite rocky scree were equally scared young men from Pakistan, many of whom were also Sikhs. The men of a divided nation stared at each other through scopes and fired at the slightest movement. Even in the moonless night with the starry eternity spread above them, the brothers could see each other's breaths curling around the sights of their rifles. Each breath reminded Gurpreet of steam rising off a plate of fresh naan. Had they been home at that moment, their mother would be setting the naan between them as they tore into the flat loaves and broke it apart like so many things in their lives that had been ripped to shreds.

Instead, that night, they stared into the darkness. Snow was falling. The moment was beautiful. The flakes falling like petals appeared as if they had just been born. The entire world wanted to begin, fresh and new, in the purity of the mountain air. He closed his eyes and could imagine a serving dish of *saag paneer*. If he closed his eyes for a moment – if his sergeant did not catch him and jab his buttocks with a bayonet to wake him to duty – Gurpreet could imagine his mother mixing the ingredients in metal bowls, the aroma in the steaming room that was their kitchen and their sleeping place, and the windows crying with condensation. The their mother would finish making dinner before a blackout rolled over their neighborhood. Blackouts were common when tensions grew on the border. Chandigarh would vanish in the night. The stars would roll through the endless sky. And when they reached the hillside where Harpreet was killed, their officers had told them, "Don't even breathe. The enemy will hear it and know where you are." Better to be in darkness. But even in their darkened room, he could see the food that was set before him, not with his eyes but with his nose: onion, garlic, turmeric, and garam marsala, sautéed tomatoes, and mustard oil, the tang of small hot chilis in handfuls...the beautiful glories, the spice of life.

Gurpreet thought he had seen the future. He was certain he and Harpreet would survive. They'd go out in the evenings to the brightly lit kiosks; they would sit in restaurants and tell girls of their glories at the front; would stop in clothing stores and buy new shirts. Songs from loudspeakers would compete with each other, and cool night breezes would weave like taxis through the snarl and chuff of the traffic. The sounds of life would be everywhere. Light and life and everything they believed were worth fighting for. Spirit and life, hand in hand exactly as the Nine Gurus had taught. One body seeking grace and truth.

There were so many worlds in which Bhakti made life, so many that there was no singular time or place. *Anekāntavāda* as the Jains believed. Many places in one place, one time. Many eternities in one moment. There were so many realities to which he could flee, and the more places he drifted off to, the more places he wanted to be – anywhere but on that valley slope where he and his brother and their company waited for something, anything, to happen. *Tan. Man. Dhan.* The three services would lead him home. And home would be as it always had been.

Someone in their ranks said they had heard the news on a transistor radio, a contraband item in the front lines, but a necessary item, nonetheless. The governments were about to back down.

The stand-off was easing. This time there wouldn't be any nukes. The United Nations had the matter in hand. The eyes of the world were on that valley. While there was still daylight, Gurpreet had seen the sun reflected in the scope on the western side of the valley. They had seen two glass eyes staring back at them. Harpreet thought they looked like frightened cats peering from beneath a tangle of leaves. He told Gurpreet the eyes were not menacing. "We can deal with them if we're given the chance. They look like farm boys, not like tigers, and we are from a lineage of fearsome beasts."

Their great grandfather had distinguished himself in Egypt and Gallipoli during the First World War before falling to a sniper's bullet in France. Neither brother nor their father knew where their decorated ancestor had died or was buried or even if there had been a body to bury. The British set aside a day of remembrance but never mentioned the soldiers of India, the Sikh regiments who dipped deeply into their warrior blood and stood their ground against machine guns and mustard gas.

Their father made a pilgrimage to Flanders to seek the name of their great grandfather among those inscribed on the Menin Gate, but their great grandfather was not there. Nor were the others in his regiment who fell in Turkey not far from the walls of Troy or had vanished to attack the Turks in a fog with the gardeners from the King's estate at Sandringham. The Trojan side story was an embellishment of their father's. He loved literature and read until his eyes became bad. He also felt shame that his past had gone missing, and he often wondered why his people were pushed aside by history.

Shame ran deep in their father. Not only had he witnessed his comrades betray their oath to serve their country, gunning down an unarmed woman as she strolled in her garden, but he also knew that no matter how cruelly she had suppressed the holdouts in the

Golden Temple, Mrs. Gandhi had not deserved to die that way. She had been shot first and then hacked to pieces.

But the pain ran deeper than the omission of their great grandfather's sacrifice in Flanders. Although neither father nor sons had any say in the matter, their grandfather had been a Sikh nationalist, or rather an Indian nationalist working for an independent Punjab, a fierce believer that the nation's greatest enemy was not the Japanese or the Communists, but the 'bloody British' as he called them. Winston Churchill thought so little of those who were giving their lives to keep Japanese expansion in check, he had starved the Indian people and three million died of hunger. That was before the debacle of independence. Another six million would die as India burned.

Their father's father had disappeared from his Anglo-Indian regiment. A photograph of him surfaced years later in a history book. An officer and a talented soldier, he had run off to become one of Hitler's Indian SS men in Chandra Bose's Azad Hind, the Reich's ill-fated Tiger Brigade. The last word from their grandfather had been a scrawled letter in which he described the peaks of the Swiss Alps only an hour's march away. He said the mountains reminded him of the snow-capped stations of Northern India, those places in a country of heat where the snow could fall at any time. He said he felt he was on his way home. That was, presumably, his last vision. The boys considered their service in Kashmir as a way of atoning for their grandfather's failure. *Dhan.*

Now, as irony would have it, Guranjpreet Singh's grandsons were told to hold their ground on a snowy valley slope. Harpreet whispered to his brother that he was certain he could feel the *bhūta* ghost of their grandfather staring at them from the Pakistani side as the brothers made ready to stand their ground. For India. For motherland. *Dhōkhā jām kō'ī dhōkhā nahīm.* Betrayers will be betrayed in the end. The sons of the turncoats will suffer for the deeds.

Gurpreet struggled to focus on his duty. It was too enormous for his mind. He took comfort in having one God in his heart. One God, *Akal,* one heart, one mind, one truth made sense. The Pakistanis also believed in a single God. Singularity was what set them apart, pointed them armed against each other. There was one world, and in that world, everyone shared one hunger, one need to be fed, although there were only so many things that could be eaten. Warm things.

Gurpreet had traveled more than Harpreet. He'd won a scholarship that took him to Kerala. He'd seen the south, had been to Dacca and Calcutta. A woman in a nightclub had him walk her home. In her tiny apartment, as her parents slept on mats in the next room, he lay down beside her and they pressed their ears to a cassette machine, and she had played an odd Western song. The musicians, she said, were called Led Zeppelin. Only a day before, the brothers had heard the song on a Walkman and danced before descending the side of the valley because they were in 'Kashmir' and were part of the song.

Harpreet turned to his brother. Softly, on the tip of his breath, he made the sound of the Led Zeppelin song and started moving his head. Gurpreet smiled. "A little dinner music," Harpreet whispered. "All we need now is dinner. *Rāta dā khā⊠ā.*"

Harpreet should not have died that night. He was a beautiful dancer. He loved bhangra. He would bounce on his toes, spinning, laughing, and spreading his arms as if to fly.

Gurpreet promised his parents he would look after his older brother. Harpreet was physically strong but not wise to the ways of the world. He was apt to make poor decisions. When his jitney collided with a police car, Harpreet had almost punched the policeman. Gurpreet arrived at the station to post bail for his brother. His mother had sent the duty sergeant a basket of food, not as a bribe, but as a kindness of persuasion: tandoori chicken, hot mango chutney, and a bowl of *saag paneer* because, as

Gurpreet was instructed to say, it was his mother's specialty that no one could resist. Harpreet was released. As he walked by the duty sergeant, the man did not look up, but after draping his arm around his younger brother, he turned, looked over his shoulder, and said, "Man, that smells like Mom's."

"You know, you idiot," Gurpreet said to his brother. "Mom just paid the price. There's a price for not thinking. Five thousand rupees, and that's before you even go to the magistrate. Think what we could have done with five thousand."

Harpreet smiled. "There are five thousand stars in the sky at night, and that's with all the lights of the city. Think of what we'd see if we were staring into complete darkness. That would be a moment worth remembering, hey, brother?"

And when they sat in utter darkness, a darkness of death, beyond life where there was no hunger and no way to answer the dreams of the world that haunt a person until he finds satisfaction in the stomach or the flesh, Gurpreet looked at his brother in their foxhole. Harpreet was squirming.

"Guri, I have to pee," he said, "and I'm so cold. So cold, and we're just waiting around here for something to happen." Then he glanced up into the sky. "I used to dream of seeing the stars like this, stars as they are, not clothed in the city lights, but naked and beautiful as a girl I've dreamed of screwing. She could be anyone, but she, for one night, would be mine. Do you think the eyes behind those stars have to go pee, too? Do you think they're going to make something happen? They probably want to be asleep instead of staring at us in the darkness. The Pakistanis probably have those American night scopes on their rifles, watching us writhe in our little foxhole while we lie in our own piss. They are probably waiting for me to stand up and pee."

With that, Harpreet stood up. He was reaching for the zipper in his trousers when the sound of a shot echoed off the walls of the valley. Gurpreet reached up as if to hold his brother and keep him from falling over the lip of the foxhole as he spun around. And then, as if he had decided not to stand up and relieve himself, Harpreet sat down.

"Guri, I see a beautiful naked girl. There she is. Among the stars. They like it when we tell them their eyes are beautiful as the end of a long day." Harpreet's eyes fixed on the sky. Gurpreet held him, but his brother's body would not grow warm.

He closed Harpreet's eyes. He raised an arm over his own eyes so the fellows of his regiment would not see him weep. Gurpreet could picture the streets of Chandigarh crowded with traffic on a dusty, sweltering summer night, and he reached forward to sound the horn on his cab so shufflers and laggards in the street would get out of the way and get on with the business of their lives, though what he heard may only have been the signal siren sounding the alarm of an attack that never came. *Ti'āra'tē.* At the ready. Always at the ready.

When he arrived home, Gurpreet sat down beside his father at the dinner table as his mother put the serving dishes of the evening meal before them. The food had the same aroma as every dinner he and Harpreet ate during their childhood. The scent of spices and onions, the hard feel of the chair beneath his buttocks and legs, and the peace at the end of the day – all the memories of his life were there and waiting for him to open their door and step in.

On the wall behind the place where Harpreet sat with his back turned to the framed faces, hung photographs of the family's generations of soldiers. Gurpreet and Harpreet in their uniforms had been added by their mother while they were away in Kashmir. The brothers had joined the lineage of tigers. They were warriors from the loins of warriors.

Everything stands still, Gurpreet thought. Nothing changes. Not the taste of food or the names that no one remembers to inscribe on gates or gravestones. Gurpreet looked up as he wiped his plate of *saag paneer* sauce with the last swath of *naan*, weary after a long day of navigating the streets. Harpreet was just beginning his meal, a feast of dishes spread before him as if he was a prince, and he dug into the food and fanned the rising steam from the *saag paneer*, so it filled his nostrils with the perfume of eternal life.

Merry Midnight

As he slid into the pew beside Fred, he leaned over to wish his friend a Merry Christmas.

"I should be home with the missus. She's been cleaning and cooking all day, but I figured if I stuck around, I'd just have to listen to that god-awful choir from the Vatican that sounds like a train wreck set to music and the commentator, the same guy year after year, who sounds like some guy whispering into a microphone on a televised golf tournament."

"You shouldn't be here. I smell the liquor on your breath."

Already Fred's wife was facing in the other direction. She didn't want anything to do with Mike.

"I can be here if the Lord lets me," Mike said with a slightly mocking indignation.

"Father McCaw says that liquor does something to the host. It negates it. It makes the taking of the sacraments into something they shouldn't be."

Mike jabbed Fred.

"Sure, and with a little cheese, it would be just the right kind of party, eh? Just the right kind of party. Besides, can't you smell it? The whole place is lit up like a Christmas tree, and why not? Jesus turned himself into alcohol. It is not antithetical to the divine nature of the holy sacrament," Mike said in an imitation Barry Fitzgerald voice. "It's Christmas. I tell you, Fred, it's a miracle I'm here. What a year. You know as well as I that growing up Catholic was no easy business. Like when I was ten. Here's a story for you. Fr. Paul, you remember him at St. Hubert's, said, "Boys will be boys," when Mick kept crushing my bicycle spokes. He did it right in front of Fr. Paul, but would Fr. Paul say or do anything? No. Mick was always walking around with a back pocket full of

Tootsie Rolls just like the ones Fr. Paul kept in a glass jar on his desk. I wanted justice. I didn't get any, though."

"You should have had it. Who wouldn't want justice?"

"When I finally tried to get even with Mick, it didn't work. Mick had gotten the better of me again. I squealed on the little bastard."

Fred's wife glared. "You're not supposed to say *bastard* in a house of God."

"I'm telling your husband a story," said Mike who lowered his voice to a hush. "Besides, your spouse was there. He knows what happened. The best person to tell a story to is someone who understands what's going on in the plot. So, I sat in Fr. Paul's office, watching the clock on the wall, listening to its hard fist of a pendulum knock the innards out of time. I wanted to hear Mick's whimpering through the door. But no. Fr. Paul didn't punish Mick. He called me into his inner office and told me I should be ashamed of myself for being the little rat I was and told me I'd be poisoned someday not by rat poison but by my own evil suspicions of Mankind. A regular little Judas. I didn't deserve that. He dismissed Mick. Stuck his Tootsie role in the little bastard's back pocket. I wanted to but didn't grab the ram's head brass letter opener for self-defense or the black-handled leather strap almost bare of its polish Fr. Paul had sitting on the edge of his desk. He set them right in front of me. Temptation, I tell you. Then Fr. Paul came around the desk, made me stand up, and struck me and struck me across my palms twelve times on each, once for every apostle and two extras for good measure. The priest said, 'This is what it feels like to be dead to Him. Now go and give your trespasser a second chance.' But later, when I got home and fell down on my bed to cry until my eyes went red and swollen, I questioned why it was so important that I give a trespasser or Mick or even God a second chance. Tomorrow it would all be the same. God made the world that way and there was nothing I could do to change it, though, if I could I've always wondered what power might feel like, the power not to turn an eye to all the crap that passes for justice but is just injustice done up as authority, especially if I could've crushed Mick's skull between my aching palms, and God's, too, if He had a skull."

Fred moved closer to his wife. Mike was not only drunk. He was blasphemous and on Christmas Eve. And in church.

"Now, saints alive," said Mike, "I have to sit here and listen to a priest named after a parrot. Fr. McCaw-caw-caw."

"That's enough, Mike. That's enough, way too much enough. You've got a drinking problem."

"Only when I can't get a drink."

"Mike, leave now. No. Wait. Don't leave. You're in no state to drive. Come with me."

Fred grabbed his friend by the elbow and led him out down the center aisle as the organist began to play the prelude from Saint-Saëns' Christmas Oratorio. The service would be starting shortly, and Fred felt that absence was the better part of discretion. His friend might sober up in the cold. There was a bench on the church walk and both men still had their coats with them, though Mike wasn't sure when he got outside where one of his gloves had gone. They walked past Father McCaw. Mike tucked his hands in his armpits and was about to make a cawing noise when Fred wished the priest a Merry Christmas.

"I know it's been hard on you Mike. It's just a year now tonight. Losing your father and your daughter's fiancé on Christmas Eve, that's tough. I know it isn't easy being someone's son. The closer one gets to morphing into one's father, the harder it is to let go. It's like losing part of yourself. You two played catch in the backyard. You two went to ball games and cheered loudly together. You posed with your arms slung over each other's shoulders, holding fish in your free hands with a dock in the background and a boathouse with a wooden launch tied up to it, the gunwales rubbing against the buffer tires."

"So?"

"So, I know you're wrestling with the dark angel of losing your father and then your daughter's breakdown. You had a father that a man could be proud of, a father who would listen, who'd be there, an 'old man' who would tell you what's what but in a kind way. You had a father who took you out for a damned fine steak on your eighteenth birthday because you were a man, and steak is what men do even though it eventually kills them. The mystique kills them. Do you want to talk about it?"

Fred drew in a deep breath.

"The day he died and how he died was a mess. Something was wrong with the hospital generator, and the power had to go to places in the building, the intensive care and neonatal wards, the operating rooms, the machines, and monitors. The last place light needed to be was in the lunchroom where my wife and I sat in the dark. A nurse named Macklin told us he'd hang on for the rest of the afternoon, and a can of warm pop and a questionable meat slapped between two slices of dried-out white bread was the respite we needed from the dark hallways and the stinking wards. I said we should go down, down all those flights of stairs because the elevators were off. My old man, up on the seventh floor, the top floor, so he could be closer to heaven, my wife joked one night while he was still conscious. That last day, when we needed lunch and went all the way to the ground floor down the dimly lit stairs, he didn't know whether we were there or not."

"It is hard losing someone."

Mike looked up at his breath circling his head. The choir was singing the processional, "O Come, All Ye Faithful." He pointed with his thumb at the doors of the church.

"Listen to that. There's got to be a joke in it somewhere," Mike said. "I never told anyone that just before we left his room, I opened one of his eyes. His face had collapsed in on itself, his false teeth taken out for mercy's sake, and the round 'O' of his mouth was caked with what looked like dried oatmeal but is the crap that comes out of the mouths of the dying. I looked in that one eye of my father's, the eye he wasn't seeing me with then and probably never saw me with while he was conscious. It was just there, staring. But as we climbed up the fourteen flights, I felt myself growing short of breath, huffing and struggling as if I was emerging from a pit. When we got there, the nurse, Macklin, just says to us, 'He's gone. He went just after you left.' All the time we'd been sitting in the dark and eating those dreadful, dry sandwiches."

"That's rough, Mike. That's rough."

"It is not that I wasn't proud to be his son. It is not that I didn't love him. I did and I do. It's in the contract, as they say. But after he passed, I wished we'd gone fishing together just one time. I never got to ask him everything I wanted to know. Lord knows I tried. He was a failure at conversation. Wouldn't touch a drop to loosen his tongue. No, sir. He was dry as a desert even before he went stiff as a board. No long conversations. No steak on my eighteenth birthday. No card, no call. I made all that up. And then, about a month ago, I got up one morning and looked in the bathroom mirror and I didn't see my face. I saw his. He was staring back at me, and I realized I'd become him, and I was as much or more a failure with my own kids as he was with me."

"How is your daughter doing?"

"Doing? She's not doing. Paul's funeral was hard on everyone. There was the December wind tearing at our faces. The ash cross on the casket was carried away as if nature were telling us we had nothing to hold on to. Everyone blamed me. I was the one who poured then let him drive home. I should have ordered him to stay on the couch or slashed his tires or something."

"So, are you drinking because you have taken his place?

"Hell if I know. Is this some sort of AA meeting?"

"No, but we can talk about it at the next one if that would help.'

"Ah, Freddy, Freddy. What have we become? Why has love failed us, not just love in the general sense, but the love we receive and the love we give. It is all so small and fragile and can never do enough. Sometimes I think it is like a hummingbird cupped between my palms. I can feel its wings buzzing against my lifeline and I want to keep it warm because the world is always just like tonight, even on the good days. It is always midnight when everyone is on the verge of rejoicing that a new day has come, yet it is still cold, still dead with its own stillness and nothing we can say, not a shout, not a sharp word, can wake it from its curling breath that hangs over our prayers and threatens us with everything we say and do."

"Well, Mike, it is not on you. You are a good man to bear it. You carry it even though the way is one way, and no one returns from the hill of the skull. But just think, each year we have the illusions of a beginning, the image of a child, the idea of crossing some imaginary line between the past and the future in order not just to leave something behind but to find something on the other side."

"And that is?"

They stood together. They walked over to the crèche and stared in silence.

"I swear every year that kid needs his nose repaired. He's supposed to lead us not into temptation and deliver us from evil and he hasn't got a nose he can follow."

"You could fix it, Mike.

"The nose?"

"No, you idiot, the world."

And when they were certain the service was in full swing and no one was leaving before the big blessing, they turned to each other and began to cry. They wept into the shoulders of each other's overcoats that were stained not just from carrying the weight of life, but from the large fresh flakes of snow that were coming down on them and that they had not brushed aside.

Jenny

THE LIGHTS WERE SO CLEAR that he could see the future played out in the ribbons of the Aurora Borealis as if he was watching a movie. Some of what he saw made sense. Most of it did not. In some scenes were things he wished for and promised himself he would achieve. But there were other images that defied explanation: someone banging on a window, a long table with empty chairs around it, men walking ahead of him through dense brush, two little girls in red dresses, and a chessboard in which he was a knight that had just been taken. He lay bundled in his sleeping bag, his limbs stiff from the cold, his stomach aching from lack of food.

He refused to die that night or the night after. And when he thought he would fall asleep, the Arctic sky clapped him awake. He'd heard legends about the sounds emanating from the Aurora. The stories were true. The Northern Lights really did make sounds. He would wait for someone to find him. He couldn't fly out. The tank in his Jenny was empty and the oil in her engine congealed in the frigid temperature. Her body lay twisted in the snow and one wing drooped as if it was an injured bird. Everything in the cold and dark told him that he was going to die.

And why shouldn't he die? He'd done everything wrong in preparing for the Jenny's flight. Hugh Denver should have been with him on the flight, but the bushman begged off because his wife had just given birth to a son. Shortly before he took off from the frozen surface of Kildare Lake, Hugh had appeared at the hut they used for sorting specimens and piling elk hides. His business partner, a large, bearded bush-hand who knew nowhere better than anyone he'd ever known, held his newborn son wrapped in a Hudson's Bay blanket. The child's hands were pale and delicate and reminded them of crayfish they found in the lakes where they set down during the thawed months.

In the excitement over the baby and the gulps of grog to celebrate the son's arrival, he neglected to collect his charts, though they weren't really maps but someone's guess of what might lie beyond the edge of the known world. Hugh once joked that a cartographer could draw a lake no one had seen, and there would be people hovering in the deckled edges of photographs the following summer. The Northern Lights held such specters.

Hugh asked if it wouldn't be wise to wait a week or two, but he had replied that the winter would be deeper by then, and the Carswell brothers, their competitors in the find and stake game for the rumored goldfields in the area, would probably have registered their claims by then. The Carswells had been gone by snowshoe for more than two weeks and might well be sitting on their superfinds by now. He told Hugh that the Jenny would cut his travel to nothing, and he'd wave as he flew over the trudging competitors or dip a wing – some gesture that would break the Carswells' hearts.

Hugh and he had purchased the Jenny from the War Surplus Yard. She wasn't in the best of shape. The gum skin on her left wing was torn. The connecting rod between the cockpit and the right rudder had snapped. Hugh asked the yard keeper why that particular plane hadn't already been purchased as a crop duster, or a barnstormer, or a training aircraft. The yard keeper simply shrugged. They'd been assured that the Jenny hadn't seen combat duty, though when they took the engine apart, Hugh pointed out the synchronizing mechanism for a front-mounted Vickers machine gun. The machine had been a weapon. On closer inspection, they found the screw holes from the mounting of a Lewis gun swivel on the rear compartment. The aft seat had also been turned around and the underside of the body had been patched. The thought that the plane had seen active duty only added to an aura of luck and fortitude that the plane held. He told his friend. "After all, someone had given her a happy landing."

There was a man on Great Slave Lake who also owned a Jenny, but after his crash, he stayed on the ground and was only too happy to sell the pair of greenhorn prospectors a pair of pontoons and a set of skis for their plane. Between landing on water and landing on snow or ice, there was nowhere they couldn't go. That gear in itself would give them a major advantage over the Carswells. He joked to Hugh there'd be no more paddle blisters on their palms. They retrofitted baskets and hanger racks on the fuselage – one to carry a canoe and the other to carry their supplies. They could survive in the bush for weeks and, if the pickings got slim, they could simply fly out.

The area where the tree line peters out to meet the Arctic tundra is deceiving, especially so if winter arrives early, which it did in September 1939. How could he have been so distracted by the baby, Hugh's joy, and the desire to beat the Carswells to the other side of Great Slave that he'd neglected to pack enough supplies? There was snow on the ground. Being alone, he had thought, would have its benefits. He could enjoy the vistas, the deep indigo horizon, and the rises and falls of the terrain below without Hugh interrupting him to point out things that he didn't want to see. But what he met up with as he flew over the lake took him entirely by surprise.

A half-hour into the flight, he ran into a blizzard. It was too high to fly over and too low to duck beneath. There'd been no sign of it on the horizon as the darkness settled on the treetops by late afternoon. The monotony of flying into heavy white flakes – so many flakes their multitude mesmerized him, and he almost fell asleep at the stick – made him want to set the plane down, but he was certain he'd fly through it, that the weather had to have another side, and the lake was below him, vast and cold, if he stayed true to his compass bearings and kept a northerly path. But the plane was rocked as if it was a toy.

Headwinds turned the snow to ice. He fought the rudder as the plane began dipping to one side because the wing that had taken the repairs held onto each flake and turned the clusters solid. The wires became ice-encrusted vines in the darkness. He had to put down. Then, almost as quickly as the storm had come upon him, he flew out the other side. He took the nose low and searched for a place to land.

The skis bumped along the snowdrifts. One snapped, and the Jenny spun before the tail collided with a drift and came to a halt. How long had he been in the air? He'd lost all sense of time in the storm. His face was a mask of ice. The situation was hopeless. The Jenny was not going to leave its resting place. It was part of the landscape, a dot on the map.

And where was that? When he reached for his charts, they weren't there. He stood up in the cockpit and opened the engine hood. The pistons were still steaming and reminded him of a runner at the end of a long race on a winter day: the moment they stopped to cool off, vapors rose from their bodies. Now the pistons, the heart of his plane, were still. All he heard was the wind. He didn't remember what happened next. One of the struts or perhaps a chunk of ice had struck him in the head. He'd had enough clarity to crawl into his sleeping bag.

He woke. Was it the morning? How long had he been asleep? The sky was dark, though a veil of grey-green hovered above the direction his feet pointed, and he assumed he was facing east. He opened his eyes and stared for hours. The stars behind his head were infinite. There were more stars than he had ever seen. The universe spread itself before him as if he was God and they were an offering brought to him. He was watching a movie and the movie in the Northern Lights was about him. As the movie ended, he closed his eyes. If he was to die, the images he saw would be illusions, fiction, a good story that would never be told.

He was roused from sleep by the sound of an airplane skiing across the snow in front of him. The letters RCMP were painted on its side. "You're one lucky sunnuvabitch," Hugh said, leaning over him and shouting to be heard above the search plane's engines.

Miraculously, he did not lose any toes or fingers. He had pulled a wool muffler tight around his face and though it was caked in ice around his mouth and his eyebrows had almost frozen together, there were no black spots on his cheeks. "One lucky sonnuvabitch."

When he arrived at Kildare Lake, the first thing he said to Hugh was that he'd seen the future, his whole life, a movie where he was the star, the hero, as a kind of newsreel when he stared at the Northern Lights.

"I've heard of people looking at them long enough to go mad. You probably think I've lost my mind. People aren't supposed to see visions of their lives in the sky. That's Old Testament crap. But I saw my path forward. You were with me part of the way. Sometimes you were not. The lights even looked like strips of film. People moved about in them. They make sound, those Lights. I think they were speaking to me. I am certain I saw my future."

"I hope you saw *us* up in the sky. We're going to be fighter aces," Hugh said. "War has been declared. They'll be looking for pilots, guys who can fly by the seat of their pants and who won't break down even if their planes do. Just imagine the two of us getting medals pinned on our chests by Billy Bishop."

A month later, he and Hugh were in Edmonton taking their physicals for the Air Force. He kidded Hugh. "You'll look snappy with wings pinned to that grey-blue."

But Hugh was turned down. The doctor said his vision was bad and he had flat feet. The presiding officer repeated the facts to him. Hugh didn't take the news well. "Why the hell do I need feet to fly?" his friend asked.

Hugh was hauled out of the line-up and lectured on air force manners by several sergeants. By the time Hugh caught up with him, he had to break the sad news. Neither of them would-be pilots.

"We don't have licenses. Sure. I told them I knew how to fly, that the two of us had taken turns flying our Jenny in and out of the Arctic until I got lost in a snowstorm and crashed. I told them that I was such a great pilot I'd even crashed. They didn't like the idea. Good pilots, they said, don't crash. I told them, 'So what?' But one way or another, I still want to get up in the air again and take out my frustrations on the Germans, and they said, 'Not with our planes you won't,' so they're making us both gunners. They gave me a map test. Seems I don't know north from south."

"That's why you kept flying in the middle of the blizzard?"

"I said that to them, but I think my undoing was when I added that I knew I'd come down eventually. They don't like humor. They just looked at me, frowned, and asked for the next man to be sent in. They also said we were too old for the cockpit."

Gunnery training wasn't about shooting. They could both shoot. Gunners had to be able to work cranks and the rotator mechanisms with their feet and their hands at the same time. Hugh proved completely uncoordinated. The Air Force assigned Hugh to guard duty.

But unlike Hugh, he discovered he had an aptitude for the cranking, spinning, and the mechanical work of lining up a target in a sight and making sure the belts were feeding. And while Hugh would be marching up and down beside a barbed-wire fence, he would be flying in the 428 Squadron, the "Ghosts," whose symbol was a Death's Head wrapped in a black shroud. The 428 motto was *Usque ad finem*. To the very end. He had the feeling that it was going to be a long war and it was. After training for almost three years, the crews of the Wellington bombers became so accustomed to each other that they worked together like a machine. The younger men in his crew admired him for the adventure stories he told about the north. He'd been tested, not by battle with a human enemy but by nature itself; and they, having encountered neither a German foe nor an Arctic night considered him battle-tested, a father figure who knew how to survive and how to help them through the worst of it.

The training and the waiting, the constant gunnery practice, the spinning in imitation turrets, the hot brass shell casings of blanks falling around his ankles and burning holes in his socks, and then test flight after test flight so that the men became one with their machines, were all a blur to him. He had not seen those days in the Northern Lights, though he thought he had caught a glimpse of a training bomber, an Oxford Airspeed, taxiing down a flat Saskatchewan field and dipping its left wing just as it was about to lift off, and the men of the squadron running toward the burning wreckage as the fire crews fought the flames and one survivor tumbled from the twisted metal with his skin coming off as a fiery flight suit clung to the writhing body. The vision had been a momentary flash. The wingspan, the shadow of the plane as it left the ground, was just a snippet of what the lights had shown him.

There were nights when he would wake, believing he was still caught in the drifting blizzard, and moments in those dreams where he saw his Jenny with her arms spread out like a lover pleading to be held. He imagined Jenny would be growing old by now, torn apart by the wind, the shreds of her rotting flesh hanging from the struts, the fuselage split open by passing polar bears. He missed the feeling of the wind in his face and envied the flyboys as they climbed into the cockpits of their yellow Harvard trainers and pushed back the canopy and closed their eyes once they were airborne to feel the voice of the wind in their ears. He was certain he had heard that voice before. It was the sound the

Aurora Borealis made, a sound like sandpaper, and some said they heard angels galloping past them in the Prairie sky.

Those days were followed by the voyage overseas. He wondered if he had seen the image of waves in the cold night sky, the seascape rolling and tossing and changing shape in a ribbon of grey. And when he arrived in Dalton and he and his crew climbed aboard their Welly and he felt the ground fall away beneath him as he sat in the cramped tail gunner's compartment, he felt close to his long-lost bush plane stranded in the fly-infested tundra by summer and the frozen timeless winter the other ten months of the year.

When their bomber got shot up badly while on a run to drop their load on a submarine nest in Brittany, they returned to their base in Yorkshire to find a new plane, a Halifax, waiting for them. He cursed as he tried to climb into the tail gunner's perch. It was even smaller than the Wellington, and his six-foot-two frame ached as he straddled the hand controls and rotated the guns. The long night-flights left him unable to open his knees, and he had to be lifted down through the hatch and bent back into shape, remembering the same pain when Hugh and he tried to paddle too far in their canoe.

Looking down at the carpet of stars of targets alight below him, he wondered if the vision of the heavens behind the dancing lights had been a foretaste of the burning cities. Factories, military installations, and people's homes burst to shining points of light through the low cloud cover, and he tried to persuade himself that the lights were constellations aglow until the pilot turned the Halifax into the darkness for the run back to base.

More than anything, he feared the flak, the bursting shells from ack-ack guns with their muzzles pointed skyward. When the Ghost Squadron's bombers were near their targets, either coming or going, shells would burst around them, blinding him with flashes of shrapnel spraying in all directions. He had seen other planes in his squadron with their tails blown off, the gunner gone, the rudder jammed, as they landed badly on the home field. The crews would return just as dawn was breaking, having spent a night of terror in the sky, hungry for a meal – they were served steak for breakfast – and dog-tired so they missed most of the day as they slept off their previous mission, waking in time to shower, dress, and present themselves for another sortie, they would climb into their machines for another run.

That was when the next clear vision from the Northern Lights appeared to him --an image of someone pounding on the outside of his glass bubble, looking in, and fighting for his life to hold on. The images had been dark for a long time. He should be relieved, he told himself, that the frames of his story from the dancing sky had returned, but the more he thought of it the less he wished for that snippet of his future to come true.

They'd been raiding positions on the far side of the Rhine in an even newer bomber – the Lancaster – and he was grateful that the tail gunner's pod had more space. The only problem with the new plane was the frost build-up on the inside of his canopy. The Lancaster had a higher ceiling and a higher ceiling meant colder temperatures. He found himself continually scraping the glass so he could see through the frost made by his breath if his plane came under attack from the rear. He had just finished clearing the canopy when his flight was set upon by a dozen Focke Wulf FW 190s, fast and dangerous German fighter planes leading a support group of older Junkers bombers.

As the Ghosts flew into a storm of flak, the fighters and their escort bombers followed them. Some of the German planes were hit by their own ground fire and he could see chutes opening. The men firing at the sky made no distinction about whom they shot down.

A burst of flak exploded so close to the nose of his Lancaster that he was sure his plane had been hit. The snap was like the sound of the Aurora clapping its hands above him to wake him from the edge of somnolence and death.

That's when the man thudded onto the fuselage above him and was pulled onto the outside of the turret.

The man – he wasn't sure if he was a Canadian torn from one of his squadron's planes or a German who bailed out after his aircraft was hit – was scratching to hold onto the narrow rim of the frame between the gunner's chamber and the fuselage of the Lancaster.

The man pounded on the glass, demanding to be let in.

He stared into the man's face for an instant.

He saw the horror in the man's eyes.

There was no way he could reach him, and if the outsider let go of his tenuous hold, he would fall into the burning abyss below.

Then another shell, this one closer and aft of the Lancaster, exploded and blinded him with its flash.

The man, who appeared to burst open, loosened his grip, let go, and sliding down the canopy for a few seconds, clung to the barrel of one of the four machine guns, then fell into the darkness.

He stared at the spot where the falling man had held on. A spider web of fracture emanated from a blood-stained center. The falling man had saved his life by taking the impact of a piece of shrapnel that would have killed him where he sat in his gunner's perch.

Just as he looked away, he saw a Junkers approaching fast behind him, its yellow tracers eating at his Lancaster's wings like ravenous fireflies. He pulled on his trigger with a rage he had never felt before as he stared through his sight and emptied his guns into the attacking bomber's cockpit. He had never been that close to the enemy – close enough to see the outline of men's hands and heads as they were engulfed in flames.

Red-hot brass shell casings fell at his feet and seared his boots. The turret filled with smoke from the guns, but through the pall, he could see each shot glowing like meteors and he could not stop firing and shouting at the thing that wanted to kill him. He watched as the Junkers spewed flames from both its engines, rolled to the right, and exploded into fragments of fading light.

Someone else got credit for the kill that night.

He was fine with that.

He had the deaths of the German aircrew on his conscience, a group of men like those who surrounded him in the darkness on every mission and who were as much a part of him as he was of them, but officially he wasn't to blame.

He should have been accorded an honor. His name was never mentioned in dispatch though the men on his Lancaster knew what he had done.

When they landed at their home field, now in the south of England to prepare for the D-Day invasion, his crew were gathered around the tail gunner's hatch to pat him on the back, but when his feet touched the ground, he bent over and was sick to his stomach.

During the raid, the 428, the 'Ghost Squadron,' lost five of its planes. There were empty seats in the mess hall. Orderlies were packing up the personal effects of the dead and preparing their rooms for replacements. That night over the Rhineland was the zenith of the Ghosts' service and the low point for the morale of the survivors of basic training in Saskatchewan. The seascape of wheat fields felt like a lifetime ago. But more than the empty chairs at breakfast, absences to which he had grown accustomed, he was haunted by the image of the falling man. He knew it was coming, but the future was never real until he lived it.

He fell asleep that morning telling himself that the man on the other side of his turret had been a dream. The fiery cockpit of the Junkers with its glass nose shot up, a small, cramped space where men were ablaze and struggling to survive as it rolled from his view and fell in the darkness the way a meteor burns bright before it burns out –even the shot stopped by a someone who had owned a life and gave it for what he believed in – all of it was beyond belief and if he told anyone, a commander, a mess buddy, or even Hugh, no one would believe him. He had learned from the Arctic lights that the future is transfigured into the past and when it yields to memory, a memory never lets go of a person's mind.

In the next image from the Northern Lights, he had seen a woman with one rubber boot, her arms reaching out to him, begging him to carry her, and Hugh and another man walking ahead and disappearing along a trail into the overgrowth of dense bush. He recognized the woman the moment he met her. She would become his wife. Clara was short and delicate, someone as unsuited to the bush as much as he and Hugh had been born for it.

He met Clara in Toronto at a prospectors' meeting. She was working as the secretary for a new company that was searching for something in the ground far more precious than all of Solomon's Mines. Hugh and he were contracted along with a man named Pulsifer to blaze a trail from the north shore of Lake Huron and find radioactive ore buried beneath an interlace of hills and lakes. The directors of the company said that uranium held the key to the future, and the directors made him swear an oath of secrecy because Canada was now locked in a race with the Soviets to claim prominence in mining the radioactive mineral.

"Imagine," Hugh said as they walked along Bay Street, both baffled and amazed at how unlimited energy could come out of a rock, "we may be doing something historic for once."

The two prospectors purchased Geiger counters, small boxes with wands attached. The dials on the box would move and they'd hear a whirring or clicking if they came upon a deposit of what they'd ignored in the past as pitchblende, an amalgam of stones surrounded by compacted puce-colored dust.

They were shown top-secret films about what uranium could do. After all the freezing night flights over Germany, where he watched cities burn beneath his bubble at the rear of a fuselage, and after all the losses of men he knew – most no more than boys – a small amount of the rock had set off a chain reaction in which atoms, the particles that made up everything in the universe, had been split in half, and in a flash above two Japanese cities, the world had changed forever.

The world changed shape as if it had been a vision in the Arctic night sky. They set out with everything they needed to walk into an area forty miles north of Lake Huron's North Channel.

The first day of the trek had been arduous. Clara insisted on accompanying her new husband, supposedly as a cook, but secretly because she feared he would meet a beautiful woman in the bush and never return to her.

"Heaven knows if there are hussies just waiting for you out there in the middle nowhere."

She kept insisting that the men stop so she could rest her tired feet. Clara complained about the mosquitoes. They were thick. The spring had been rainy. The lakes overflowed into the marshes, and the marshes were deceptive because no one knew how deep they were. Hugh and Pulsifer agreed that the best way to cross a wetland was to go directly to the other side. He carried Clara across twenty bogs, and at the twenty-first, she decided she could cross it herself, saying, "It doesn't look that hard."

But she was wearing rubber boots, what the British called Wellies, the kind with the red toes and red upper rims that were a size too small for her because she wanted to wear heavy socks. She was halfway across a muddy bog when the muskeg, the bottomless clay in the murk, grabbed her left boot and wouldn't let go.

He tugged and tugged at the boot, but the mud would not give it up, and the more he worked to free it, the deeper it sank, so by the time Hugh and Pulsifer had joined in the tussle, the boot was lost forever.

He carried his wife to the shore and set her on a rock.

"What are we going to do with you? You can't go on. I'd have to carry you all the way in and then out. Hugh suggests we set up a camp for you here and promise to come back for you."

"No!" she screamed and began to weep. "Carry me! Please! Don't leave me alone. I'll be eaten by bears. I've never been alone in a public park, let alone the bush."

He hoisted his wife for the next ten miles but eventually grew too weary from her weight and set her down. Hugh and Pulsifer shook their heads.

"You've got a problem there, old chap," Pulsifer said, having assumed an air of Englishness during the war when he was a liaison officer for the Canadian army.

Hugh put his hand on his friend's shoulder.

"It is probably best if you two wait here until we come out. My Geiger counter doesn't seem to be working. You wouldn't mind if I borrowed yours, would you?"

Reluctantly he took the box and its holstered wand off his shoulder and handed it to his friend. He watched as the two men disappeared into the bush, and although he was angry and despondent that he couldn't go with them, he realized the moment was one of the visions he'd seen in the frigid sky when he crashed the Jenny.

Hugh and the borrowed Geiger counter found the motherlode. Pulsifer and Hugh took the credit and the lion's share of the profits for the discovery. His moment in history had been lost because of a rubber boot. Hugh tried to console him. There would be other, smaller claims they'd stake, and those would set him up for a comfortable life, but not the life he had wanted to live. Hugh and Pulsifer found the motherlode of yellowcake. They became celebrities of the nuclear revolution.

The town that rose around the uranium mine-head had streets named Dover and Pulsifer. He didn't want to complain to Hugh about his lack of recognition. Hugh and he heard they'd appeared in a movie being shown to school kids, "The Miracle of Light" without realizing they'd been filmed as they set off to find the motherlode of yellowcake. Fame was fleeting and it gave him no joy when, within two generations, the mine was shut down and atomic energy became the pariah of the energy industry. The street named for his friend was bulldozed to let the townsite fade back into the bush.

Hugh gained greatly and lost greatly yet appreciated the humor of watching his triumph fade into nowhere.

Pulsifer became a broken man and lived long enough to see his achievements vanish before ending his life by his own hand.

"Cheer up. You can do better than having a ghost town named after you, although ghosts seem to keep popping up in your life," Hugh told him one day over drinks. "Friends don't let friends believe in transparent success."

The Northern Lights had been transparent, though. The images were ghosts, and the ghosts came to life. He could say he had seen through them, had looked upon the stars beyond the shadows and the stars were steadfast and real. And when life began to remind him again of the scenes he had seen in the green and yellow projections above him, twisting like ticker tape or spools of film in the Arctic sky, he saw what he knew was the second to last image – his daughters.

The little girls were primed for a party in red puffed sleeve dresses with smocked fronts and crinoline underskirts that flared their pleats. They were wearing white knee socks and black patent Mary Jane shoes with red bows attached to the toes. The older and the younger were dressed the same, and instead of running to him as he spread his arms after entering the front hall of his house, they stood and argued, each blaming the other for getting something better as a homecoming gift from their father.

"You have your nerve," Clara shouted at him. "Don't you know how it sets them off if one gets something the other wants? You know damned well they each have to have the same thing."

He looked ashamed. "I forgot," he said. "The crystal horse reminded me of Debbie and the porcelain elf tree of Dawna."

With that, each girl snatched the other's present and smashed it on the floor. He stood for a moment, broken-hearted at what the girls had done, then turned, closed the door behind him, and drove away. When he arrived in the bar, he wanted more than anything for Hugh to be there, to tell him a story about the bush or even explain how the girls had been spoiled by his desire to please both equally, blurring their personalities to the point where any differences between them – a crystal horse and a porcelain elf tree – were magnified thousands of times, especially in Clara's eyes.

But Hugh was thousands of miles to the northwest in the middle of nowhere. His wife had passed away. His son was in England studying Eighteenth-century books, and the bush gave him a quiet refuge from his grief. He envied the peace Hugh must be feeling where he could almost hear the wind passing through the trees or a river lapping over smooth stones as it rushed down from a hillside.

He recalled one summer afternoon when Hugh and he had the pontoons on the Jenny and were lake-hopping between possible claim sites. In his mind, he made a mental note to tell Hugh when they landed how being in a place and creating a record of their presence transformed a void on a map from a nowhere to a somewhere, and if Hugh ever wanted to go back to it, it wouldn't be a nowhere anymore.

"You know, Hugh, there's a part of a person that doesn't want to be in a place, at least not in a known place. Nowhere is a beautiful idea, but the moment a person arrives, it is no longer a vacant, ephemeral, idea. It becomes a point on a map, and God knows there are too many places already and each of them carries its own set of sorrows."

"Do you ever think about our Jenny?"

"Yes. Sometimes. There are moments when I see her sitting there, or at least what's left of her, as the stars and the Northern Lights look down on her and wonder how she found that particular spot. I saw a map not long ago, on which someone had detailed the terrain north of Great Slave, and whoever made the chart put a tiny 'X' where the Jenny lies. I've wondered if I wanted to go and see her again, but I can't bring myself to do it. I can't bring myself to look at that map. I want to believe she has ceased to exist because she found that silent, magical place that is beyond knowing."

"We had some good times flying her into nowhere."

"That we did. That we did."

As he drove home, one of those times, a moment the Lights never predicted or even noticed, entered his mind because it had been his moment and no one else's.

He recalled the day that he saw the bald eagle. The bird flew astride the Jenny. The plane's top airspeed was only 75 mph and the old engine had just enough push to keep the wings aloft at a slow pace. Flights of geese and the odd raven often caught up with them and kept pace with the plane that was flying with the wind against her.

The eagle drew close.

He turned to point out the bird to Hugh, but his friend was asleep in the rear cockpit, the sun on his goggled face and the wind tousling his hair and beard. The hum of the engine had lulled his friend to sleep. He leveled the plane and kept the flaps steady as the creature beat the air like a sculler with its wings, looking over until, after exchanging glance for glance, the bird peeled off and vanished in the Jenny's slipstream. The Aurora Borealis had not foretold that perfect moment of joy, but the sight spoke to him saying, "This is what you've always wanted. This is what your life has been."

Despite the silence from those in the mining industry, the prospecting community hadn't forgotten him. They knew the story of how he'd carried Clara on his back through the bush and how he'd flown a Curtis JN in and out of the most remote places in the north while searching for the land's hidden wealth. His work had laid the foundations for others who followed hunches that came true and who developed an uncanny ability to read a landscape for what lay beneath it.

The Association of Prospectors made him their first honorary president. He had not only made history: he was the living past, a kind of ideal of what miners wanted to be with a pick hammer, an old plane, and a burlap bag sagging from the weight of samples chipped white and raw from the earth.

He was supposed to be upstairs at the luncheon where he'd be honored, but instead, he waited in the bar on the ground floor for Hugh, who wasn't a city person and had gotten lost. When Hugh finally arrived, they ordered double bourbons, a habit he'd picked up in Kentucky, where he spent weeks persuading investors to back his search for the legendary lost Carswell claim that had never been filed. He'd begin his pitch to the wealthy Americans by saying, "They never did find the motherlode and they never discovered the fate of the Carswell brothers, but they knew and I know that there is gold out there waiting with your name on it."

Hugh smiled and told him he was full of shit, that there was nothing there.

"The land doesn't roll right. You're not going to get gold out of a rock," an old joke of theirs.

The Carswells, having set off on foot two weeks before he crashed the Jenny, had tried to cross Great Slave Lake and had run into the same blizzard that spelled the end of the biplane. The Carswells might even have heard the sound of the Jenny's engine as it passed over them, but frost-bitten, starving, and out of supplies, the anxious brothers who had refused numerous offers of partnerships with men who knew better than to tempt winter storms with ambitions, could not have signaled for help even if they had wanted to. They never carried a flare gun.

Hugh and he ordered another round of doubles for old time's sake. Hugh sensed his friend wasn't eager to get upstairs for the award ceremony. When the waitress set the glasses down in front of them, they swirled the liquid and stared into it as if they were auguring a vision.

"What do you see?" Hugh asked.

"Not much, but I know what I saw," he said. "You know, Hugh, the nights I was alone after the crash of our Jenny, the sky was absolutely clear, and I lay there, hungry and freezing, and staring at the Northern Lights. I saw the course of my entire life like a movie in those twisting lights. I saw moments, frame by frame, that came true, and I've seen everything except the last image – a checkerboard floor, and I don't know what that was supposed to mean. I wish I did. Any guesses? I saw my Air Force service. I saw you and Arthur Pulsifer walking ahead through the bush as I staggered under the weight of Clara after you told me to turn around and head to base camp. I saw my daughters, and I saw us as we're sitting here. I'm not sure if seeing the future is a blessing or a curse. Maybe it is both."

Hugh smiled and pulled on his beard.

"You never did find a motherlode to call your own, and maybe that's why you didn't see it. Your treasure has been your life. That's the claim you've struck. You've staked a claim to everything you have known. You are as you are, and that's the lot of it. Did the lights call you by name?"

"No."

"There you have it. The lights don't say anyone's name. The future doesn't care who we are. It just wants us to show up, live it, and be part of it, and we aren't permitted to know its value until we have lived it and made it our own. Even then, names don't stick. I drove up to the town site last summer. I found the street they'd named after me. The only thing there was a tree growing up between the arms of an umbrella clothesline. I thought I had everything and then I lost it all. I think the future is just about showing up for it because it happens anyway, whether you want it to or not. My mother used to say, 'Hugh, the future is what you make it,' but I'm not sure she was right. I believe it is already made for us and we just step in it like a heap of musk ox shit. Maybe you really were given some kind of gift the night the Jenny crashed. I've seen those lights. I've stared at them and wondered what they were trying to tell me, and I could never make head nor tail of their message. They're pretty, but I never saw the movie of my life up in the sky. So, my friend, you are about to be honored by the Prospector's Association, not for what you found but what you didn't find, and the guy at a podium upstairs is about to call your name and give you a plaque so you can remember what happened and who you are. I guess they don't trust us to keep track of the past ourselves."

Clara was pacing back and forth outside the door of the Grand Ballroom, afraid he would miss his cue or not show up at all when everyone had gone to such trouble to honor him. If Clara had accepted the award on his behalf, she would have told the story about her boot, and he had other things he wanted to say.

He wanted to tell everyone he'd seen his future after he'd crashed his biplane. He wanted to explain that the Northern Lights have seen queer sights, and not just the ones Robert Service wrote about, but realities, hard truths, and things impossible to speak of because they are either too awful or too wonderful. He could hear voices chatting inside, the clink of glassware as the audience was summoned to attention with the preamble to his award. Hugh held the door for him and everyone in the room stood, turned, and applauded.

And as he was about to hear his name called, his knees buckled beneath him, and he sank to the checkerboard marble floor. A pain snapped inside him and reminded him of the lights cracking to keep him from drifting off into a cold, eternal sleep, only this time the sound was inside him and he felt his heart splitting in two as a windstorm tore the remains off the upper wing of his Jenny and carried it across the northern darkness where it disappeared from view.

Hugh loosened his friend's tie and collar as Clara stood over her husband, screaming for help, and weeping in fear and surprise.

"Do you want me to turn you over?" Hugh asked, and though he was unable to speak, he motioned 'no' with his free hand as he lay on his side.

He'd seen the view across the cold marble squares one night long ago. It reminded him of the horizon beneath the first snow of the season where the lakes and veins of rivers, as far as the eye could see, had not yet frozen over. If he pushed the Jenny just a little more, coaxing another few miles from her tired wings, he'd find a good place to set her down, make a camp for the night, and lie back and watch the stars as they twisted to show him the shape of things to come.

Roosevelt Dimes

During the last months she spent by herself in the house, my mother would wake at night to the sound of footsteps in the kitchen or the basement. The wind would rattle and whistle around the corners of the eaves, and she would listen in the darkness and wonder if someone was trying the lock on the back door.

I stayed with her when I was in town for meetings.

My old room seemed cold and empty. Devoid of the books that had once lined the shelf, the room echoed. I had the sense that there was something in there watching me. My father had spent his final weeks in my room, having moved out of the space he'd shared with my mother for fifty years. She desperately needed rest.

Even though the dementia and heart problems were wasting him both mentally and physically, there was still something in him of the father I knew. It was buried deep beneath the confusion, the fears, and the moments he gasped for breath. He remarked how awful it was to suffer from Alzheimer's, and how he was afraid of dying, especially in a hospital. He said more about himself in those final weeks than he'd said during his life. He was a man of few words, and almost impossible to know. Had I not been so busy, I might have sat down to listen, but that did not happen.

He would take my hand as I was leaving at the end of a visit and say, "Don't let your mother sell the house." I worked to reassure him that she would stay put. He knew I wasn't telling the truth. My father considered the house to be the sum of his life's work. It was the post-war dream of suburbia come true. Now it was too costly for my mother to keep up. The house had to be sold.

A week before he died, I had dinner at the house. I wanted to be with him as much as possible. I wanted to talk to him. But what wasn't part of his confusion was rushed. As I said goodbye to my mother in the front hall, my father cried out from the back room. He was crumpled in a heap on the floor beside my old bookcase.

"I am going to die exactly a week from now."

I objected. When a person suffers for a long time, as my father did, those around him keep up a flood of absurdly positive wishes that cannot possibly come true.

I helped my father to bed.

"The specter in the corner told me I will die a week from now." He pointed across the room, but there was nothing there.

The night before he died in hospital six days later, his situation was stable. The doctor said my father would probably be sent home in a few days. I told my father that my wife's grandmother was about to celebrate her one-hundredth birthday and that we would be gone for a day or two for the celebrations out of town.

"I'll see you when we get back."

"I won't be here," he said, without looking at me. He sat staring at a reality show on the television.

"Yes, you will. Just stay put. Don't go anywhere. We'll be back, and I'll come to see you in two days."

His last words have haunted me: "Much you care."

He never looked at me again. Not, "I love you, son, I'm proud of you, or you've been a blessing to me, or even have a nice life and a safe trip." *Much you care.* Three painful, dismissive words that repeated in my head.

I tried to tell myself the words were his illness talking and not him. But what was said was said. There was a sense of the factual about them, a clinical tone that stung me. I left the antiseptic corridors and the pinging machines shaken.

As my wife and I were loading the car the next morning, the phone rang. It was the hospital. We had to come at once. When we arrived, my mother was holding my father's lifeless hand.

A week after my father died, my mother and I stood on the front sidewalk, trying to see if we could spot the leak in the shingles over the living room. A glint caught my eye on the pavement. I looked down at an American dime.

"Pennies from heaven?" my mother said, her hand still shading her eyes as if she was saluting.

I stared at the coin.

"It's a Roosevelt dime."

"People said your father always reminded them of Roosevelt. The way he backcombed his hair, the way he would tilt his chin."

I put the dime in my pocket.

That night, as I emptied my pockets while undressing, the dime fell on the floor underneath my bed. When I bent down to pick it up, there was another American dime beside it.

"What are the odds of that," I thought and stared at the two heads in my palm.

There is a determination in Roosevelt's jaw that intrigues me. He is looking off to the left as if gazing into the future or facing a setting sun for a vision of how to mend his nation. My father's chin was more rounded, and the only time it protruded enough to be noticeable was when he was angry.

Fathers are supposed to maintain some mystery. It is in their code. I had hoped mine would tell me more about his life, but he kept everything to himself. I tried the phrase, "a penny for your thoughts," many times, but he'd respond, "It'll cost you more than that." He took his stories to his grave, and the life he had experienced would not be shared at any price.

I have to accept that my father loved me. I had a home to live in. He paid for my clothing, my education, and the food my mother prepared. My father was, as appearances suggest, a good man. I don't doubt that. At his funeral, his former colleagues came and told me how lucky I was to be his son.

"You remind me of him," several of the old men said. "He must have loved you a great deal."

I would have given anything for a fireside chat. I would have loved him to reassure me in times when I was troubled or afraid. I wanted to hear him say, "The only thing we need to fear is fear itself." But he never entertained such grand thoughts, and even if he did, they remained bottled up inside him. He was the man I never truly got to know, the one man I should have known better than any other. He was the epitome of mystery.

He was no Roosevelt.

I put the two dimes I'd found in with my pocket change and determined that I would spend them on something, anything, the next time I was in a store.

But the dimes started to turn up with increasing frequency.

I found three under my bed at home.

I asked my wife if she had spilled the bottle where we saved loose change for nights out when we didn't have enough in the weekly budget to spend on fun. The jar hadn't spilled.

American dimes appeared on the floor of the car, in the elevators at my office, and on the floor of my dentist's office, and the coffee shop next door to my work. I kept looking down but one day I decided to look up and I saw a man leaning off a balcony and reaching for something that fell from his pocket. He called down, "It's yours now." A Roosevelt dime bounced on the sidewalk and rolled toward me.

I was frightened by the dimes. They were not merely appearing; they were coming at me. I didn't live in the States. They were foreign currency. They were the pocket change of another place, so I decided against spending them and saved them up in an old ashtray that I kept in a desk drawer at home.

The more I looked at them, the more I wanted to shout back at them. I wanted to demand that they tell me their secrets. I wanted them to open up and speak to me, not about FDR but about the man for whom they were becoming a dime-store persona.

They seemed almost bewitched. I wanted to take handfuls of them and toss them into the deepest part of the city's harbor. The more I hated the image on the coin – not the president, but the father who everyone said looked like the president – the more they kept appearing.

I slipped on one while entering a country club for a wedding we had to attend. My foot rode out underneath me as the dime slid on the terrazzo floor of the hallway. I threw my back out. Even when I was recuperating, flat on my back for several days, I looked up at the doorframe of my room and realized the previous owner of the house had left one sitting on the top ledge of the doorframe. They were everywhere and had been for years and I just hadn't noticed them.

And while I was on the heating pad one afternoon, I dozed off and had a dream about my father. He was standing at the foot of my bed. In one hand he had a bag of dimes, and he was throwing them at me, one by one, as if wanting to wake me up. It was a childish gesture. They were striking me between the eyes. In the other hand, he had a needle, and he jabbed it into my big toe.

"Son of a bitch!" I screamed as I woke. My wife came running.

"What's wrong?"

I was in tears. "My father jabbed a needle into my big toe. Please make it stop. He won't leave me alone. He's dead and he won't go away. He's been dead for weeks and everywhere I go he keeps appearing."

"You mean, you see him?"

"No. I keep finding Roosevelt dimes."

I showed her the stash. The old ashtray overflowed. They now filled half of my drawer.

"I even slipped on one at the wedding."

My wife picked them up, sorted through them in the palm of her hand, and spread them on the blanket.

"Wow," she said, "You've hit the jackpot."

She picked them up, one at a time, and squinted over the top of her glasses.

"I don't know whether you've noticed or not, but none of the dimes have the same date." They seem to begin with the year of your birth, and you have almost every year up to now. Some have a D after the date and others have a P or an S."

"Those are mint marks," I told her. "Denver, Philadelphia, and San Francisco. They are minted across the country and their point of origin is stamped on each one so you can tell where it began its journey."

"How did you come by all these?"

"They keep appearing. Everywhere I go. They're all over the place. Some I get in change, but most are just lying there waiting to be found. If I found dimes with the Bluenose on them as often, I'd say, 'that's just people being careless with their pocket change.' But in this case, the Roosevelt dimes are just too much of an odd coincidence. They aren't even the currency here. They're foreign change."

"You've got about eight or nine dollars here. We should add them to our savings jar."

"No!" I answered vehemently. "I mean, I want to spend them, but I can't let them go. I keep wanting to hold on to them. I don't know why. Maybe my father is trying to tell me something."

"Your father? Yes, I can see a slight resemblance, especially when he got mad at something, but for what it's worth," my wife said as she got up to leave the bedroom, "I never really saw the Roosevelt thing in him, though everyone talked about it. He just seemed angry, silent, and set in his ways."

"Since he died, they've been everywhere. They dimes are messages. They're not just pocket change. They are trying to tell me something. Too much of a coincidence is not a coincidence. It is a statement, a communication, maybe a warning."

"A warning?" she asked and looked at me, puzzled. "Well, let me know if they tell you something."

"I wish I could have known him differently. I wish we could have had long talks with him, enjoyed the same things, played catch. He never liked sports, even though I did. He'd come home late after working long hours. I'd want to ask him things and he'd just close his eyes and pretend I wasn't there. I wish he'd known how to have a conversation, maybe not just about himself but about the world. I wanted to see things through his eyes, and he never let me. I feel as if I only knew the tip of the iceberg, the man, but not the person behind the man."

"Maybe you should see a therapist. You could go through my EAP and the people at your job wouldn't know. It isn't good to have this hanging over you."

The therapist did not see any "unseen force" at work in the appearance of the dimes. He dismissed the coins as a fantasy I was having.

"Transference," he said as he coughed into his elbow. "You need to come to terms with your father. You should count yourself lucky. He gave you a good home. You can't do anything about him now. He got away with it. He did what he did and that's that."

My second appointment was my last. The dimes kept turning up, although less frequently. I suspected my father knew I was on to him.

When spring came, mother said she'd had enough of the family house. "There's only the past here," she sighed. "I want a fresh start."

Ruffians from the neighborhood were banging on the windows at night. She was besieged by real estate agents. The place became more than she could handle. Roof, lawn, the snow-covered driveway, a cracked foundation, plaster damage, a garage door that slammed shut and broke its window, and the constant noises of unknown origin troubled her.

"I've got to get out here for so many reasons. Financial. Physical, but mostly I need to get away from the memories and start over," she told me over tea one morning.

She sold the house for a good sum of money and purchased her condo. My sister, wife, daughter, and I pitched in. We all wanted her to make a clean break of it. She is a good person. She deserves her happiness. For the first time in her life, she had enough to live on, enough to make her new place what she wanted it to be. She was close to the few relatives and friends of hers who were still living, and the building was secure, the rooms easy to maintain, and the people in the building caring and friendly. She found her place.

My task on the final afternoon in the old house, after the movers had taken away the last boxes and pieces of furniture, was to walk through the empty rooms and halls, and check the closets in case something had been left behind. The June day was hot. It was the sort of day when my father would have been cutting the lawn or tinkering with something in the garage.

I closed all the windows. Every interior door was open, and the house felt as if it had become a ghost. The carpet was indented with shapes of table and dresser feet. Faded squares on the walls, empty hooks where pictures had once hung, showed how the walls held the ghosts of what had once been there and real. I stared at the spaces and began to forget what had occupied the patterns. I thought of birthdays, the family gatherings when there was laughter, nights when I lay awake in the darkness with a fever and my mother would come to me with a cool cloth to place on my forehead, and the mornings I ate my breakfast and saw my shadow on the kitchen floor. Every room held a secret that would remain a secret forever now that we were gone and no one would be there to remember the old days. And even though the house was emptied of every stick of furniture, I could see my father in every room and I saw his shadow in my old room.

On the final pass through the basement, I heard footsteps upstairs. At first, I thought my wife must have come in to use the bathroom. She'd been waiting outside so we could take the key to the lawyer's office. But through the basement window, I saw her legs on the lawn. The footsteps became angry stomps. I shouted, "Who's there?"

Doors began to open and slam. I got to the top of the stairs and looked the length of the hallway to my parent's old bedroom. I could not see who was running through the house, though I could hear someone searching for something breathlessly from room to room.

I went into the bedroom at the back of the house, the room that had been mine for years and where my father had his vision of his death. As I entered, the curtain rod came undone at one end, and the drapes we had left for the new owners slid to the floor. I bent and gathered them up, folding them neatly, and laid them on the closet shelf for someone else to sort out.

"Temper, temper," I said out loud. The doors continued to slam. My wife called in through the front door.

"What is going on in there? Are you coming? We have to drop off the key. Let's go."

As I got to the front door, I noticed three dimes in the middle of the living room floor. They hadn't been there ten minutes before, on what I thought was my final pass. I bent down, scooped them up, and left the house, pulling the front door behind me. I turned the key and the setting of my early life vanished with a soft click.

My mother decided to thank us for helping her move. She treated us to Christmas in New York City. She'd said she always wanted to spend Christmas in New York, "just like in the movies."

Snow was falling on Bryant Park as I stood in a Japanese/English bookstore and read the titles of recent bestsellers while I killed a half-hour before meeting up with my wife and mother.

On a shelf against a pillar, I spotted the "Collectors Craft" section, and among the volumes, I found a slim, red book with *Roosevelt Dimes* written on the spine. It was a folder for collecting coins. Each page had rows of empty, round slots in which to nest a dime. Beneath each circle was a date, the place the coin had been minted, and the quantity of each issue. It was only a few dollars, so I bought it. I had the feeling my father wanted me to sort the coins – at least that was the convenient fiction I invented so I could close the book on the past.

When we returned home to Canada, I sat down at the kitchen table one Saturday afternoon with the large jar of dimes. I had asked my wife what she thought they all added up to as I searched for meaning in the coincidence. "About fifteen dollars would be my guess," she answered. I had hoped she'd say something else.

A heavy snow was falling on our garden. It was a sad weather day to try to see what my childhood amounted to.

I peered through a magnifying glass at each minuscule date, some with 'P's after the numbers, others with 'D's for Denver, or 'S's for San Francisco. I squinted. My eyes were not as good as they used to be. I was getting old, I thought. I was becoming my father. I needed reading glasses, just like the ones he wore when he was the age that I am now. I saw my reflection in the toaster, and my hair had turned white.

Having sorted the dimes by decade and created stacks for each of them, I began to press the coins into their niches, and as they nestled into their slots, I recalled the day we settled my father's ashes.

The cemetery workers had dug a deep, round hole in the green lawn of the family plot and surrounded the round maw with pieces of artificial grass. I had to get down on my stomach to lower the mahogany box into its resting place, and as I did, it slipped from my hand and fell down the rabbit hole.

"Much you care," I heard him say. In the end, he simply got away from me.

I wiped the dirt from my hands, rubbing them together lightly, as they passed each other, but barely connecting.

When I was four, my father did a magic trick for me at my birthday party. I had forgotten he knew how to do sleight of hand things with coins. He showed me his empty hands. There was nothing in them. The sight of his open palms must have frightened me. I could see his lifeline, his heart line. I was looking into his future. When he convinced me that there was nothing up his sleeve, he reached up to my ear and pulled out a dime. It was a Roosevelt dime.

"Your father is magic. He can make dimes appear out of nowhere." one of my aunts said as the grown-ups applauded. I wished he had told me how he did it.

Maybe it was something I imagined. Maybe it never happened. I think I sat there for a long time and felt my ears to see if there was more where the dime had come from. Then the cake arrived.

After about ten minutes of tedious work inserting dimes by date and mint in the coin collector's card, a pattern began to emerge on the cardboard pages. On the first fold-out, the dimes spelled out a Y. On the second, they took the shape of an E, and on the third page they formed an S.

YES.

What was meant by YES?

I turned over the back of the coin book. On the back cover of the collector's book was a series of famous quotes from FDR that I hadn't noticed when I purchased it.

"The only thing we have to fear is fear itself," announced the first quote. I was not impressed.

"Much you care," I said under my breath, as I turned over the coin book to study the large, Roosevelt dime on the front cover. He did look like my father, though the chin was more pronounced. I did care about him, but neither of us knew how to break the silence. Language is not merely what one says but how one finds the right thing to say, the bridge across the gap of wordlessness.

That's when I looked up from the book and saw the coins I hadn't included in my collection. The Roosevelt dimes I didn't want as being too badly tarnished to be included, dimes I would cast into the loose change jar, though they trailed off in an ellipsis as if someone was listening, waiting patiently for a reply, and wanting to initiate the conversation by saying…

Thine Is the Kingdom

My grandfather entrusted me with his trench diary, but I had to promise that I would never open it. The old man had gained some notoriety among historians of the Great War because he said he had been witness to one of the conflict's atrocities. He'd signed up with the Third Toronto Regiment, Company C, Platoon 7, and saw what he called the "worst of it" at Vimy Ridge, where he made it to the crest of the summit and Passchendaele where the Vimy survivors disappeared in the mud. He insisted he was the sole survivor of the platoon that had discovered a young Australian soldier crucified on a barn door.

Historians who interviewed him contested his claim. They said there was no record of the men of Platoon 7. The Aussies, on the day he described, were miles down the front. According to my grandfather, his platoon had lost their way in a fog that hovered over the quagmire and had been haunted by the sound of men screaming for help as they were sucked under and drowned in shell holes.

He told the scholars that Platoon 7 had bivouacked in the remains of a farming hamlet named Petite Sainte. Those who studied the war said that there was no Petite Sainte, not before or after the lines shifted like tides leaving nothing in their wake. But my grandfather was adamant that he knew what he knew, and as much as it pained him to talk about it, he would not back down from his story.

"The Holy Spirit speaks not only to us but through us," he told me on the last night of his life. He took my hand and said he would soon stand before his Maker and would have to tell the Father Almighty he had killed his beloved Son as the only begotten died for the sins of Mankind a second time. My grandfather was no centurion dicing for robes. He was a boy from Toronto who wanted to go home.

"You don't know the burden I am taking with me," he whispered. "He can forgive all the wrongs of humanity except the one that took his Son. I should have hanged myself when I had the chance, but there weren't any trees for miles. When I finally saw chestnuts in Paris, I hadn't the heart or rope to bring more death into the world."

The story the historians contested was a piece of grizzly apocrypha of the Western Front. It ranked with the Germans chopping the hands off Belgian babies. According to men who studied records, the Germans were human, too; that despite introducing poisoned gas, despite using flame-throwers on the Allied lines and bombing the streets of London in the night, they did so only because they knew for certain that the Allies were planning to do the same to them. Being pre-emptive is a cold fact of war.

My grandfather went on the CBC and told his story. I have a recording of the broadcast on an old reel-to-reel tape. I can hear how he fought the tears to get the words out. The night was raining, "filthy weather," as he put it. The rain was mixed with sleet. They had taken Vimy on Resurrection Day and emerged from their tunnels to surprise the Germans behind their lines.

Their sergeant, a carpenter from Cooksville in his previous life, spotted some farm buildings in the shadows. There should not have been any structures left standing in that area. The area had been the target of heavy shelling for three years. The platoon made for the barn, broke open a side door, and threw themselves down on the hay. Someone lit a small fire so the men could remove their tunics and de-louse them over the open flame. They heard nothing. Even the lookout, denigrating his duty – and who could blame him under the circumstances – fell asleep. The guns were silent. One of the men thought he heard a nightingale.

They woke before dawn to the sound of someone moaning and crying out in agony for a mother.

"Here is your son," the voice said.

They'd grown used to such sounds, to the voices of their mates caught out on the wire, shot, and shot again as they struggled to free themselves, then falling silent because no one came to help. But the voice was near, almost beside them, if not among them. One man in the platoon said he couldn't stand it and, putting on his gear, crawled around the barn to the large, gated door on the opposite side from where they had entered. He screamed and pushed so that the door opened into the barn.

My grandfather sat up. He wasn't sure if he said it or if someone else uttered the word, but the name "Jesus" hung in the rancid air. A Catholic boy, new to the unit from St. Michael's College, crossed himself. The Australian soldier, his hands and feet nailed to the door, his arms spread, his breathing labored, was hanging there.

He called out to the awe-struck Canadians, "I thirst." The sergeant reached for his canteen and ran to the tortured soul, but the Aussie was nailed too high to reach. He looked around and shouted that someone needed to "Get the lad down," or "Where's a scythe so I can reach him?" But no one was certain of what the sergeant said. The moment was silent, and the silence bordered on holy awe.

The historians said that the crucified suffocated after only hours when their pectoral muscles tore, and the weight of their bodies choked them to death. They argued that they would have heard the dying soldier's moans the minute they arrived at the barn, that he could not have suffered all night long without the Canadians knowing that he was there and that they would have been called to action immediately to help a wounded comrade had the story been true. What was true was that they would have done anything to help the lad. He called out to them, "Please, please."

"Raise me up!" the corporal of the platoon shouted. "For Christ-sakes, lift me up and let me try to pry him loose." My grandfather said he was among the men who held the corporal up so that he could grab the nail heads with his fingers, but the more he wiggled and worked them, the more the Australian screamed. The nails would not give up their grip on the wood. Just before my grandfather and the others weakened, and lowered the corporal down, he looked into the eyes of the dying soldier, and fell to the ground weeping.

My grandfather drew his bayonet and screamed to be lifted up. He said that if he couldn't loosen the nails, he could try to pry the door boards apart; but they were old oak and would not budge. He thought for a moment he could pull on the Aussie, that the nails might slip through the stigmata and release him, but the heads were broad and had been hammered into hooks and they held the man fast and in his pain, as he cried out with sounds my grandfather said he had never heard from a human voice.

He'd heard men explode with agony when they were hit. He had cradled the dying in his arms and said that even they never made a sound like the crucified soldier. The radio host asked him what the sound was, and my grandfather replied that it was the voice of a million demons being crushed beneath the weight of an avenging hand.

"Isn't there anything we can do?" someone in the platoon yelled. The men stood in stunned silence. Some began to weep. If the moment had been intended to send a message of shock and horror to Allied soldiers, it had achieved its purpose.

The historians said that such an atrocity would never have been permitted, not according to the articles of war, and not according to the meticulous records kept by commanding officers. They said that despite hundreds of thousands, if not millions of men whose bodies were never recovered from the Western Front, the offices of the command knew where their men had fallen, could pinpoint the exact locations within inches. And in a war where men had fought and died for inches, every patch of mud, every step, every footprint marked a moment in the conflict.

"You are wrong," my grandfather told the expert in the radio studio who was there to refute his story. "You are the devil because only the devil would deny the death of the Son of God."

The expert laughed. So did the radio show host.

I could tell from the recording that my grandfather, already on the verge of tears, was ready to explode with rage. But he did not. He sighed. It was not a sigh of exhaustion or even trepidation, but a sound I never heard him make. It was a sigh of someone confronting a darkness while asserting that there may be light in it somewhere beyond the scope of the eye.

"So, what did you do?" the host asked almost mockingly to cast doubt upon my grandfather's story. "What did you do then?" he repeated.

"We all knelt. We knelt as if we were standing on the skull of Golgotha. We knelt as if the sky had turned black at noon, and we felt such sorrow. I looked up at that young man, his hair blowing across his forehead, his breaths laboring, his pain unfathomable and his suffering the embodiment of everything I had witnessed in the carnage of the front. Old soldiers are not supposed to talk of what we have seen. It is the unspoken code among us, and I am breaking it when I tell you that I knelt with all the others and closed my eyes. I closed my eyes and saw the faces of all my mates who had perished. I saw them staring at me and reaching out from the muck with outstretched hands and trying to speak to me. But the dead live in an eternal dream, and in dreams a person cannot speak. They can only imagine they are making sounds and those sounds are nothing but muffled moans and cries, the sound of souls attempting to call out from Hell to the living who cannot hear them."

"Do you mean you were all praying?" asked the expert. "That sounds very extraordinary."

"There was nothing we could do. All of us, the Catholic boy, the corporal, the sergeant, we all broke into the Lord's Prayer, and when we reached those words where the Protestant version carries on after the Catholic one has finished, I stood. I had brought my rifle with me from the hayloft in the barn because a soldier is never, or should never be, without his rifle. I stood. And just before we reached the words that offer Heaven and Earth to the Father, I stood and drew the bolt back on my Enfield."

"You were going to murder him?" asked the radio host.

"We shot our own to stop their suffering. They begged us to. Yes, we shot them. In a world without quarter, we made our own mercy. The Aussie knew what I was going to do. He looked at me. His eyes said. 'Yes.' Then he raised them to the sky and cried out, "Father, forgive them, for they know not what they do."

I raised the barrel and said out loud so everyone could hear, 'Thine is the kingdom, the power, and the glory, for ever and ever,' and as the platoon said 'Amen' in unison, I pulled the trigger. I shot the poor lad to put him out of his suffering. Amen."

The radio host and the expert were silent. Then the host interrupted with the name of the program and the names of my grandfather and the historian in the studio.

The historian added, "Nice story, but it never happened."

The last thing on the tape of the broadcast is my grandfather saying, "How the hell would you know?" Then dead air.

I have remained true to my word. I have not opened and read my grandfather's diary. It is sealed with a small brass lock. My grandfather said he bought the diary in a fancy stationery store in Salisbury when they were stationed on the plain for their final training before crossing the channel. It still has grains of mud that were caught where the pages meet the spine. There is a brownish-black streak along the bottom edge of the book, and when I try to put my fingernail between the pages, they are stuck together. The stain is probably my grandfather's blood. Not long after the events of Petite Sainte, he was wounded by mortar fire. He claimed that the same shell killed the sergeant and the Catholic boy. My grandfather was sent, as he said, "To Blighty."

If the truth is written in that diary, it is not for me to know. It is not my truth, but I am certain that the events were real to my grandfather. Often, just before men were wounded, especially if they had not been sent down the lines for rest after extended duty, they saw and imagined things that rose from the horrors they experienced around them. It was called 'shell shock' by the troops. My grandfather would never have admitted to that state of mind. He was an enlisted man. If an officer suffered shell shock, the proper scientific name for the malady of the mind being neurasthenia, he would be sent to a quiet English garden in the countryside to recover his nerves before being returned to the front and likely to death. If an enlisted man said he was suffering from nerves or trench fatigue, he would be shot. My grandfather was determined to survive, and he could have hidden in his mind.

As he fought the Angel of Death for weeks in a Toronto hospital, I wondered why he simply didn't give up. His wounds coupled with his intestinal cancer put him through a torment I cannot imagine. I watched him being crucified by his own life, heard him calling out for the Lord to take him, heard him forgiving a Maker who would make his creations suffer and kill each other either for King or country but usually in the name of God. I am not preaching, but I cannot forget what he said.

He drew me close the day before he died. "Will I go to Hell for what I did?"

I wanted to tell him that he had eased someone's suffering, that he would have cured the dying soldier had been able to do so. So, I said, "No."

Then we prayed together. We reached the end of the prayer, but he could not utter the word Amen.

A Lovers' Moon

The American Civil War photographer, Matthew Brady, fell on hard times when the fighting ended. His final portrait of Abraham Lincoln cracked in the upper left-hand corner as Brady was developing it, and he set it on a shelf and forgot about the one image in which the war president is smiling. Peace had come to the land. Several hours later, Lincoln was shot at the Ford Theatre. Most of Brady's glass plates ended up as panes in a greenhouse. The light faded them until the spirits they contained melted into thin air.

Life is never kind to photographers, perhaps because they make their greatest art when they capture a moment, and moments pass. Everything changes except a photograph. In Brady's case, peace ushered in a new way of looking at the world. No one wanted to see the bodies of slaughtered Northern and Southern soldiers twisted in attitudes of despair and suffering with hands upraised, clutching at the emptiness of heaven. Little Round Top became a distant memory. War no longer held its place in the public imagination. Love followed war and became the ethos of a new era.

Love is the most difficult subject of all to depict. If it is portrayed in a tawdry manner, it becomes lurid or worse, pornography. Naked men and women caught in each other's embrace stare at the camera without a hint of personal connection. Female figures prone on fainting couches, revealed in their corsets with their bodices open and their legs splayed with lasciviousness, plead to be loved and not just admired for what they depict. That plea is visible in the eyes of the women in French postcards. They want something more than what life can give them. They speak of pity instead of pleasure, no matter how hard they try to smile.

When love is missing from such a work, the souls of men and women fail to say what they are living for, and the image cannot speak of love, let alone utter the lost word for the spirit that binds two people together. Perhaps there is no word other than love itself that precisely defines that ethereal power that transcends both life and death. That is why I found the greenhouse of the old Jadot estate so fascinating.

As had been the fate of Brady's glass negatives, so the conservatory between the house and the garden of Emile Jadot's home has become a repository for the photographer's glass negatives. Jadot was the Matthew Brady of love.

In Paris of the 1880s, he was the spokesperson for what draws two people together and binds them, body and soul, against the world. His figures stare into each other's eyes. Some are seated together on courting couches, others on the single plank of a swing hung from a wisteria in full bloom. All are clothed. They can easily be misconstrued as sentimental; in the way a Watteau couple could be perceived as naïve on the verge of the Revolution. Instead, Jadot's figures capture a tenderness, and that is why few of his prints, popular in their time, have failed to survive. They are considered the junk of fin de siècle art. But they are far from being kitsch. They reveal tenderness.

Jadot's home, a derelict ruin, has been a time capsule for many years. I discovered him by chance when I was shooting a feature on the abandoned houses of the Parisian environs for a magazine in New York. The editors wanted me to show grandeur with vines and trees growing through bedframes. Instead, I found shadows of figures cast by the setting sun on the conservatory's flower benches.

Whenever I had the time, I would visit it during the year I lived in Paris. It was an overgrown, haunted place, the floors of the upper bedrooms collapsing on the drawing-room and library beneath. What had once been the carpet of his study was green with moss and strewn with moldering books. I went inside the house only once. It was more than I could take. Walking through the hallways, I felt as if I had opened the door to a crypt in the Père La Chaise and was staring at the body of someone who had once held society in the palm of their hand, only to watch it run through their fingers like water or life. It was a tomb. It frightened me, for it was the antithesis of everything I knew about Jadot. It was a disappointment grown into a despair.

The First World War and the slaughter of Verdun and the Somme brought an end to Jadot's love of love for love's sake. If people fell in love, and undoubtedly they did, regardless of what hardships or finalities they faced, they still managed the mysteries of love, but the age of sentimental gardens festooned with bougainvillea and wisteria had passed.

By 1917, bankrupt, Jadot had closed his Paris studio, the door of his home, and the gate to his miraculous garden. He must have struggled to hold back time. The glass plates, suddenly archaic in the world of newsreel photography and paper pictures of mass casualties, were used to repair the greenhouse ceiling. With shells landing hourly on Paris, glass was hard to come by. It was as if Jadot was trying to hold back and hold onto the delicacy of life, the butterfly wing dust that is the spirit of an orchid, a frail symmetry of life that would never come again.

What kept drawing me back to Jadot's abandoned home was the greenhouse that opened onto the garden. Jadot's garden had been famous once, perhaps almost as famous as the water lily pond and the Japanese bridge of Monet's Giverny. It had been the backdrop for photographs that honeymooners would purchase and take home with them from Paris to show their friends that Paris really was a place of romance and, keeping the card-backed images imprinted with the signature of Jadot himself, passed the portraits on to their children who cast them aside to the amnesia of time. My hunt for Jadot consumed years of my life as I sorted through antique shops in upstate New York, as I tried to imagine what lay beneath a tangle of branches and thorns that surrounded the conservatory in a witch's spell of overgrowth.

The benches where Jadot had grown orchids and camellias were collapsing from age. There were notes lying on the shelves, and several ceramic signs like the ones the French place on their doors and street corners to indicate what had once grown in a world where he controlled the light and climate, coaxing blossoms from thickets of fingers as the snow fell outside.

One summer evening, the light deceived me. I had been so enamored with the ghostly shadows in the glass that I forgot time existed. I missed the last train back to Paris. I decided to wait out the night in the conservatory when the most miraculous thing happened. A full, round, midsummer moon appeared through the trees and rose glowing toward the stars. This is what astrologers call a lovers' moon. It was as if the moonlight was plucking the stars from the heavens and embracing it in the glow. And that is when the images came to life.

I could perceive the fragile shadings that had been the shadows of men and women holding hands, leaning shoulder to shoulder beneath a bower, or facing each other on an s-shaped courting couch. The sentimentality of their shadows, the tracery of a background garden, and the Monet-style footbridges on which they met, spoke of a gentility between men and women that was both charming and sad because it all happened in a moment that was shattered by extremes of inhumanity. They, too, were staring into the future of a falling blade, and not one of them could see it coming.

I could almost hear the old man speaking to me among the shadows and the decaying benches, a pair of pruning shears in his hand, the occasional snip of an unwanted branch. He was telling me to look up through the faces that had lived once and whose traces were shining for one last moment of devotion, the men and women staring into each other's eyes, as if the luminescent distance between them, perhaps only a millimeter or so, as they were about to kiss, was about to pronounce the unspoken word for love that is impossible to know by daylight.

THE END

Acknowledgments

"The Ghosts," appeared previously in *The Hong Kong Review* and was nominated for a Pushcart Prize in 2021.

"Urineworts" won the Anton Chekhov Prize for Very Short Fiction from *New Flash Fiction Review* (UK) in 2019.

"Candlemas" was a finalist for the Bath Short Story Prize, 2020, and was published in the *Bath Short Story Anthology, 2020.*

"Mack the Knife" was shortlisted for The Mogford Short Story Prize (UK), 2020.

"A Narrow Space" appeared in *Paris All Lit Up* (US).

"Skating" appeared in *Time of the Last Goal*, Black Moss Press, 2015.

"The Star-Maker Machinery" appeared on *Vocal*, 2021.

"Thine Is the Kingdom" was published on *Passenger Journal*, 2021.

"A Lover's Moon" was published in *Fiction Southeast* (US), 2021.

A very special thank you to Lewis Slawsky, the editor of this book, for his keen observations and care with these stories, and Alex Wall of Crowsnest Books, for believing in these stories. Another very special thank you to Rosanna Micelota Battigelli for her keen eye and assistance with the Italian language and for her enthusiastic response to these stories. Thank you to Ben Berman Ghan for pointing me to Crowsnest Books. The author expresses his thanks to the Wallace Collection (London, UK), Tony Huang of *The Hong Kong Review*, Trasie Sands of *South Shore*, Angela Readman, Meg Pokrass, Halli Villegas, David Bigham, Antonia Facciponte,

Marty Gervais, Michael Callaghan, Margo Lapierre, and Michael Mirolla for their support, encouragement, and suggestions. And a very special thank you to Dr. Carolyn Meyer, Margaret Meyer, Katie Meyer, and Kerry Johnston for their love and support, and to the author's writing companion, Daisy Meyer.

Author Bio

Bruce Meyer is the author of more than sixty books of poetry, short stories, flash fiction, and literary non-fiction. His stories have won or been shortlisted for such prizes as the Carter V. Cooper Prize for Short Fiction, the Thomas Morton Prize for Fiction, the Tom Gallon Trust Prize for Fiction, the Fish Short Story Prize, among others. His broadcasts on The Great Books with Michael Enright of CBC Radio One remain the network's bestselling spoken-word audio series. He has been Visiting Writer/Writer-in-Residence at Dobie House in the University of Texas at Austin, and the University of Southern Mississippi at Hattiesburg. He is professor of Communications and Liberal Studies at Georgian College in Barrie, Ontario, and has taught at Victoria College in the University of Toronto, Laurentian University, the University of Windsor, Skidmore College, Humber College, and Seneca College. He was the inaugural Poet Laureate of the City of Barrie from 2010 to 2014. His most recent collections of short fiction are *Down in the Ground* (Guernica Editions, 2020) and *The Hours: Stories from a Pandemic* (Ace of Swords Publishing, 2021). He lives in Barrie with his wife, retired CBC journalist and researcher Kerry Johnston, their daughter Katie Meyer, and his pal Daisy Meyer.